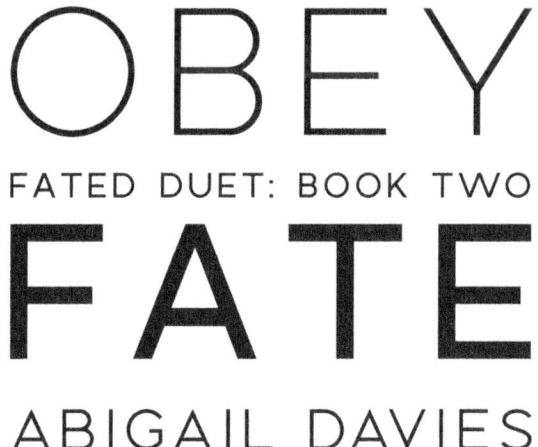

OBEY

FATED DUET: BOOK TWO

FATE

ABIGAIL DAVIES

Obey Fate
Fated Duet: Book Two
Copyright © 2019 Abigail Davies.
All rights reserved.
Published: Abigail Davies 2019
www.abigaildaviesauthor.com

Editing: Jennifer Roberts-Hall
Proofreading: Judy's Proofreading
Photo Credit: © Regina Wamba
Cover Design: Pink Elephant Designs
Formatting: Pink Elephant Designs

Chapter One

ARIA

It started with the tingling in my fingers. I stared down at my hands as it traveled up my arms, and then it dispersed throughout the rest of my body. I wasn't sure what was happening, but I was...*feeling*. I could physically feel the strength flowing through my body and making me stronger and stronger by the minute.

A gasp left my lips at the sensation, and I glanced up at Cade. It was because of him. I'd been searching in all the wrong places to feel normal again. Nothing else had worked but the caress of his lips against mine and his whispered promises. I just hoped it didn't dissipate this time.

"Cade," I murmured, but he wasn't looking at

me, his attention was focused on the door, his face draining of any color. I frowned at him and glanced over at the door.

I wished I hadn't.

I wished I'd stayed in my own little bubble where everything was starting to feel okay.

My eyes widened when I saw Miss Simmons standing in the doorway. Her gaze met mine, and I blinked. Had she seen what we did? Had she witnessed what we'd kept secret for so long? Her heels tapped on the floor as she stepped inside fully, and my breath caught as she closed the door behind her, the click of it ringing out in the otherwise silent room.

"What are you doing?" Willow asked, her voice deceptively soft, but I could see the anger swirling in her eyes and the way she held her shoulders back. She wasn't happy with what she'd seen, but the question was whether it was because me and Cade kissing was wrong or because she wished it was her.

My fingers drifted to my lips as I remembered the way Cade's lips had softly touched mine. My waist still burned from the feel of his hands on it even though he was several feet away from me now. I was caught up in my own head, not really under-standing what had happened. Not until I shuffled on my seat and winced from the sharpness of the wound on my thigh.

I'd cut again, but this time I'd done it in school. I never thought I'd go that far, but what made it even worse was Cade had noticed. I was losing myself, more than I ever had before, yet he was there, offering me his hand to bring me out of the darkness and back into the light. And now…now Willow was blocking the light.

"Willow," Cade started. He held his hands up in front of him like he was surrendering to her. "It's not what it looks like."

She raised her brow, her blue eyes narrowing on me and then Cade. "It looked like you were kissing." She paused, waiting for either one of us to say something, but when we were both silent, she continued, "But that can't be right. You wouldn't be having sexual relations with a student, would you, Cade?"

"I—"

"That would be absurd." Willow laughed, but I could tell she was trying to convince herself she hadn't seen what she had.

"She…I…she…" Cade trailed off, and I felt his eyes burning a path over my skin. I flicked my gaze to his, my stomach dropping at seeing his dark-blue eyes focused entirely on me. It always felt like too much for me to handle when he stared at me like that. His eyes swirled, a muscle in his jaw ticked, and my heart beat faster. He'd made up his mind, and as soon as he took a step toward me, I knew what he was going to do.

He'd made me a promise, and this time, he was intent on keeping it.

But I couldn't let him destroy everything he'd built just for me. His determination was as clear as day, but I refused to let him do it. I couldn't let him take the fall. This was my fault. If I hadn't cut at school, he never would have touched me, he never would have kissed me.

Ford's words echoed in my mind, the warning he'd given me when we were in the hospital. It wasn't only about Cade losing his job. He would lose so much more than that, which meant I had to save him. I had to do to him what he'd done to me, even if it meant I'd lose him all over again.

"It was me," I croaked out. My hands flattened on my desk and the coolness of the wood seeping into my palms as I looked over at Willow. Slowly, I stood, bringing my bag with me. I was doing this. I was protecting the person I cared about most in this world, and I didn't think twice about it. "I came on to him."

Willow blinked as if she hadn't heard me, but I felt Cade move a step closer. "Aria," he warned, his voice low, but it was too late. He may have broken my heart, but that didn't mean he wasn't the one who had made it whole in the first place.

"I'm sorry, Mr. Easton," I murmured and stared

up at him. I tried my hardest to convey to him what I was doing—that I had his back—but the swirl of his dark-blue eyes warned me against it. I knew the line I was drawing—but it was all for him, everything would always be for him. "I shouldn't have tried to kiss you."

"You shouldn't have," Miss Simmons cut in, her voice razor-sharp. I turned to face her again, steeling myself for what she would say to me. "It's girls like you who cause people like us to lose our jobs and ruin our reputation." She stepped toward me, her shoulders pushed back. "I knew you were trouble the first time Jasmine mentioned you."

My nostrils flared at the sound of her sister's name. Jasmine was good at getting people to believe in her and follow what she said, and it looked like it wasn't any different with her sister. Either that or Jasmine had learned it from her to begin with.

"I'm sorry," I whispered, not meaning it in the slightest. I'd never be sorry when it came to Cade. *Never*. "I shouldn't have done it."

"No, you shouldn't have. And if I had my way, we'd be marching to the principal's office right now." I heaved in a breath and hoped to hell she wasn't going to. I could handle it, but it would mean Cade would be investigated and then— "But seeing as Cade is a very close friend of mine, I'm going to let this slide."

I swallowed against the lump in my throat as I

ABIGAIL DAVIES

soaked in her words. Were they close? Had I missed something? I frowned as I thought about when I'd seen them earlier today in the hallway. Her hand had been on his chest…

And he hadn't moved it.

My body begged me to turn and face Cade to see if my thoughts were true, but I knew I couldn't, not if I wanted Miss Simmons to believe what I was saying. "It won't happen again, Miss Simmons." I took a step toward her. I needed to get out of this room, I needed to get away from them before my act wasn't good enough, and she saw right through it. The thought of them being close was making me feel sick, and if I weren't careful, my mask would slip, and she'd see the truth.

"I know it won't," Miss Simmons replied, her lips curving up into a smirk. She was so sure of herself, and part of me wanted to blurt out what we'd done to throw it in her face, but it wouldn't help the situation, so I simply nodded and walked past her.

My hand connected with the cool handle on the classroom door, and I pulled on it. The creak of the wood echoed around us, and just as I was about to step out, I turned back one final time. Miss Simmons was staring at Cade, her mouth moving, but I wasn't sure what she was saying because she was talking so low.

His stare connected with mine, but it was locked down, preventing me from being able to see what he was thinking. He'd tried to bring me back from the brink, and he'd succeeded, but in the process, we now had a target on our backs, and I knew one thing as I looked at him.

I'd never tell the truth.

I'd lie to save him—to save us—even if it meant I'd never feel his touch again or hear his voice whispering promises to me. He'd rescued me from myself in this classroom, now it was time I did the same for him.

———

CADE

My body was frozen, my joints locked in place, my muscles motionless. I'd let her take the fall. I'd allowed her to lie for me, and the worst thing was, I'd done nothing to stop it. I should have interrupted her and told Willow the truth, even if it meant going to jail and losing everything I'd worked toward.

Because Aria was worth it.

She'd always be worth it.

But as Aria stared at me from the classroom door, her eyes clearer than they had been when she'd first entered, sheer determination shining in them, I knew I couldn't admit what had happened to Willow. I'd made a mistake. I'd allowed myself to forget who and where I was. I'd given in to the temptation again, but I didn't feel an ounce of remorse for it. The only thing I regretted was not following Aria out of the room as she walked out.

She closed the door behind her and walked past the classroom windows, and my heart raced in my chest. It felt like so much more than her walking away from the situation. She was walking away from me, and I couldn't do a thing to stop her, not if I didn't want everything to explode in my face. She disappeared from view, and a finality settled over me. That was it. We could never go back, not now.

"So pick me up at eight?"

I blinked several times, trying to clear the fog around me. Everything was happening too quickly, and my mind wasn't able to catch up. Minutes ago, I'd had my lips pressed against Aria's. Seconds ago, I was making silent promises to her. And now I was here, more alone than ever.

"What?" I frowned down at Willow and backed up a step. She was too close for my liking, and she knew that. She'd been cornering me every day for the last few days, but now she had something on me, and I wasn't sure I could deny her advances any longer.

The way her blue eyes swirled, I could see she knew what had really happened in here, but she was pretending. The only difference was Aria had covered for me, but Willow was doing it so she would get what she wanted.

"You and me, Saturday night, a date." Willow placed her hands on her hips and pushed her chest out. "You can pick me up at eight."

"I…I can't this Saturday," I told her.

She was silent for a beat, her brows rising high on her forehead as she stepped away from me. Her movements were slow and methodical. "I guess I could just go and see Mr. Smegly," she commented, her voice sounding bored. "Tell him what I saw in here." She looked at her nails as if she wasn't concerned. "I'm sure he'd be very interested in what I had to say."

She was threatening me, and there was nothing I could do about it. If I wanted to keep my job and not go to jail, I needed to go along with her. I had to follow the path she was creating, no matter how much I hated it. She had me backed into a corner, and it felt like there was no way out.

"I meant…" I cleared my throat and shook all my thoughts from my head. Now wasn't the time to get caught up in everything I was feeling. It was time for self-preservation. Time to slap a Band-Aid over the situation I'd found myself in. "I meant I have to look after my little brother and sister this Saturday. What about"—I stepped toward her and pulled my lips up into a grin, sure it would get her to melt —"next Saturday? I know a great Italian restaurant in town."

She smiled at me, her cheeks pinking as she replied, "That sounds perfect."

"Good." I shifted past her and placed my hand on her arm as I did, hating the way her skin felt against my palm, but knowing that small touch would make her think there was more to it. She was playing a game, but she didn't realize I was adept at playing them. "Are you leaving? I'll walk you to your car."

I grabbed my laptop and pushed it into my bag then shouldered it. My nostrils flared as I pulled in a deep breath, preparing myself for the way I was going to have to act around her. I'd made my bed, and now I was going to have to lie in it, whether I liked it or not.

"I'd like that," Willow's sickly sweet voice said, and when I turned, she was staring at me like I was her Prince Charming coming to save her. She was delusional, but so was I for doing this. Did I really think I could win at this? I wasn't sure I would, but I'd try my damn hardest. If I had to pretend just so I could keep what Aria and I had secret, then that was what I'd do, whether I liked it or not.

I waved my hand in front of us, signaling for her to exit first, and then I followed her to her classroom. She put an extra sway into her hips, and any other time, I'd have loved the way her skirt gripped her ass, but that was before…

Before Aria…

Before I'd fallen in love with her.

Shit. Fuck.

I couldn't think about that, not now. Not while I was trying to push it all aside just to cover our tracks. I needed to hone in on my game face and not let a single crack appear.

Willow collected her things, and together we walked down the hallway and out of the school. My gaze landed on the steps, the same steps Aria would sit on while she waited for her mom or Sal to come and pick her up after school, but she wasn't there.

My gut churned at remembering the last time she'd sat on the concrete steps. It was the first time I'd seen her scars—fuck, she'd cut today at school and I'd tried to fix her. I was trying to make her better when all she had needed was me to be there. I'd abandoned her after Ford's warning, and I hadn't stepped up when she needed me the most. I'd let her down, but more importantly, I was still letting her down. I was failing on all the promises I'd made—words I'd said and thought I'd meant, but I hadn't followed through.

I tried to steady my breathing as we halted next to Willow's car and attempted to pull a smile on my face to mask the way I felt as I looked down at her, but I wasn't sure how successful I was.

"I'll see you tomorrow?" I asked.

She nodded and stepped closer, her hand landing on my chest as she lifted up onto her tiptoes and placed a kiss on my cheek. She hovered longer than necessary, and I closed my eyes. That was a mistake because the first thing I saw was Aria's face. Her beautiful features with freckles dotted over her nose. I imagined her blush as I stared at her, and the way her eyes would spark when I touched her.

But it wasn't Aria's lips pressing against the stubble on my jaw. It was Willow's, a woman I would have wanted a year ago, but now held nothing to the woman I really wanted—*needed*.

"Thank you, Cade," Willow whispered, and pulled away. I wasn't sure what she was thanking me for. Maybe for saying I'd take her on a date, or maybe because I'd agreed to take part in her game —as if I had a choice in the matter.

"You're welcome," I murmured and stepped back as she got into her car. I didn't move from the spot I was standing in as she turned the engine on. I stayed glued to the ground as she reversed and exited the parking lot.

Once I knew she was out of sight, I yanked my cell out of my pocket and clicked on my messages. I was typing one out and sending it before I even realized what I was doing.

Cade: We need to talk.

Aria: No, we don't.

I gritted my teeth at her reply and sauntered across the lot to my car. We couldn't leave things the way they were. I needed her to know I meant each and every word I'd whispered to her. I needed to make sure she was okay. *I just needed her.*

Cade: Yes, we do. I'm coming over to your place.

Aria: I'm not there. Just let it be, Cade.

Aria: Just let it go. She'll never know what really happened. Not from me.

I pulled my car door open and read her messages over and over again. I knew what she was saying, but I didn't want to let go. I didn't want to think about the possibility of her not being in my life. I didn't want to imagine what my days would look like without her face in them. But I didn't have a choice. I never had a choice, no matter how much I thought I did.

Cade: Thank you.

Cade: For covering for me.

Aria: Us. I did it for us, Cade.

Us. There'd never be an us again. I knew that. But it didn't mean I liked it.

Chapter Two

ARIA

Everything weighed me down as I walked down the school hallway and toward my locker. I had to pass Cade's classroom on the way, but I tried not to look because, if I did, I wouldn't be able to keep the mask on my face I'd perfected since yesterday.

I was doing this for him. I was making sure my demons didn't catch him because he didn't need my darkness in his life. So I'd do what I always did. I'd pretend everything was okay. I'd go to class, I'd run on the track, and I'd be the best student I could be.

We were only three months into the school year and already so much had happened. Life could change in an instant. I knew that better than anyone else, which was why I was doing all of this. I wouldn't let Cade take the fall for something we'd both taken part in.

I opened up my locker, put my books away, and grabbed my lunch. Any other time, I would have met Hope, and we would have sat under the bleachers, but things had changed—I'd changed them. I'd cut everyone off. I'd pushed Hope away, scared she'd see through everything that was happening, but now it was time I fixed what I'd broken.

Pulling in a deep breath, I pushed through the students milling in the hallway and kept my head high as I moved closer to Hope's locker. I had no doubt she wouldn't let me get by easily. I had some explaining to do, but I wasn't sure how much I'd actually divulge. I couldn't tell her everything. I couldn't tell her what I'd been doing to myself, but I could skirt around it. I could amend what I was telling her and give her the cut-down version.

I swallowed as I halted behind her. "Hope?" Her back straightened at the sound of my voice, her shoulders pulling back, but she didn't turn to face me. "Please, Hope. Can we talk? I'm…I'm sorry."

She slammed her locker door closed and spun around. "Sorry? Are you serious right now, Aria?" I opened my mouth to reply, but she didn't give me the chance. "You've flat-out ignored me for weeks, and now you think you can just come up to me and say sorry and everything will be okay?"

"I…" I frowned as a sinking feeling washed

through me. Her face was angry, but that didn't hurt. It was the sadness echoing in her eyes that gutted me completely. "I'm really sorry, Hope. I've had some things going on and—"

"Like what? Knocking Jasmine out?" She crossed her arms over her chest. "You could have told me you were going to do that. I didn't even get to see it."

My brow rose, my lip quirking at the corner. I wasn't sure how this was going to end, but the fact she was pissed about what had happened with Jasmine was a good sign. "You're mad because you didn't get to witness me hit her?"

"Hell yes, I am! She deserved it, and I missed it." She threw her hands up in the air. "What the heck happened, Aria?"

I blinked several times, knowing exactly what had happened. I was trying to feel something—anything—and I had for a few minutes. When Jasmine had hit me back, she'd allowed everything to come rushing forward. It had only been a glimpse, much like yesterday with Cade, but it was enough to keep me going.

"I'm not even sure where to start," I told Hope, genuinely not knowing. She was my best friend, but I hadn't treated her like one. I'd let her fall by the wayside and allowed myself to drown in my own sadness instead of reaching out to her. I hadn't been able to perfect my mask, but now I didn't have a choice. "Can we go to the bleachers and I'll explain?"

Hope narrowed her eyes at me, and I wiped my sweaty palms on the side of my jeans. She was making me nervous with her long pauses. I hoped she would give me the chance to explain, not only because she was my best friend, but because I missed her. I missed her constant rambling. I missed how she'd distract me.

"Fine." She puffed out a breath. "But don't think you're forgiven. I expect the full story, missy." She pointed at me in warning, and I nodded. I'd tell her as much as I could without destroying myself in the process. "Come on," she said, her voice sounding bored, but I could see the small lift of her lips as she spun around.

Hope was a forgiving person, sometimes too forgiving. I'd witnessed over the years when she'd let things go and forgave people too soon—like her own parents—and I'd told her she shouldn't keep doing it. She needed to put her guard up some-times. The problem with Hope was she never had her guard up, and now, it would help me. Her being so forgiving would allow me to be her friend again.

We walked side by side down the hall and out into the quad. Cheerleaders and football players were being rowdy, but for what felt like the first time, we went by unnoticed. Not one of them looked at us, and none of them said a word. We were invisible.

The track and field were empty, but I couldn't stop my gaze from wandering over to Cade's office windows. I couldn't tell if there was anyone in there, but I didn't need to remember what we'd done inside those four walls. The way he'd touched me. The way he'd kissed me. The way he'd made me feel—like I was the only person in the entire world he cared about. There was nothing like it, and I was under no illusion I'd ever feel that way again, not without Cade.

"Hey!" Hope's hand waved in front of my face. Her head turned to see where I was staring, and then she looked back at me. "Hmmm…I think someone needs to start talking." She raised her brows, waiting for me.

I swallowed and nodded. I did need to start talking. I needed to tell someone what was going on. I needed to share what I'd done and the way I felt. I needed my best friend.

"Come on." I grabbed her wrist and searched around us, making sure no one would be able to hear us, and then pulled us under the bleachers. There was a reason we found this spot—for its inclusion. No one would know we were here, and more importantly, they wouldn't be able to hear.

We both settled on the dying grass, and I placed my lunch on my lap. I wasn't sure I'd be able to eat, not until I told Hope everything I could. "I lost my virginity," I blurted out at the same time she was taking a drink of her water.

Water spurted out of her mouth as she choked, her eyes watering as she stared at me. "Holy shit, Aria. Give a girl some warning."

My cheeks burned. "Sorry. I just needed to get it out." I let my shoulders sag, already feeling like some of the weight had been lifted off them.

Hope blinked and then her brows lowered. "Wait, wait"—she held her hand up—"you need to start from the beginning."

I bit down on my bottom lip and looked above me to the underside of the bleachers. I wasn't really sure what the beginning was. I suppose it all started with my dad—all roads seemed to start and end with him. "So…I met Cade when I was eight—"

"Cade?" Hope shouted as she dived at me and grasped my arms. "As in Mr. Easton?" Her eyes were as wide as saucers, her mouth opening and closing like a fish.

"I…yeah." I pulled in a breath and held my hand up so she wouldn't interrupt me. She slowly backed away, so I continued, "I had a huge crush on him back then, but I hadn't seen him since I was thirteen. And then he just…turned up here." My pulse thrummed when I thought about the first time I'd seen him in class. I had no idea we'd end up where we were now. "We…I…damn, I can't even explain it. I fell in love with him, Hope. I...he..."

"Oh my god, you're having an affair with a teacher." She slapped her hand over her mouth and looked around us. "This is so scandalous." Her lips spread into a wide grin her hand couldn't cover.

"Was," I told her. "I was." I cleared my throat, determined to be able to get this all out. "Long story short, he ended it and then a load of crap happened." I blew out a breath and started to mark things off with my fingers. "Mom and Sal got engaged, I got into a fight with Jasmine, we moved from the apartment and into a new house, and then..." My eyes filled with tears at the finality of what had happened yesterday. There was no going back, not now. "Miss Simmons caught us kissing in his classroom yesterday."

"What?" Hope leaned forward again. "I thought you said he ended it?"

"He did but..." I couldn't tell her why he'd kissed me in his classroom. I couldn't explain to her what I'd done to myself in the school bathroom. That part would stay secret—it would always stay secret. Only a small shuffle had the cut on my thigh stinging, and it was enough to get me to focus on what I had to say. "We kissed after class, and Miss Simmons walked in."

"Holy. Shit." Hope fell back a little and stared at me, but her eyes weren't really looking at me as opposed to looking through me. "Jeez, Aria. You've had a shit load happening, and all I wanted to tell you was someone asked me on a date. Now I feel stupid for being pissed that you ignored me."

"Someone asked you on a date?" I didn't want to acknowledge what else she'd said, because all it would do was remind us of what happened. I needed to move past the last few months. I needed to pretend none of it happened, both for my head and my heart. If I locked it all away and didn't entertain any of it for a single minute, then I wouldn't have to feel the agony at losing Cade. I wouldn't have to think about the loss I was suffering. I wouldn't have to remember it was me who drew the final line. It was me who shot the final bullet.

"Oh my god, yes! So, you know the drummer in Lisha's boyfriend's band?" I didn't, but I nodded anyway. "He wants to take me out for pizza!"

"Isn't he, like, twenty-one?" I asked, concerned for her. I didn't want her to get hurt, not the way I had.

"Psssh, coming from you who lost her v-card to someone in their mid-twenties." She had a point, so I kept my mouth closed. "We're going this Saturday, and gah! I'm so excited."

I smiled and leaned back on my hands, listening to her talk about what she was going to wear and what the drummer was like. There was a silver lining to having Hope around. She distracted me, and right then, I needed it more than anything.

————

CADE

I picked up my bottle of beer and glanced down at my cell for what felt like the thousandth time. I'd never been impatient, but this was different. I was caught in a trap with no way of escaping and had no idea what to do.

Willow had talked my ear off in the teachers' lounge today at school, and I'd felt obligated to sit there and listen to her. All it would take was a few words from her, and everything would be over. She held my life in the palm of her hands, and it was a feeling I detested with a passion.

There was only one person I could ask for advice, the same person who had been there for me when I'd lost two of my best friends and my girlfriend in one fail swoop. He'd been there when I needed him, but most importantly, he knew about Aria and me.

Aria…

God. She'd taken the blame. She'd put it all on her shoulders, and I'd let her. I'd let her dig me out of a hole she hadn't created, at least not on her own. I was an asshole.

"Hey," Ford's gruff voice greeted. I whipped my head up to face him as he slipped onto one of the barstools. I'd chosen a table toward the back of the sports bar so we could talk properly, but I didn't want it to look suspicious. I was overthinking everything, I was aware of that, but I couldn't stop it.

"Hey," I grunted as Ford lifted his hand to one of the waitresses. We stayed silent while we waited for his drink, both of us looking up at the screens littering the bar and playing various sports. And when the waitress finally placed his bottle of beer in front of him, I blurted out, "We were caught."

Ford's gaze slid to mine, but he didn't say a word. He was watching me in the same way he did to everyone else, assessing and reading my body language. Eventually, after what felt like hours but in reality was minutes, he asked, "What happened?"

"I—" I cut myself off and shook my head. I couldn't tell him why I'd made promises to Aria in my classroom. I couldn't tell him why I was so worried about her. It was yet another secret I was keeping, but one I would never tell. "I fucked up. I kissed Aria in my classroom."

"Jesus," Ford groaned and took a pull of his beer.

"I know. And…a teacher walked in on us." Ford's nostrils flared, but it was the only indication he'd heard what I said. "This teacher, she won't give the hell up." I drummed my fingers on the wooden table, trying to keep myself calm. "She's been coming on to me since I started at the school."

He tilted his head to the side. "Did she report you?"

"I…" I blew out a breath, hating the words which were about to come out of my mouth. "Aria took the blame. She said it was all her." I gritted my teeth and gripped my beer bottle tighter. I hated she'd taken the blame. It wasn't only her, it was me too. She had enough shit going on, and now there was this added to it. I was meant to make it easier for her, not harder.

"Of course she did," Ford grunted. "She's trying to look out for you."

"She doesn't need to—"

"I told her." Ford leaned forward. His attention was solely on me. "I told her what would happen to you. I told her you broke the law. I told her—"

"Are you kidding me?" My voice rose and caught the attention of some of the people around us, but I couldn't bring myself to care. He'd crossed the line. There had been a reason I hadn't told her. My eyes bore into his as I ground out, "Why the hell would you do that?"

"The question is, why wouldn't you?" he shot back. "Why were you not honest with her in the first place?"

"Because she's…fragile."

Ford raised a brow and lifted his finger to point

at me. "That's bullshit, and you know it. You didn't tell her because you wanted to find a way to be with her. Newsflash, Cade, there is no way, and now you're fucked because someone else knows."

I closed my eyes and rubbed my palm over my face. He was right, I hadn't told her because I always thought deep down we'd find a way to be together. If she didn't know what could happen, then she wouldn't protect me from it. It was ironic that now it was precisely what she was doing: protecting me.

"What the hell am I going to do?"

"What did the teacher say?" Ford asked, and when I looked up at him, gone was the fury and emotion in his gaze and features, and in its place a mask he'd perfected over the years. He was putting a plan together in his head, finding a way to make something work, but I wasn't sure there was a way out.

"She…" I frowned when I thought back to how Willow had acted. She'd taken Aria's word at face value and not even doubted it for a second. "She…I…I'm taking her out on a date next Saturday."

"What?" Ford frowned. "Jesus, how did that happen?"

"I'm not really sure." I pushed my hand into my hair and gripped it, needing to feel the burn on my scalp. "I was listening one minute, and then the next she was telling me to pick her up at eight and I…agreed?"

"So she's blackmailing you."

"What? No, she wouldn't—"

"She is," Ford cut me off and placed his arms on the table. "And you have no choice right now but to go along with it. She has something on you that could ruin everything, and not just for you. Imagine what it would be like for Aria. I get the feeling she doesn't have it easy in that school, especially after what happened with that girl—"

"That girl." I laughed and shook my head, not believing what was happening right now. "That girl is the teacher's sister."

Ford's mouth opened and closed, but he didn't say anything. For the first time ever, he was speechless, and I wasn't sure what to make of it. It definitely wasn't a good sign. "The girl Aria knocked out is the sister to the woman who caught you kissing?" Ford said, summing it all up in one simple sentence.

"Yep."

"Well, fuck." He leaned back, his eyes glazing over. "Then you have no choice at all. Butter this woman up, make her feel like a million dollars, because there's no way this won't come back on both you and Aria if you don't. I warned you, Cade. You messed with fire, and you're getting burned."

I knew what he was saying, but that didn't mean

I liked it. I didn't want to be in the situation I was in. Taking Willow out on a date didn't appeal to me one bit, but he was right, I had no choice. I had to do what was best for both me and Aria. I was doing it for us. Everything I did from now on would be for us, she just wouldn't know it.

"I'm so fucked," I groaned, downing the last of my beer. It wasn't strong enough for the situation I'd found myself in.

"That you are, Cade. That you are."

"Jeez, thanks, Ford."

"What?" He shrugged. "I'm not gonna blow smoke up your ass. You fucked up, and now you have to deal with it. Life isn't fuckin' rainbows and unicorns."

"I know that."

"Do you?" Ford asked. He tilted his head to the side. "Because from where I'm sitting, you're bitching like a little girl who didn't get a goddamn pony. You're a fuckin' man, Cade. Start acting like one."

My heart beat faster in my chest, anger rushing through my veins at his words. He knew I hadn't had it easy growing up, or while I was away at college. Shitty things had happened to me in my life, but as I sat across from him and really took in what he was saying, I realized I hadn't had it half as bad as the people who I considered family.

"You're right," I told him, pushing my shoulders

back and resolving on what I would have to do. I needed to suck it up and play the cards I'd been dealt.

"Damn right, I'm right. You need to protect yourself, Cade, but you need to protect her too."

"Her?" I asked.

"Aria. I know you were there when she had that meltdown in her apartment. You heard the shit she said." A muscle in his jaw ticked. "I don't know the ins and outs, but from what I can see, she's fuckin' lost." He paused and pointed at me as he stood. "But you can't be the one to make her find her way. You gotta cut your losses, for her sake and yours."

He flung some money on the table and pushed the stool back under it, then sauntered away without another word. He'd thrown so much shit at me in such a small amount of time, but he was right.

I needed to protect her too, even if that meant pushing her so far away she'd never be able to come back.

Chapter Three

ARIA

We'd been living in the new house for a few weeks, and we had yet to have a family dinner here. Mom and Sal had been too busy finishing the decor and organizing everything to do with the new diner and new house, so I'd barely seen them.

I wished I could say it was a change, but it wasn't. The only difference was the family dinners not happening. But as I walked into the house, the smell of a pot roast drifted toward me, and my stomach growled.

"Aria? Is that you?" Mom called.

"Yeah!" I placed my bag at the bottom of the stairs and ambled through the living room and the into kitchen adjoining it. "What are you doing?" I asked Mom.

She spun around, and I widened my eyes at her. Her hair was a mess, her cheeks flushed, and she had…

Was that flour on her apron? And why the heck was she wearing an apron?

"I'm cooking family dinner," Mom said as if it were obvious. And when I glanced around, I saw that it *was* obvious, but the last time she'd cooked, she'd burn everything to a crisp and Sal had told her she had a skill for cremating things.

"Should you really be trying to cook?" I asked her with raised brows, silently reminding her of the last time.

"Hey!" She pointed the spatula at me. "This is going to be delicious, and if it's not, then you and Sal will still eat it. Okay?"

I held my hands up in surrender, a smile flashing on my face. "Okay." Simply having her home was enough to make me feel less alone.

We hadn't really spoken since we'd moved out of the apartment other than the usual good mornings and good nights when we saw each other in passing. But now we were having an actual conversation, and it felt good.

Until she said, "Why are you home so early?"

And just like that, the smile dropped from my face. I backed away a step. "Cade canceled practice. Something about him needing to attend a meeting."

"Oh." Mom frowned and started to turn back to

the stove but then paused. "Do you call him Cade at school?"

"No." I pushed up onto one of the breakfast stools lining the counter. "I call him Mr. Easton or Coach. Why?"

Mom shrugged and finally turned completely back to the stove. "Just wondered. You two seem to have gotten really close lately."

My breath stalled in my chest, my throat burning at what she was saying. "No more than we used to be," I told her, my voice breaking. I was trying to keep up pretenses, but I was afraid she'd see through all my cracks. Keeping a secret had never been tough for me, but this one was getting harder and harder the more time went on.

"Right," Mom said, but she didn't look at me. She kept her focus on what was in front of her. "How has school been this week after…" She trailed off, but I knew what she was asking: after I got suspended. I wasn't really sure how she felt about what had happened with Jasmine, but that was the crux of it all. She pushed things down and hid things, exactly like I did. I'd learned from the best, and I'd perfected it.

"Good," I said as the front door opened and closed. Footsteps pounded through the house, and then Sal walked into the kitchen, his eyes narrowed on Mom.

"Are you cooking, Jan?" he asked in his gruff

voice and halted near me at the counter. His gaze slid to mine, silent concern echoing in his eyes. We both knew what a disaster Mom was in the kitchen.

"I am." She twirled around, her lips flashing him a bright smile. I couldn't remember the last time I'd seen her smile like that. I couldn't remember the last time *I'd* smiled like that. I didn't take my eyes off them as they continued to talk, but I wasn't really listening, I was watching them. Each one of their movements, each spark of their eyes, each smile. Was that how Cade and I had looked at each other before everything exploded in our faces? Did he stare at me like Sal was at my mom right now?

My stomach dropped, and my hands started to shake. I wasn't sure I'd ever be looked at like that again—not now, not after everything that had happened. I wouldn't be stared at like I was the only person in the room. I wouldn't be held like I was a precious diamond.

I was too broken, and all anyone would want to do was fix me. Cade hadn't, though. He hadn't wanted to mend a single piece of me, he'd just… promised to be there. But now he couldn't be. I'd put a stop to it the second I took the blame for the kiss in his classroom.

"Ri?" Sal's gruff voice pushed through my thoughts, and I blinked. How many times had he called my name? I glanced up at him and realized both he and Mom were staring at me. "You okay, Ri?" he asked, a frown marring his brow. He was concerned, and I wasn't surprised. I'd let loose the day we'd moved here. I'd exposed pieces of myself I'd never be able to get back, but I'd do what I always did—pretend I hadn't done it.

"Yeah." I pushed off the stool. "I was just thinking about a paper I have to write."

Sal tilted his head. He was trying to analyze me, but it wouldn't work. My wall was steel enforced and impossible to get by.

"Can you set the table, honey?" Mom asked. "Dinner is almost ready." I glanced at her. She knew I was lying—only liars could spot liars—but she wouldn't say anything. She never said anything. I wasn't sure what was worse: having her not confront me because she didn't want to bring the past up, or having her stay silent when I was falling apart inside.

There was nothing I could do about it now, though. It was how we were. I walked across the kitchen and collected everything I needed to set the table: cutlery, placemats, glasses, water. The task consumed me, taking all of my attention and letting me forget about everything else going on around me.

By the time the table was set, Mom was dishing up our dinner, and then we were all sitting around it for the first time as a family. Sal and Mom continued to talk as I dug into the food. It wasn't bad considering Mom had cooked it, but I thought anything would have tasted good since I'd forgotten to eat lunch.

I caught bits and pieces of their conversation: the new diner, the wedding plans. Mom talked nonstop, and I was kind of glad she did. At least that way I didn't have to say anything. I'd get by unscathed and retreat to my bedroom as soon as I could. And once I was there, I could find the relief I so desperately needed.

"What time did you say we had to meet them, Sal?" Mom asked, and I lifted my head after taking my last mouthful of food. It would only be minutes until I was alone again.

"Seven." Sal lifted his cell. "In an hour."

Mom leaned back in her seat and bit down on her bottom lip. "Do you want to come with us, Aria?"

"Come where?"

"To the new diner. We have to meet the contractor to talk about the plans. I thought you might want to come and see it."

"I…" I shuffled on my seat, willing to feel the wince from the cut several days ago, but it was nonexistent now. It had disappeared, and it made my breath catch. I needed to feel it. I needed the physical pain to center me and get me through the day. "I have a paper to write," I blurted out and stood. I took my plate to the sink. "I'll do the dishes while you're gone." I didn't wait for either of them to say anything as I rushed out of the kitchen.

I grabbed my bag from the bottom of the stairs and then took them two at a time. My ears buzzed the closer I got to my bedroom, and by the time I closed the door behind me and sat on the bed, the world was spinning.

My hands shook as I pulled my jeans off and placed them on the bed next to me. I could just barely hear Mom and Sal talking downstairs as I reached into my bag where I'd been keeping my case. I fumbled with the zip and sighed when I got it fully open. The row of razors had my breath slowing down, and once I plucked the first blade out, I already felt better.

I focused entirely on the blade and my legs as I sat on the edge of the bed and parted my legs. Cordoning off a section of skin on my thigh, I pressed the blade to my skin, about to puncture it when a knock sounded on my bedroom door.

"Aria?" Mom asked, but I didn't shift from my position. I couldn't move the sharp metal away, not now that I was so close to feeling the pain it would cause. I couldn't give it up. "We're heading out. We should be back around ten."

"Okay," I croaked out, only loud enough for her to hear through my closed door. I put more pressure on the blade and closed my eyes as it finally pierced my skin.

"You okay in there, honey?" Mom asked, her voice now a little closer.

"Yeah," I told her, knowing my voice didn't sound normal. I was getting a high as the blade scratched along my skin, and I couldn't look away when the bright red started to flow out of the cut. "Just getting changed," I said as an afterthought, my attention solely on the blood.

"Right." I heard Mom clear her throat. "I'll see you later then?"

"Bye," I whispered as the echo of her feet sounded across the hallway. I let the blood drip down my leg, watching it with fascination until it hit my ankle. The front door closed, an engine roared to life, and yet, I couldn't stop. I allowed the blood to hit my carpet, knowing it would stain, but not caring. I was doing a lot of that lately—not caring. Until it came to Cade.

I closed my eyes and wished I hadn't because the first thing that appeared was his face. *His handsome, chiseled face.* He'd once asked me to reach out to him when I felt the need to cut, but that had disappeared along with everything else. Now my only salvation was the blade I held in my hand and the pain it could cause.

My fingers trembled as I cleaned the razor off on my jeans next to me, and my breath stalled in my chest when I placed it back in my case. I usually felt a little better after I'd cut, but there was something different this time. Energy buzzed through my body as I stood, and my attention zoned in on the stain on the carpet. The urge to clean it was overwhelming. I hadn't cared while I was cutting, but now it was the only thing consuming me. I had to make it disappear, so I rushed downstairs and grabbed all the cleaning supplies I could manage in one trip.

My legs were exposed, with small trails of blood still trailing down the skin, but there was no one around to see. I had to get this blood out of the carpet no matter what. The stain had to be invisible, so I sprayed it with bleach, and put every ounce of effort into scrubbing.

I kept my gaze fixated to the spot, using both hands to grip the sponge I was using. Bleach permeated through the air and stung my eyes, but I simply sprayed more so the stain would leave.

A door banged shut somewhere, voices and footsteps echoing throughout the house. Someone called my name, and I wasn't even sure I answered them, all I knew was that the stain was now gone, but the rest of my room needed to match the cleanliness of this spot. Maybe that was what I needed to feel comfortable in this new room? Maybe I needed to cleanse it, just like I cleansed myself of all my thoughts.

Time started to move in chunks. I stripped my

bed, cleaned all my furniture, pulled all my clothes out and reorganized them into acceptable piles. I scrubbed the walls and left watermarks all over them. But I didn't care. All that mattered was cleaning my room and making sure it was acceptable for…

I blinked, the fog clearing as the sun started to rise. Birds chirping and singing echoed through my open bedroom window. I stared down at my hands, the red skin peeling in places from all the bleach I'd used. A breath left me in a puff of air as I spun around on the spot and stared at my half-clean room. I'd made a pile in one corner of things I hadn't gotten around to, or that just didn't fit inside my drawers. I had a mismatched room, half pristine and half a mess, and it was now morning.

I'd been up all night, and I didn't even remember most of it. And now footsteps were sounding out inside the house, and it would only be a matter of time before Mom and Sal left for work.

The cloth I'd been using dropped from my hand, falling to the floor like a flag at the start of a race. My shoulders slumped, tiredness setting in at a rapid pace. My legs carried me to my unmade bed, and as soon as my body dropped onto it, my eyes closed. For the first time in what felt like forever, the thoughts in my head were silent, and I fell to sleep with a small smile on my face.

CADE

Two weeks had flown by since Willow had walked into my classroom and witnessed Aria and me kissing. I'd been trying to keep her at arm's length, hoping she'd forget about the date I'd promised her. I didn't want to take her out, but it didn't mean I had a choice in the matter.

Aria hadn't spoken a word to me. Not in class, and never when we saw each other in the hallways. I'd tried to keep distance between us so I wasn't tempted, which meant I hadn't been over to my dad's house. It left me alone more often than not, and alone was never a good place for me. I overthought everything, but worse than that, I relived memories, memories of Aria and me. Remembering the way her lips had felt against mine. Hearing the echo of her laugh. Seeing the smile on her face. It never stopped, and part of me didn't want it to.

But I couldn't think like that, not when I was waiting for her to come out onto the track. I hadn't been alone with her since that day in the classroom, and I needed to hear her voice. I needed to make sure she was okay.

I leaned against the metal fence surrounding the track and kept my attention on the doors to the building. Finally, she came out with Reagan beside her. She wore her dark-blue athletic leggings with a tank top, but it was her hair thrown up into a bun on top of her head that held my attention. The closer she got, the more I couldn't stop staring.

I'd pressed my lips against that neck. I'd pushed my face into the crook. I'd tasted—

"Hey, Coach," Reagan said, and I darted my gaze to her.

I had to stop. But I couldn't. *Fuck.*

"Afternoon, ladies." I took a breath and looked over at Aria, surprised by the small smile on her face. Maybe this wouldn't be as bad as I thought. Maybe I'd built it up in my head to make it become something it wasn't.

"Coach," her soft voice greeted, but there was something I couldn't put my finger on. She didn't sound like her, she almost sounded *too happy*.

"You both ready to practice?" I asked, trying to fill the time. I didn't know what I was doing. I usually barked orders at them, telling them what they needed to work on, and then we'd get on with it, but today I felt the need to get Aria to talk. I needed to hear her voice and have her eyes focused on me, even if it was only for a little while.

"Yep," Reagan said as Aria nodded.

I begged her with my eyes to give me more. Say something, do something, anything to make me feel like I wasn't losing my mind any longer, but all she graced me with was her small smile.

"Should we warm up?" Reagan asked.

"Yeah." I blew out a breath and glanced over at her, finally breaking eye contact with Aria. I'd never felt as empty as I did at that moment. There was always something keeping me tied to her, something pulling on the end of the rope, but now…

Now it was lost on the wind, never to be found again.

They both backed away and started to jog around the track as I tried to get my thoughts in order. I'd pushed everything aside the last couple of weeks so I could wade through what was happening, but I hadn't gotten anywhere. No reasoning or solutions had magically appeared, which meant I was in the exact same position I was from the moment we'd gotten caught.

I stared at Aria as she started her first of five full laps to try and get her times down, and realized how well she was taking all of this. She'd managed to push everything we had to the side and keep surviving, but that was what she did best—she always pushed through, determined to come out on the other side. Maybe it was time for me to do the same?

"There you are!" I winced at the brash sound of Willow's voice and pulled in a sharp breath. There wasn't any escaping her. I'd managed to avoid her as much as possible, but I knew she would only sit back for so long. She held my life in the palm of her hand, I knew it, but most importantly, *she* knew it.

"Hey," I said, pulling my lips up into a smile as I turned to face her. She swayed her hips as she sauntered toward me, her tight skirt leaving little to the imagination.

"Hey yourself," she purred, coming to a stop a couple of feet away from me. She fluttered her lashes and placed her hand on my chest, and I couldn't help but glance over at Aria. She wasn't watching us, though. Her attention was solely on the track in front of her and the beat of her feet as they pounded the ground.

My skin crawled, my fingers twitching with the need to get her hand off me, but I knew I couldn't. I had to play this game with her, at least until I could find a way to win. The problem was, I wasn't sure there was one. She held all the cards, and I was fuckin' helpless.

"What are you doing out here?" I asked. I tried to sound casual, but I had a feeling I wasn't coming across like that at all. My acting skills were awful, and if I wanted to not have my life completely crushed, I needed to hone in on them and make them the best they could be.

She shrugged, acting at ease, but I could tell she wasn't that at all. "Just thought I'd come and say hey." She turned a little, looking out on the track. "I didn't realize Aria Sayer was on the track team."

Her voice had changed. Gone was the sweet and innocent Willow she tried to portray, and in its place the true version of her. The one who let her anger show in her voice. The one who wanted what she wanted, no matter the cost.

"Yeah." My nostrils flared, anger coursing through my veins at having to explain myself to her. "She and Reagan have the best track times in the school."

"Hmmm." She paused, and we both watched as Aria sped up for her last lap. Her arms pumped in time with her knees, her gait getting better and better the quicker she ran. "I'm sure Jasmine tried out for track too."

"She did," I grunted.

"Well?" I glanced at Willow and raised a brow in question. "Why didn't she make the team?"

"Because her lap was a minute longer than both Reagan's and Aria's."

Willow's eyes narrowed on me, and I could tell by the flat line of her lips she wasn't happy with my answer, but it was only the truth. I hadn't allowed Aria on the team because of what had happened with us. She was on the team because she deserved to be there. Period.

"Coach?" Reagan called, slowing down and coming to a stop. "I beat my time by half a second."

"Well done." I high fived her, and Reagan

grinned at me. "Stretch out and cool down. I'll be over there in a second."

She nodded and moved into the middle of the field. After practice, I usually talked to them separately about their times and the way to improve them, but they were level pegging now, and after what had happened with Aria, I knew I had to switch things up. So I planned to talk to them together, at least that way we would be safe from any…*mishaps*.

"I better head—"

"The date, Cade," Willow interrupted, her voice demanding. "You said you would take me out on a date, but you're going back on your word." A sweet smile pulled at Willow's lips, and my stomach sank. "I can go back on my word too, you know."

I knew what she was saying. There was no way I could get out of this. Ford was right, I didn't have a choice. "Saturday?" I asked, stepping away from the fence and catching sight of Aria walking toward Reagan with her hands on her hips. "I'll pick you up at eight?"

"Make sure you do." She spun around and then paused to look back at me. "I'll message you my address. Don't be late."

I didn't say another word, and I didn't take my eyes off her as she walked toward the building. I didn't trust to have my back to her. She was a snake, and I had no way of getting away from her—not yet at least.

Shaking my head when she was out of sight, I turned on my heels and headed toward the girls. They were both stretching out on the grass, talking, but when I halted a few feet away, they went silent. "Well done today," I said to both of them. "We need to up our practices, so I'm going to add another day."

"Another day?" Reagan asked. "Why?"

I crouched down in front of them and let my arms rest on my thighs. "I've heard some chatter about track meets. I don't have anything concrete yet, and as soon as I do, I'll let you know, but in the meantime, we need to get those times locked down and your endurance up just in case. Does Friday after school work for you both?"

"Fine with me," Reagan said, stretching her leg out in front of her and reaching for her toes.

"Good." I glanced at Aria, but she wasn't looking at me. She was staring down at the grass between her open legs, mid-stretch. "Aria?" She didn't move a muscle to indicate she'd heard me, just kept staring. "Aria?" I repeated.

"Huh?" Her head whipped up, her gaze clashing with mine. There was a fraction of a second where I saw something swirling in her eyes and then...

Nothing.

It was gone, almost as if it wasn't there in the first place.

"I asked if you're okay adding a Friday practice after school?"

She blinked and pulled her legs together. "Yeah, I'm good with that."

"Okay," I said.

"Okay," she repeated, but neither of us looked away. We were caught in a stare-off, but I wasn't sure what she was seeing when she looked at me. Did she see the man who thought the world of her? The man who had fallen head over heels for her? The man who had promised so many things? Or did she see the man who let her take the blame? The man who let her walk away and didn't fight for her?

I should have fought for her.

I knew what I saw when I stared at her: nothing. I saw nothing behind her beautiful eyes. Not a spark, not an inkling of how she was feeling, just a whole lot of emptiness. Was she hiding it from me, or was she protecting herself? I wasn't sure, but either way, there wasn't a thing I could do to find out.

We'd drawn the line—a line we couldn't cross no matter what.

I cleared my throat and looked away from her, intent on getting her out of my head any way possible. Maybe going on a date with Willow would be a good thing. Maybe having her fill some of my head-space would erase Aria.

But as she stood and walked across the field with Reagan, she turned her head to look at me, and I knew it would never happen. I couldn't erase her because she was a part of me. A part buried so deep nothing could eradicate it.

———

ARIA

I was trying to get back to my routine—the one I'd had before Cade—and part of it was babysitting Belle and Asher as much as possible. Now that we lived so close, I could be there earlier and leave later, but going to the house Cade had spent years growing up in—and where he still had a bedroom—wasn't exactly escaping him.

But somehow, I felt more at ease. Like the thought of him turning up anytime made me feel safer. It was one thing Cade had never failed to make me feel: safe. He was a master at calming my inner worries, and now that he wasn't around in any capacity other than being my teacher and coach, they were going haywire.

I'd gotten so used to the way I felt and the way I coped, that having Cade come and change it up was a relief. But now the relief was gone, and things were getting…worse. Each day was a battle I had to wage, and when night fell, I almost always lost it.

Today wasn't any different. I'd gone to school, followed by another track practice Cade had added to our schedule, and then right to Uncle Brody and Lola's. Lola was pulling into the driveway when I turned the corner to their street, and by the time I was walking up the drive, she was opening the back door for the kids to get out of the car.

"Aria!" Belle shouted and darted toward me, her hands outstretched. I didn't think twice about wrapping my arms around her and lifting her up off the ground. "I missed you!"

"I missed you, too!" Asher shouted, wiggling out of Lola's arms and then running toward me too. I barely stayed upright as he bashed into my legs.

"I missed you guys, too," I said, a lump forming in my throat. I hadn't seen them since the classroom incident, too afraid I'd cause more trouble, but it wasn't until this moment I realized I shouldn't have done that. It had been two weeks, and so far, Cade was still working at the school and wasn't being carted away to jail, which meant Miss Simmons had believed me.

I'd seen her around him more, especially at practice on Wednesday. I hated the way she smiled at him, but more than that, I detested the way he grinned back at her. It was too much to bear, so I pushed all the feelings down, along with everything else.

"Hey, I want in this group hug, too!" Lola shouted, her heels clicking on the driveway as she walked toward us. She wrapped her arms around all three of us and sighed. "Ahh, that feels better." Her hazel eyes met mine. "We all missed you, sweetheart."

"I'm sorry," I whispered. "I've…I had some things going on."

"You don't have to explain," Lola said, pulling back a little. "But if you want to talk, you know I'm here, right?"

I nodded and swallowed. I did know she was there, but I wouldn't even know where to start. She'd never look at me the same, none of them would. I wouldn't be Aria the quiet one. I'd become Aria the delicate one, or even worse, Aria the crazy one.

"I'm hungry," Asher groaned and squirmed away from our group hug. "Mommy, I want juice and chips."

Lola raised her brow and whispered, "He's so much like his dad." She rolled her eyes and turned to follow Asher. "Don't you mean: Mommy, may I have some juice and chips, please?"

I heard his huff as I took Belle's hand and together we walked up the driveway toward the front door. "May I have some juice and chips, please, Mommy?"

"Why, yes, Asher, you may have some juice and chips." Lola grinned wide at him and unlocked the door, and I couldn't help but smile at them. This was always the one place I could come to for refuge, and that was part of the reason why I'd been staying away. It was easier to wallow in sorrow than to pull yourself out of it.

Once we were inside, Lola set Asher and Belle up with a snack and let them watch TV. I wasn't sure if Uncle Brody and Lola were going out tonight now that I was here, but either way, I wanted to be here.

"Uncle Brody is on his way home," Lola commented as she opened the refrigerator door. She pulled out a couple of bottles of water and handed one to me. "We have about fifteen minutes of girl time." Lola raised her brow and leaned against one of the counters in her huge kitchen. "So, talk."

My eyes widened, and I cleared my throat. What did she want me to talk about? Surely she didn't know something was happening with Cade. What girl time were we meant to be having? I—

"Aria." Lola chuckled and took a swig of her water. "Don't look so scared. I just want to know what's been happening these last couple weeks. It's been weird without you coming by all the time."

"I…" I let out a breath and looked out into the

backyard. The last time I'd been out there was the night I'd stayed at Cade's. The same night I'd given him a piece of me no one else had. And then it had all disappeared, just like everything else in my life. "I've been adjusting to the new house."

"It can be jarring to move out of the home you lived in for so long and into somewhere new. I get that." I glanced over at her, but she was staring into the backyard too. "The house I lived in after my mom died was full of memories, mainly bad ones, but it was still sad to leave it behind when I moved here." She shrugged and looked at me. "It's hard to leave things like that behind."

I blinked, not sure what to say. "It is hard." I pulled in a deep breath. "Mom is hardly home, Sal either."

Lola frowned. "So you're home alone most nights?"

I shrugged, acting like it didn't matter. "It's nothing new. It's been like this for years. It's just I'm not used to having a big house all to myself."

"You know you can stay here anytime, right? You can sleep in Cade's room."

My heart started to race, and I tried to keep my features schooled. There was no way I could stay in his room, not after everything that had happened. It would be too much, too raw. I couldn't do it, but I wouldn't tell Lola that. Instead, I said, "Thanks."

"Sweetheart, are you sure there's nothing else—"

"Dad's home!" Belle shouted. Her footsteps pounded across the house, and the whoosh of the front door opening rang out. "Ford is here too!"

I wasn't sure how to act or what to say. The last time I'd seen Ford was when I was in the hospital. I waited with bated breath as the sounds in the house got louder, and when Lola exited the kitchen, I stayed put. I couldn't move my feet, no matter how hard I tried. I'd made a mistake coming here. I should have stayed away, at least until everything settled down, but now I was going to have to face Ford, knowing he knew what Cade and I had done.

It was too much. The weight of an elephant was on my chest, and I wasn't sure when the last full breath I had taken was. I needed to breathe. I needed to center myself. I needed…

I needed to leave.

I needed to get out and get home, but when footsteps neared the kitchen, I didn't have time to escape unnoticed.

"Hey, baby girl," Uncle Brody's deep voice greeted. He wrapped his arms around me, and I allowed him to pull me to his chest. I couldn't speak, afraid of what would tumble out of my mouth if I opened it. "You're staying for dinner, yeah? Gonna get takeout."

"I vote pizza!" Ford shouted, causing Belle to groan.

"You always vote pizza," Belle whined. "It's boring to always have pizza."

"Nu-uh," Ford replied. "Pizza is always a good choice, Baby Belle."

We weren't the only ones in the kitchen now, but I had yet to move away from Uncle Brody's chest. I was scared to death they'd all witness me falling apart. "Hey," Uncle Brody whispered and pulled away. He grabbed my chin and forced my gaze to his. "What's going on? You're shaking."

"I…need the bathroom," I managed to croak out and pulled away from him. The kitchen spun as I stepped toward the door, faces blurring, voices fading. I was losing my bearings, and there was only one way I could get them back: cutting.

Chapter Four

CADE

Part of me had wanted to be a couple of minutes late for the date, if only to show Willow I didn't adhere to her demands, but I knew it wouldn't bode well for me. I had a feeling she wouldn't be patient much longer.

The jeans and T-shirt I'd thrown on were a definite rejection to her. She was expecting this to be a proper date, and for all intents and purposes, it would be, but I wouldn't dress like I wanted to impress her. There was only one woman I wanted to impress, and it was the one I couldn't have.

I pulled up outside her house at two minutes to eight and turned the engine off. I spotted a curtain twitching in one of the living room windows, no doubt making sure I turned up. Inhaling a deep breath, I pushed out of the car, but hadn't even made it to the end of the path leading to her front door when it swung open.

"You're here," Willow sang, almost as if she hadn't expected me to turn up. It crossed my mind what she'd actually do if I hadn't. Would she have gone to the principal? The police? Even if they didn't have any evidence—which I had no idea what they could unearth if they were really trying—it would still be a black mark against my name.

A black mark I'd never be able to scrub clean.

"I am," I said, pulling a smile onto my face as she walked toward me on heels so high I had no idea how she was managing to balance. I glanced down at the red, tight dress she wore, but I didn't feel a thing. This time last year, if I'd have seen that on a woman, it would have been my mission to view it on my bedroom floor, but now…now I was indifferent. I wasn't sure what was worse: feeling a certain emotion toward something, or feeling nothing at all.

I pulled the passenger door open for her, and she gripped my hand as she slid into the car, staring up at me like I was her Prince Charming. Was she really so clueless?

Slamming her door shut, I closed my eyes, and took a breath. I wasn't sure how I would get through tonight. I wasn't good at sheltering my emotions or schooling my features, but I needed to become better at it; otherwise, this wouldn't end well.

Neither of us spoke as I drove. Luckily, it was only fifteen minutes until I was pulling up outside the restaurant and parking in an empty space. The growl of the engine and low music I'd had playing stopped as I turned the engine off, basking us in silence. I waited a beat, trying to pull myself together fully, and then exited the car.

I walked around to the passenger side and opened her door. I held my hand out to help her out. She didn't let go of it when I shut the door, and even though I wanted to move my hand away from hers, I didn't. I needed to put an act on. I had to give her the date she wanted. Maybe that way she'd be satisfied and I could put all of this behind me.

Her heels clicked on the sidewalk as we walked toward the restaurant, and I glanced over at her. She came up to my shoulder, taller than Aria, and I cursed myself for comparing the two. Aria was small and delicate, whereas Willow was harsh and in your face. It wasn't only that, though. It was the history. Aria and I had a weaved web, but Willow and I were just colleagues.

Willow stared up at me as I pulled open the door to the restaurant, her smile showing her teeth. "Thank you." I nodded in reply and let go of her hand as we entered.

The restaurant was full to bursting, exactly like I

hoped it would be on a Saturday night. At least with other people around to distract us, we wouldn't have to share too much conversation—I hoped.

We were shown to a table toward the back and placed between another two couples who also looked like they were on dates. Part of me wanted to ask to be seated in the area it looked like had been cornered off for families, but I refrained and sat down.

I was acting like an asshole not pulling her chair out and not asking what she wanted to drink before I ordered myself a beer. I wasn't here because I wanted to be, and I wanted Willow to know that. She could slap her makeup on her face all day long and wear the tightest clothes she could, it wouldn't make a difference to me. I still wouldn't want her. But I had to walk a fine line. If I let my true feelings show, it could all be over within seconds, and then I'd be truly fucked.

The waitress handed us the menu, and I read over every item twice, trying to distract myself long enough to hone in on what I had to achieve tonight. I needed to get Willow off my back, but also Aria's. She could turn our lives upside down with only a few words, and I couldn't forget that.

I ordered a pasta dish while Willow ordered a salad—who the hell ordered salad at an Italian restaurant? Once our drinks were placed in front of us—beer for me and wine for her—we had nothing to occupy our attention which meant…

"So, Cade, tell me how you became a teacher."

It was the obligatory get-to-know-you question, but I found myself not wanting to answer it, and it was so much more than just explaining it to her. It was revealing parts of me I didn't want to reveal—at least, not to her anyway.

"I was a lacrosse coach back in college, and I found a love for it."

"So it's coaching you prefer?" she asked, leaning forward in her seat and taking a sip of her wine. Her lipstick left a mark around the rim of the glass, and I couldn't help sneer at it.

"Yeah," I replied, I knew I needed to say something else, but I was falling flat. I wasn't usually this bad at conversation, but apparently my body and brain refused the idea of Willow sitting opposite me. "What about you?"

Her face lit up, her smile growing even more, and I realized this was what she wanted. She wanted me to ask her questions so she could tell me all the things she could about herself. At that moment, a light bulb went off in my head—the perfect way to keep her occupied: let her talk about herself.

"Well, I went to college when I was seventeen after graduating early, but I always knew what I wanted to be." I nodded like I understood her. "A principal."

I blinked, not having expected her to say that. Who goes into this job not wanting to teach kids but to just run a school? "Oh, so, you never wanted to teach?"

"God, no." She waved her hand in the air as if she was swatting away a fly. "I can't deal with a classroom full of kids who don't want to learn. I'd rather be in a beautifully decorated office running the entire school."

"Right." I tried to keep the grin off my face, but it was impossible. I was sure she thought I was grinning at her, but it was so far from the truth. I was grinning at the absurdity of it. "And you're on track to do that?" I asked, glancing around and wondering when our food would be here. The quicker it came, the sooner I could drop her home and then go and open a six-pack of beer and watch TV.

"I was." She sighed and took another drink of her wine, nearly emptying the glass. "Until Jasmine moved in with me."

"Oh?" I was giving her just enough to keep her talking about herself.

"Yeah." She rolled her eyes and looked so much like her sister doing it that I raised my brows. "She got into some trouble at home last year, so Mom and Dad kicked her out, which meant she had to come and stay with me. Not that I can control what she does— she basically uses my house as a hotel." She blew out a breath and drank the last of her wine as our plates were set on the table in front of us. "Can I have a refill?" she asked the waiter, and he nodded in reply.

I stared down at my pasta dish, groaning at the smell of the creamy sauce and pasta combination.

"What about you?" Willow asked, impaling her fork on some lettuce leaves. "Do you have any siblings."

I twirled my fork into my pasta. "A brother and a sister," I told her and then filled my mouth with my food. The creamy sauce tickled my taste buds and the pasta was perfectly cooked. The food would definitely be the highlight of my evening.

"Really?" I could hear her crunching on her salad, but I didn't take my eyes off my pasta. "I'd have pegged you for an only child."

It was on the tip of my tongue to tell her I'd lived the first sixteen years of my life as an only child, but that would mean giving her more infor- mation about me, and that was something I didn't want to do. "Nope," I said instead, and looked up at her. "My sister is eight, and my brother is four. They're cool kids."

Willow grimaced, and I had no doubt she didn't think any kind of kids were cool. She hadn't met them yet, though—and if I had my way, she never would. "That's…nice."

I hummed in agreement and shoveled more pasta into my mouth, trying to think of anything I could ask her to keep her talking, but I was coming up empty. I was quickly finding out that I wasn't the best conversationalist, and it was completely fucking me over. Why the hell couldn't I push everything aside and pretend I was on a real date?

Placing the last forkful of pasta into my mouth, I then leaned back in my seat and closed my eyes. There was nothing that compared to the feeling pasta gave you. It almost always made me want to take a nap.

"You looked like you enjoyed that," Willow commented, and when I opened my eyes, she was smiling at me. She was beautiful, there was no denying it. Her almond-shaped eyes were bright and wide, and her small straight nose led down to full lips painted red, but…she just wasn't for me.

"I did," I told her, smiling back. "How's yours?"

"Delicious," she said, and the way she said it made me wonder if she really meant it. She was staring at my empty bowl with envy. If Aria had been here, she'd have had the pasta without a second thought, and she wouldn't have worried about the bloating sure to come afterward. Nope, she'd just eat what she wanted and not have a care in the world.

My stomach dipped, my palms starting to sweat. I shouldn't be thinking about Aria while on a fake-date with Willow—I shouldn't have been thinking about her period. But it was so goddamn hard to get her off my mind. An impossible task.

Willow finished off her salad while I nursed my beer, and when the waitress came back and asked if we'd like to see the dessert menu, Willow declined. I was glad she didn't want dessert, but my stomach didn't fully agree.

"Are you ready to go?" I asked, surprised at how short this date had been.

Her eyes hooded, and she tracked her gaze over my chest and then back to my face. "I'm ready." Her voice was breathy, and I realized she thought we were going to be doing…something. She'd soon understand it would never happen, but for now, I paid the bill and walked us out of the restaurant.

The car ride back to her place was as quiet as it was on the way here, and when I pulled up into the same spot I had when I picked her up, I didn't turn the engine off.

She turned in her seat and drifted closer to me, and I resisted the urge to back away. "I had fun tonight."

"Me too." I swallowed and hoped like hell she didn't go in for a kiss. Instead of waiting to see if she did, I leaned forward and pressed one against her cheek.

"We should do this again," she whispered, and I wasn't sure if she was trying to sound sexy or shy, but neither one was working for her.

"Sure," I replied, being noncommittal.

Her lips spread into the widest grin. "Next Saturday then?"

"Ahhh." I gripped my steering wheel harder, trying to keep all my emotions at bay. "I have a family cookout next Saturday at my dad's place."

"Awesome!" She pushed the door open and got out. "I can't wait to meet your family." She slammed the door shut and left me staring after her, wondering what the hell had happened. Did she just invite herself to meet my family?

———

ARIA

"And he took me for pizza and then we walked and talked for hours. I swear to god, Aria, it was perfect. Just…perfect." Hope sighed and leaned against the locker next to mine. Her arms wrapped around the books she held to her chest as she stared upward, in a world of her own. She'd been telling me bits and pieces about her date throughout the day at every opportunity she had. "I think I'm in lust."

I raised my brows and shut my locker. "In lust?" I asked, sure she was making the statement up.

"Yep." She nodded repeatedly as she stared at me. "It's not quite love yet, but it could turn into it, and it's more than just liking someone. I'm in lust, dammit, Aria. Just be happy for me." The grin on her face was a complete contradiction to the words she was saying.

I held my hands up in surrender. "Okay, okay. You're in lust."

"Damn straight, I am." She pushed off the locker as the first bell rang for our last class of the day. "We're going out again this Saturday, but in a group. Want to come?"

I winced, thinking about what I had to do this weekend. "Can't. Family cookout."

Hope's eyes widened. "As in…" She lowered her voice and moved closer to me. "Cade's family?"

"Yep." I glanced over at his classroom door in time to see him pull it open and stand to the side as pupils filed in. "I gotta get to class. I'll message you after school."

I hurried away from her and tried to keep my gaze off Cade as she shouted, "You better, ho!"

I groaned and rolled my eyes at her words, waving at her in acknowledgment, and then entered the classroom. Cade's cologne wrapped around me, warming me in the same way a hug from him would, and I couldn't stop my lips from lifting. I may have been keeping my distance and trying to successfully put a front on for everyone I could, but

I couldn't deny the way I felt when I was around him.

Slipping into my seat, I pulled out my notepad and stared at the front of the classroom. Since everything had happened, this was my favorite class. Not track where I had to concentrate on my running, and not PE where we were surrounded by so many students, but my world history class.

Here, I could stare at him and have an excuse. Here, I could remember the way he'd crouched down in front of me and kissed me. Here, I could live in a fantasy land where everything was perfect. The hour class was my own slice of heaven, and no one could take it away from me.

I watched as Cade strolled up the aisles between the desks. I didn't look away when he turned to write something on the board attached to the wall near his desk, and I kept staring as he paced in front of the class and talked nonstop about the subject we were learning.

I made extensive notes, wanting to soak in each of his words, knowing this would soon be over. I'd be back to what my life now was, diving into the darkness with only a small light to keep it illuminated. Cade was that light, one I drifted toward but didn't get too close, afraid it would burn me.

In the space of such a small amount of time, we had been through so much, and yet, it wasn't enough. It would never be enough.

As if he could hear my thoughts, his stare met mine. At first, he moved his gaze past me but then swung it back, almost as if he was surprised I was staring at him. I hadn't allowed myself to really look into his eyes, not since we'd been caught, but weeks had passed, and things were getting worse without him in my life.

I needed his salvation, even if it was only his eyes focused on me.

From here, I could see the green specks sparking inside his dark-blue orbs. I could tell from the way they widened that he was shocked I didn't look away, and when he stumbled on his words a little, I couldn't help but smile. I was affecting him, just like he did to me.

"Open up your books to page two hundred and two," his gruff voice demanded, and murmurs spread around the room as everyone did. I had to look away to open up my book, and when I looked at the title, I realized we were about to have to read. "Josh?" I heard him say, but I was now focused on his voice instead of his face. "Read those two pages."

Josh was two seats in front of me, and cleared his throat then started to talk. I looked up, expecting to see Cade standing where he was before I'd looked down, but he wasn't there. I frowned but didn't have to look far. He was leaning against his desk, his arms crossed over his chest, and his attention fully focused on me.

My breath caught in my throat at the intensity showcased in his eyes, and I wasn't sure I'd be able to breathe if he kept staring at me like that. But I couldn't turn away. I couldn't bring myself to look anywhere but at him, and when his lips pulled up into the smile I'd only ever seen given to me, butter-flies swarmed in my stomach.

He was making me feel things again—things I had no right to feel—but I didn't have any control. I never had control when it came to Cade, and I was slowly starting to realize that.

I shuffled in my seat, but it wasn't like the last time I'd done it in here. I wasn't trying to feel the sharpness from another one of my cuts. I was turned on. Turned on and needing his touch like I needed my next breath.

My lips parted, a small gasp leaving them. His nostrils flared, a muscle ticking in his jaw, but it was his hooded eyes that told me he was turned on too. He was feeling the air swirling between us as well. My body begged me to stand and saunter toward him. It craved his touch more than anything else it ever had, but there was nothing I could do. Nothing I could say. Unless…

I pulled my hand across my chest, my palms connecting with my erect nipples, but I didn't take my gaze off his, not even when he looked down and saw the outline through my T-shirt. He stood suddenly, but I didn't stop.

"Read the next two pages, Josh," Cade demanded as he strolled around to his desk and sat on his chair. He pushed it under so I could only see his chest and one of his hands. His other arm disappeared under his desk, and I bit down on my bottom lip at the thoughts running through my head. Was he touching himself while staring at me? Was he thinking about the only night we'd had together? Did he remember the way his cock felt inside me?

I was turning myself on even more with each one of my thoughts, and before I knew it, my hand was between my legs over my jeans. I needed some relief from the tension building between us, and when he mouthed, "Touch yourself," I couldn't deny him.

My lashes fluttered, and it was a chore to keep my eyes open, but I managed to keep my stare connected with his. My gaze flicked to his shoulder that was moving ever so slightly, and I realized he was touching himself too.

We were surrounded by a class full of students, and yet, it didn't matter.

I pressed harder between my legs and moved my hand, the material rubbing me in just the right way. It wouldn't take long for me to lose myself completely, not while he was staring at me. My imagination was running away with me, envisioning what he was doing under his desk. Had he unzipped his pants and pulled his cock out, or was his hand down his pants as he rubbed himself up and down?

My breath caught and then left my mouth on a loud gasp, but I had no idea if anyone noticed, not when I couldn't look away from the stare Cade had locked me in. He'd let me go several times, but in the silence surrounding us, he wasn't prepared to do it this time.

I moved my hand faster, feeling like I was on the edge of a cliff, teetering and trying to keep myself upright, but I didn't want that. I wanted to fall. I wanted to experience the high only this could give me, but it was hard. It was hard to keep control and not shout out his name, especially when the burn started low in my stomach.

I dipped my head back and licked my lips, all the while not looking away, and then finally it hit me. Keeping my moan inside was a harder task than I'd thought it would be, but biting down on my lip as hard as I could kept it at bay.

"After the Mycenaean age ended in about 1100BC, Greece entered a Dark Age. It is known as a dark age because nobody knows much about what happened—all written language and art disap-peared," Josh's voice pushed through my haze.

My body vibrated, still not fully down from the

high as Cade's mouth parted, his body stilling, and I knew what he'd done too.

We'd not crossed the line I'd drawn, but we'd smudged it a little, and I couldn't bring myself to care one bit.

Chapter Five

ARIA

I pumped my arms harder, trying to even my breaths out as I prepared for the last lap. Since Cade had added a Friday practice to our schedules, he'd upped the amount of running we did, and it had helped me more than I ever thought possible.

My times were better, but more importantly, I wasn't nearly dead after each practice. I still had energy left. I still had more gas in the tank, which meant I was building up my stamina.

I could see Reagan a half a lap ahead of me, which meant I was technically overtaking her by half a lap. She'd started a lap before me, and I never beat her times, but if I nailed this last one, I would for the first time.

Tightening my core, I put more speed into my

legs and went for it. Everything tunneled, and all I could see was the lines on the track and the finish line in sight. No noises appeared, nothing cut through to me, and it was bliss. A bliss I hadn't felt for what felt like months. It was quiet, with no thoughts racing through my head.

My quads burned, my chest heaved, but I kept going until I crossed the finish line Cade was standing next to with Reagan, who had just finished. I slowed down, and everything came pounding back. The cheers ringing out, the smell of freshly cut grass in the air, and most importantly, my thoughts. They slung at me like an arrow at a target, and I stumbled from the impact.

I'd not been able to stop thinking about what I'd done in class yesterday. I'd leaped out of my chair and practically ran out of the school afterward, and I hadn't seen Cade until our PE class before track practice. But now we were nearing the end of practice, and I knew I'd have to look at him again.

I wasn't embarrassed by what I'd done, in fact, I craved to do it again, which was the problem. I couldn't allow myself to fall into the same space as before with Cade, not after what had happened. It felt like an impossible task, though.

"Hell yeah! You better run, girl!" Hope shouted, and I spun around, spotting her running down the bleachers. She didn't stop until she was on the track and wrapping her arms around me. "How did I not know you could run like that?"

My cheeks burned from her attention, and I shrugged. "You know I like to run."

"Not like that!" She raised her brows and widened her eyes. "What are you? Usain Bolt?"

"He's not a long-distance runner——"

She rolled her eyes and waved her hand in my face. "I know that, duh."

I grinned at her and shook my head. "What are you even doing here?"

She turned, and I followed her lead, spotting Reagan and Cade as they strolled toward us. "I wanted to see the two of you together in practice."

My eyes widened and I grabbed her arm. "He can't know you know, Hope," I whispered. I hadn't told her anything else since the day under the bleachers. She'd tried to get me to tell her stories and get information out of me about what he was like, but I kept my lips zipped. The less she knew about everything, the better.

"That was your best time yet, Aria." Cade grinned down at me, his face beaming with pride. "The extra work is paying off."

"It is," I answered, and Hope pushed her elbow into my side. I ignored her and kept my attention on him. "I better go cool down." I hooked my thumb over my shoulder and started to back away. He didn't say anything, simply watched me with his intense eyes. Why the hell was he so goddamn alluring?

"Aria?" Hope called, and I whipped my head around to face her. "You're gonna fall over." She tilted her head to something on the field, and I laughed then spun around. My face burned with embarrassment, and I had no doubt it was bright red. "Oh. My. God." Hope linked her arm with mine. "Did you see the way he was staring at you?" She sighed and placed her hand on her chest. "He looked like he wanted to eat you up."

"Hope," I groaned, hearing footsteps come closer. I glanced over my shoulder and spotted Reagan catching us up so I halted. "Don't say anything. Reagan doesn't know."

"Got it." Hope saluted me as I bent down, stretching out my muscles. "Hey, Reagan," I heard her say, and when I dipped my head to look up, I saw her holding her hand out to her. "I'm Hope, the best friend."

"I know," Reagan said, shaking her hand but frowning down at it as she did. She was baffled as most people were when they met Hope. "I'm the track partner."

"Cool, cool." Hope nodded several times and stared at nothing as we got down onto the grass to keep stretching.

"You just gonna watch us stretch, Hope?"

She shrugged. "Ain't got anything better to do.

My sister can't pick me up for another twenty minutes. She's got to get her vag pierced."

I choked on my own saliva and heard Reagan cough beside me. "What?"

"Her vag, Aria." Hope signaled between her legs. "She's gone to get it pierced."

"But…" I blinked several times, turned to look at Reagan to see if she was as confused as me—she was—and then looked back at Hope. "Why?"

"Beats me." She spun around on the spot and held her arms out. "Probably thinks it'll help her keep her boyfriend or something."

"That's—"

"Stupid," Hope interrupted. She stopped suddenly and darted toward me. "Does…you-know-who have anything pierced."

"Hope!" I let my head drop back and groaned. "Whether he does or doesn't is none of your business."

"But—"

"Nope." I stood and wiped the grass off the back of my legs. "I'm not telling you anything about him, end of—"

"Anything about who?" Cade's deep voice asked.

I turned slowly, wondering where the hell he'd appeared from, then opened my mouth to answer but Hope beat me to it, "Her boyfriend."

"Her…what?" Cade asked, his voice dangerously low.

Hope may have thought she was being clever, but she really wasn't. I didn't want to make him think I was dating anyone else. I didn't want to play games. It wasn't who I was, and Cade knew that—at least, I hoped he did.

"Ignore her," I said, pushing on Hope's shoulder. "Stop it," I whispered to her.

Cade's brows furrowed, but I couldn't think about why. Too many things were happening all at once, and I could only concentrate on one thing at a time, and right now that was getting Hope away from Cade, and me away from the both of them.

A car horn honked from the lot and Hope announced, "My ride is here! Catch you later. Have fun this weekend!" She wagged her brows up and down. I was so close to pushing her over, but she escaped from my reach before I could get to her.

We all watched her skip across the field, and when she was through the gate, I heaved a breath. "Sorry about her, she's a little—"

"Weird?" Reagan answered. "It's all good. Weird is my chi."

"I…" Had no idea how to answer that. "Right."

Reagan pulled her arms over her head and let out a breath to finish her stretching. "I won't be here next Wednesday, Coach," she directed at Cade. "I've got a doctor's appointment."

My stomach dropped at her words, and I tried to keep my features schooled. I couldn't be alone with Cade. There was no way I could do that and come out the other end okay. When Reagan was here, she was the buffer we both needed, but without her...

Without her, things wouldn't go well, not for either of us.

————

ARIA

"Come on, Aria, we're only waiting for you now!" Mom shouted up the stairs.

"Coming!" I resisted looking at myself in the mirror on the back of my bedroom door as I pulled it open and headed down the stairs where Mom and Sal were waiting to walk over to Uncle Brody and Lola's.

"What took you so long?" Mom asked, glancing over at me. Her brows rose at the black jeans and flowy camisole I had on. "You're wearing that? It's like a hundred degrees outside."

I shrugged, acting indifferent when I was anything but. She'd always bitched at me about wearing jeans in the summer, and sometimes she won the battle. Like when I'd worn a dress to the last cookout, but I couldn't do that this time.

A collection of new cuts marred my thighs and the side of my knees, and I wasn't sure I'd be able to cover them enough so no one would see. The last thing I needed was for everyone to find out what I was doing and how often I was doing it. Perfecting my mask was getting easier and easier, and not one person had noticed a crack as of yet. I intended to keep it that way.

"Go and get changed—"

"She's fine, Jan," Sal interrupted Mom. "Let's go, I'm starving."

"You're always starving," Mom replied and rolled her eyes, but the smile on her face could be seen from a mile away. She was happy, happier than I'd ever seen her, and I was glad. I truly was.

Sal locked the door behind us all, and I kept a couple of paces behind them on the walk to Uncle Brody and Lola's. Each step I took rubbed against my latest cut—the one I'd made just before leaving my bedroom. They probably thought I'd taken so long deciding on what I was wearing, but the reality was, I'd been too busy preparing myself for today.

In the back of my mind, I knew I'd taken things a step further. I was no longer cutting to find relief, but instead, I was cutting *just in case* I needed it. I'd gone over the edge, but I couldn't bring myself to care. I wasn't sure whether it was a problem in itself or not, but I wasn't going to overthink it, not when I was about to head into what felt like the lion's den.

Cade's car was parked at the curb, and as we walked past it, I couldn't help but stare. The last time I'd been sitting in his passenger seat was the morning after we'd had sex. I'd watched him drive, fascinated by each move he made, but also knowing deep down that something was about to go down.

Mom and Sal walked right into the house, and I trailed behind them, hearing the voices and laughter coming from the backyard. Maybe today would be good for me. Maybe having some time with the people who cared the most would bring me back from the brink. I needed to be positive. I needed to believe I could stop cutting at any time. I was only doing it for now. In a year or two, I wouldn't need to do it so often and—

"What the hell?"

I halted on the spot in the living room, the hairs on the back of my neck standing up. I couldn't have heard who I just heard. There was no way in hell she would be here, not after—

"What are you doing here?" she asked, her voice as sharp as a chef's knife.

My fingers twitched, my body not wanting to turn and face her, but I had no choice. "I'm here for the cookout," I croaked out, my voice betraying me as I looked at Miss Simmons.

"No, you're not. Leave. *Now*."

I shook my head and felt the burning on my cheeks. "What—"

"You heard me." She stepped toward me, and I flinched when her hand lifted, but all she did was point at me. "You don't belong here."

"Excuse me?" another voice asked, and my heart hammered in my chest. Footsteps neared us, but I was too afraid to look to see who it was. "You okay, Tyson?" Ford. It was Ford.

"I…" I stepped back and away from Miss Simmons and toward Ford. "Yeah, I'm okay." I wasn't okay. I was so far from okay it wasn't even funny.

Glancing up at Ford, I saw he had all of his attention on Miss Simmons. He narrowed his eyes, and I flicked my gaze to her to see what she was doing. Her red-painted lips were in a straight line, her hands on her hips, and her anger-filled eyes were focused on me.

We were in a three-way stare-off, but for some reason, I felt safe with Ford, so I stepped even closer to him. "I didn't know Miss Simmons would be here," I said to him.

"Of course I am." Miss Simmons scoffed. "Where else would Cade's girlfriend be?"

Girlfriend? She was his girlfriend?

"Oh! Aria, you're finally here," Lola's voice broke the stare-off, and she pushed through the middle of us and threw her arm over my shoulder. "Willow, I'd like to introduce you to my second daughter." Lola paused as I stiffened at the way

Miss Simmons' eyes were narrowed on me. "She's not technically my daughter, but she may as well be."

"How…lovely," Miss Simmons commented. Lola's brow rose, and she glanced at me, her eyes asking me what was going on, but it was yet another secret I had to keep. "I'll be heading back out to Cade now, excuse me." Miss Simmons sauntered away, and I couldn't help but stare at her as she flicked her hair over her shoulder.

"I do not like her," Lola ground out, pulling me closer to her. "She has that—"

"Bitch look?" Ford asked.

Lola clicked her fingers and pointed at him. "Exactly that." She let out a breath. "Anyway." She turned to face me. "Asher is taking a nap upstairs. Could you go and check on him while I finish off the side dishes?"

"I can do the sides," I told her.

"I got it." Lola pulled away and flashed me a beaming smile. "I just want to make sure he stays asleep for a little while. He was up during the night with a temperature."

"He was?" I frowned. "Is he okay now?"

"Yeah." Lola swiped her hand over her hair. "It broke at three this morning. I think I got about two hours' sleep last night." The bags under her eyes confirmed her lack of sleep.

"I'll go check on him," I told her, already

backing away to head up the stairs. I took them two at a time, gritting my teeth at the sharpness the stretch of my legs caused against my freshest cut. It was precisely what I needed at that moment, and enough to calm me down.

I couldn't believe Cade had brought Miss Simmons here. Was this a statement he was trying to make? Was he trying to tell me what happened in the classroom this week wouldn't happen again? Maybe it was all in my head. Maybe I'd imagined what we'd done.

My hand gripped the door handle to Asher's room, and I paused. I needed to stop thinking about any of it. It wouldn't do me any good, not while I was in a house full of people who couldn't find out.

I turned the handle and pushed all my thoughts aside as I entered Asher's room. Slowly and carefully, I crept across the floor toward his pirate bed and grinned. He was spread out like a starfish, his mouth wide open, heavy snores coming from him. I had no idea how such a little person could snore so loud, but he was managing it no problem.

He turned his head, and I froze, hoping I hadn't woken him up, but when the snoring started again, I knew I hadn't. I backed away and out of the room, then closed the door softly behind me. I could feel the smile on my face as I turned around, but it dropped as soon as I saw who was leaning against the hallway wall.

"Aria," Cade's deep voice said, but I shook my head. We couldn't be up here alone. He couldn't be here waiting for me.

"Leave me alone," I demanded. My voice betrayed me, the words coming out breathy and not at all how I'd meant them to sound. My feet carried me toward him, but I had every intention of ignoring him and going back downstairs.

I saw him push up off the wall out of the corner of my eyes and flinched when he reached for me. It was a gut reaction, one I hadn't meant, and one that caused me to halt in front of him.

"Just let me explain."

"Explain what?" I asked. "You don't have to explain anything to me." I dipped my head back to look up at him, trying not to search his eyes for anything, but I couldn't help myself. He was addicting, and I had no idea how to not need him. He fueled my every thought, and my brain was out of gas.

"I didn't invite her here."

I knew who *her* was, but I shrugged as if I didn't care. "I don't care."

"She just kind of…invited herself," he gritted out, and I looked away from him. I refused to allow him to see the hurt in my eyes. I didn't know why her being here stung so goddamn much. Maybe it was because she'd said she was his girlfriend. Or maybe it was because this had always been my safe haven. A safe haven that would be ripped away from me if she had anything to do with it.

"Was Hope telling the truth?" he blurted out. "Do you have a boyfriend?"

I scoffed and shook my head. "Of course I don't —unlike you who now has a girlfriend—Miss Simmons to boot." I was getting angry, and I needed to calm down. I couldn't let him see how bothered I was about it all. *Push it down, Aria. Push it all down.* I took a calming breath, pushed my shoulders back, and told him, "I'm leaving now," then stepped away from him.

This time, when his arm reached out and his hand gripped my wrist, I didn't flinch. If anything, I sighed from the way his palm whispered along the sensitive skin and wished he would never let go.

"Please wait…" My back was to him, but I heard and felt him shuffle closer. "I just need a second."

My breaths became heavier the longer we stood in the silent hallway, distant echoes of laughter being heard, but otherwise, it was only him and me. The last time we'd been alone, he'd kissed me…

I turned, my shoulder grazing against his chest because of how close he was, and my gaze flicked up to his lips.

"Don't do that," he groaned out, and I swear every hair on my body stood on end.

"Do what?" I asked, my voice so low I could

barely hear myself, especially over the pounding of my heart.

"Look at me like that." He moved even closer, his chest now against mine, and his hand moved off my wrist and to the dip in my waist. "Fuck, I missed having you so close."

I felt the same, but I couldn't get the words out, not while he was touching me in the way I'd imagined for weeks. We'd tried to erase each other from our lives the last few weeks, but it was now evident how hard it was.

He pushed, backing me up against the wall, and dipped down. A gasp left my lips as his erection pressed between my thighs, and I stared deeply into his eyes. He had everything there on display for me. Every single thing he felt, and I was hopeless to resist any longer.

I lunged forward, slamming my lips down on his and taking what I so desperately needed. I bit down on his bottom lip, not being gentle in the slightest. I soaked in each of his moans and relished each stroke of his tongue as it dipped and flowed against mine.

I finally had what I wanted, but I knew I couldn't keep it.

I could never keep it.

CADE

I had to stop.

We had to stop.

But I couldn't.

I couldn't pull away from her sweet lips. I couldn't move my hands off her tempting body. Most of all, I couldn't separate my heart from hers. They were fused together, and no matter how much we tried to break them apart, they refused.

"Wait," Aria said, pulling away, but I followed her, trying to seek out her lips again. I needed another taste. Just one more before the earth would come crashing down around us and we'd have to go back to how things were. In this silent, empty hallway, we could be whoever and whatever we wanted to be.

"No," I growled out, pressing my lips against hers again. This time, I slowed us right down and gripped her legs in my hands. I pulled her up and used my hips to pin her against the wall. She gasped, and I took my opportunity to dip my tongue into her mouth again.

I didn't know how we'd managed to end up like this. It was inevitable, but we couldn't have it. We could never have what we wanted, not while we had everything hanging over our heads in the way it was.

There was no way out.

"Mommy?" a small voice called a second before a door squeaked open.

Aria's hands pushed against my chest, and I stumbled back, the opposite wall saving me from landing on my ass. She swiped her arm across her lips and narrowed her eyes at me. "That was the last time." The conviction in her voice told me she believed what she was saying, and I grinned. How did she not understand we were meant to be together—

"I mean it, Cade." The door opened fully now, but neither of us turned to look. "Do you want to go to jail? Do you want to lose your job?" My stomach dropped, my gut churning from her harsh words. "All it would take is a few words from your girlfriend, and it'd all be over. Everything would be over, and I'd…" She trailed off, her eyes misting over. "I'd lose you, Cade." She pulled in a breath, but I could hear how stuttered it was. "I can't lose you."

"Baby," I murmured, stepping toward her.

"Aria?" the small voice asked, and we both turned to face it. Asher was rubbing his little fists into his eyes and stumbling into the wall.

"Hey, sleepyhead!" Aria greeted, the smile on her face forced. She crouched down as Asher got closer and picked him up. "Mommy said you weren't well last night."

Asher laid his head in the crook of her neck as

Aria rubbed her hand up and down his back and stood. She turned to face me, and I froze. She looked so comfortable with a child attached to her, and I couldn't help wonder what she'd look like with our child.

Our child? What the hell was I thinking? I shook my head, trying to get rid of my thoughts, and stepped toward her. "Aria—"

"No," she commanded, both her voice and face now telling me she really meant it this time. "That was the last time, Cade. We can't keep doing this." Her throat bobbed as she swallowed. "Deep down, you know that. You know we can't ever be anything but..."

"Friends?" I finished for her, hating the word with more passion than anything I had ever disliked. The thought of only being her friend again made me want to break everything I could, but I knew what she was saying was true. There was too much at stake for us to be together. Way too much.

"Yeah," she whispered. "Friends."

I didn't say another word. I couldn't, no matter how much I tried. She walked away with Asher, murmuring something to him, but I didn't move from the spot I was in. I stared at the wall I'd pinned her against, and I pressed my fingertips to my lips, trying to savor the way her lips had felt against mine. Because she was right. All we could ever be was friends. There was no going back now, only forward, and if it meant I did everything I could for her without being what I really wanted to be to her, then I would. I'd show her I still cared, but I'd keep my distance.

And as if she knew what we'd been doing, my cell buzzed with a message from Willow.

Willow: Where the hell are you?

I didn't open the message. Instead, I pushed my shoulders back and spun around to go down the stairs. Laughter rang out throughout the house from outside. I walked through the empty kitchen and into the backyard. As if my body hadn't quite accepted what had happened, it sought out Aria. She was sitting with Asher on her lap, a small smile on her face as she spoke to Belle and Ford beside her.

"Cade! There you are." Willow's voice penetrated my stare, and I turned to look at her. "I thought you'd left me here alone." She laughed, but I could tell it was forced, made to look like she was joking, but she wasn't.

"I had to take a call," I told her, stepping toward the table. There were two open seats opposite Ford and Belle, so I pulled both chairs out and indicated for Willow to sit.

She smiled at me and slowly sat down, her gaze not moving off mine as she leaned over to me and whispered, "You better not have been with her."

I raised a brow. "With who?"

"Don't try and act like you don't know," she ground out, keeping her voice low.

"Of course I wasn't with her." I reached for a burger on the platter in the middle of the table.

"Good. Because I wouldn't want to have to tell people what she was really like." I heard her threat loud and clear, and there was nothing I could do about it. Aria was right—all we could be were friends, but I realized that was going to be hard when it came to Willow.

Willow smiled up a storm as she spoke to Jan next to her, and I kept quiet. I didn't want to talk to anyone. All I wanted was to get this over with and then drop Willow off and go home. I wanted to be alone.

"Is she your girlfriend, Cade?" Belle asked, and I nearly choked on my burger at her words. I coughed and spluttered, taking a drink of my beer to try and calm myself.

"I—"

"I am," Willow answered for me, and placed her hand on my arm. I stared down at it, hating how her long fingers looked against my tattoos. It didn't look right, but nothing would ever look right compared to Aria.

"So is this the lucky lady you were talking about

a few months ago?" Lola asked, her face carefully masked. I met her gaze, my stomach dipping at her words. She didn't know what her words would cause, and I was sure Willow would put it together if I didn't handle this right.

"I…" I flicked my gaze to Aria and then back to Lola, who raised a brow at me. "Yes."

Lola nodded but didn't say another word to me. Instead, she spoke to Ford and Belle, the conversation forgotten—until Willow's hand tightened on my arm. She knew I wasn't talking about her because we had only been colleagues a few months ago. I turned to look at her and wished I hadn't. Her blue eyes swirled, and her lips flattened in a straight line. I couldn't say anything to her here, not while we were surrounded by my family, so I pressed a kiss against her cheek, hoping it would satisfy her…for now.

The conversations slowed down around the table as I ate what was left on my plate, and just when I was about to ask Willow if she was ready to go, I heard Dad ask, "How's school going, baby girl?"

Everyone around the table knew who he was talking too, everyone but Willow. When I picked her up, I hadn't told her about Aria. I hadn't explained she was part of the family, afraid of what she'd say. It was a mistake on my end, one I knew I had to rectify because the longer we sat opposite her, the more Willow shifted and tried to gain my attention.

"It's going good," Aria replied to Dad who was next to Lola. "I got my best time in track yesterday."

"Yeah?" Dad asked, his gaze flicking to mine. "Probably be that awesome coach you have, huh?"

Aria threw her head back, her red hair flowing down her back as a soft tinkle of laughter left her mouth. I couldn't look away, fascinated by her. "Probably," Aria said, and then she glanced at me, but it was so brief, I wasn't sure I would have known if I hadn't been staring at her.

"And what about that girl? She been giving you any more trouble?" I whipped my head to face Dad, my eyes widening. Why the hell was he bringing that up in front of everyone? Not only was I sure Aria didn't want her business talked about in front of everyone, but the girl he was talking about was Willow's sister.

"It's all been good," Aria's soft voice replied to him, but when I turned to look at her, her face was down, her gaze not meeting anyone around the table.

Willow cleared her throat, and I hoped to hell she didn't—

"What girl?"

Fuck, she went there.

"Maybe we should talk about something else,

huh?" Ford interrupted. "I'm sure Tyson don't want her shi…stuff talked about in front of everyone."

A breath I hadn't realized I'd been holding whooshed out of me. Ford knew who Willow was, and not only that, but he knew I had to keep on her good side. This would definitely not bode well for me if it wasn't stopped.

"I'm sure Aria doesn't mind," Willow said in her sickly sweet voice. When I'd first met her, I thought she was a nice person, but I was starting to see it was all an act she'd carefully created. "We're all friends around this table, right?"

Aria cleared her throat, trying to gain some attention. "I'd rather not talk about——"

"Why?" Willow asked, and I gripped her knee under the table, trying to stop her, but it was no use. "Why don't you want to talk about it?" Her voice was no longer sweet and gentle, but firm and insistent. "Do you have something to hide?"

"Willow," I growled out. "Stop."

She turned to face me with a brow raised. "Why? I'm just asking a question."

"Is there a problem?" Jan asked from beside Willow.

"Actually, there is," Willow replied to her, spinning in her chair to face her. Her back was to me now, and I had no idea what to say or do. I looked over at Ford, but even he was watching with raised brows. "I'm sure you're aware of the girl your daughter assaulted at school."

"I am—"

"That girl," Willow interrupted, "was my sister." Her inhale of breath could be heard a second before she said, "My sweet baby sister who did nothing—"

"That's a lie," Ford ground out, causing everyone's attention to focus on him. "And you know it."

Willow gasped, her hand flying to her chest, and all I wanted was to dissolve into thin air and not be here. "How dare you?"

"How dare I?" Ford asked, pushing his chair back and standing. "How dare you? How dare you come here and—"

"Ford," Aria's small voice interrupted, and she placed her hand on his arm. I narrowed my eyes at it, rage flowing through me I hadn't felt before.

"No, Ri, he's goddamn right." Sal stood, his face a mask of fierce protectiveness. "What the hell possessed you to bring her here, Cade?" His gaze met mine, and his eyes narrowed on me. "We all know what that girl has done to Aria. She made her life hell in that school, and you think it's okay to—"

"Excuse you," Willow cut him off. "My sister hasn't done anything to that little bitch!"

"Mommy! The nasty lady cursed!" Belle shouted out.

"I know you didn't just call her a bitch," Lola

growled out at the same time Jan stood and flung her chair backward.

Everything was going to shit around me, but all I could focus on was Aria and her paling face. "That's enough!" I roared, slapping my hand down on the table. The table went silent, the only sounds I could hear were the thumping of my heart. "Enough," I repeated. I stood and took a deep breath, trying my best to calm down, but it wasn't working. I wasn't sure if I was angry over the fact Willow hadn't let it go, or the fact I'd had to bring her here in the first place.

It was all my fault. If I'd have talked to Aria properly after Ford had turned up at my house and not pushed her away, then we wouldn't be in this situation. I could have explained to her what Ford had said, and we could have worked through it. But instead, I'd taken it into my own hands, and now we were here, on the edge of losing everything. But it wasn't my job I was scared of losing, or my reputation. I was scared of going to jail and having to leave Aria.

Her words rang out in my head, repeating over and over again as I got myself under control. *"I can't lose you."* This was for her. Everything I did was for her.

"We're leaving," I told Willow as I stepped away from the table. "Now."

She turned. "What—"

I darted toward her and gripped the sides of her chair, caging her in as I lowered my voice so only she could hear me. "I don't care what you want right now, we're leaving. Get up, and walk out of this house with me. Now."

"Fine," she gritted out.

I moved back to allow her to stand, and with one last look at Aria whose head was down as she stared at her lap, I spun around and walked out of the house with Willow on my heels. My strides were twice the size of hers as I headed to my car, and by the time I'd slipped into the driver's seat and started the engine, she was pulling the passenger door open. My hands gripped the steering wheel so hard my knuckles turned white.

"What the hell, Cade?" Willow sneered as I pulled out onto the road.

"What?" I asked, trying to keep my temper under control. It was all her fault. She was the one threatening to tell everyone what she'd seen. If it weren't for her, I wouldn't be in this situation right now. I'd be with Aria, or maybe I wouldn't, but we wouldn't have this hanging over our heads.

"It was her, wasn't it?" She paused, waiting for me to answer, but I didn't have one for her. "She's the girl you told them about." It was a statement, one I wouldn't confirm or deny, sometimes it was better to say nothing at all. "Oh my god." She gasped. "You were having a full-blown affair."

My nostrils flared, and I gritted my teeth. Bringing her here was a mistake—I should have known better. Of course, she was going to see another side to everything. She was under the illusion what Aria had said in the classroom was true, when it wasn't, not at all.

"This changes things." Her voice was different now, less angry but not calm. "Wow…okay."

I had no idea what she was thinking, but as I pulled up to her house, I realized it wouldn't be anything good. I hadn't confirmed what she was saying, but my silence had spoken for me. I tapped my fingers on the steering wheel, waiting for her to get out of the car.

"You're not to talk to her again," Willow demanded.

"That'll be pretty hard to do considering she's in several of my classes," I told her, not willing to look away from the windshield.

"You're just going to have to find a way. If I find out you've been talking to her, I'll go to the principal, the cops, the papers. I'll out you both." I turned to face her and tracked the features on her face. The slight curve of her lips told me she knew she had me exactly where she wanted me with no way out. "Your life will be over, and I'll make sure hers is too. She may not go to jail like you, but I'll do everything in my power to make sure she doesn't get accepted to any colleges. I'll drag her name through the mud, simply for the fun of it."

My jaw was clenched so tight I was sure my teeth would break from the force. "What do you want?"

She shrugged and flipped her hair off her shoulder. "You."

"Me?"

"Yep. You. I want a real relationship, one where you take me out on real dates. One where you call me to say goodnight. One where I'm the only person you're thinking about."

"And if I say no?"

"Then get ready. I hear they don't take too kindly to pedophiles in jail."

"I'm not a…" I ground my teeth together. There was no use talking to her about it. She wanted what she wanted, and I had to do what she was saying. I didn't care about what happened to me. I could survive in jail. I could start over no problem. But I couldn't do that to Aria. I couldn't let her suffer any more than she already had.

"Fine. You have a deal."

"Good." She reached over and patted my arm. "I'll expect a call from you tonight." She flashed me a smile, one that said she was used to getting precisely what she wanted, and then pushed out of my car.

She may have gotten her own way right now,

but there wasn't a chance in hell I'd allow her to keep it that way. I'd fight to the death for the people I loved, but Willow wasn't aware of it yet.

She may have won the battle, but I'd never let her win the war.

Chapter Six

ARIA

"So it's official?" I asked Hope from my desk chair. She was lying on my bed, her arms and legs spread wide while I was trying and failing to do my homework. She'd messaged me an hour ago telling me she needed to come and check out my new digs and tell me something important. Apparently confirming your relationship status was important to her.

"Yeah." She sighed for what felt like the thousandth time. "He's just so…dreamy."

I snorted and spun on my chair to face her fully. "Dreamy? Who are you, and what have you done to my best friend?"

She laughed and pulled herself up into a sitting position. "Shut up." She grabbed a pillow off my bed and threw it at me, but I successfully managed to avoid it. "You'll see when you meet him. He's so rock and roll, and yet sweet and gentle all at the same time."

"Oh yeah?" I stood and crossed my bedroom to grab a sweater. "And when will I get to meet him?"

She looked down at her cell as I pulled the sweater over my head. "In about thirty minutes. He's coming to pick me up from here."

I raised my brows. "Oh. Wow. Okay."

"What?" Hope asked, standing too. "Do you not want to meet him?"

"No, it's…" I held my arms out to the side. "I haven't been given enough time to prepare."

She rolled her eyes and flopped back down onto my bed. "You're so funny, har har. I can't control my laughter."

I snickered and moved back to my desk. I'd been trying for two hours to do this assignment, but every time I stared at the words in the world history textbook, I couldn't stop thinking about Cade and what had happened yesterday at the cookout.

I hadn't been able to look at him as he walked out, knowing things wouldn't be the same again. I had no doubt Miss Simmons had witnessed too much. Part of me wished I knew what had happened between them when they left, but the protective side of me didn't. The less I knew, the better. I was going to concentrate on getting through each day and making it to the end.

Someone knocked on the front door, and seconds later it was being flung open, and footsteps pounded up the stairs. "Aria?" Belle shouted, and the smile on my face couldn't be stopped. I'd told her to come to my house today, and we'd make cookies, and it looked like she hadn't forgotten. "Cookie time!" she shouted as she barged into my bedroom with her arms spread wide.

"Belle! I told you not to run off!" Lola shouted from somewhere downstairs.

"I told you, Mom. Cookies are important." Belle ambled toward me and rolled her eyes. "She doesn't understand. Are you ready?"

"I…" I looked down at my homework. There was no way I would get this finished today, not while my mind was occupied with a thousand thoughts. "Yeah." I stood but halted when a throat cleared.

"And what about me?" Hope asked, her brow raised.

"Oh."

"Who are you?" Belle asked, planting her hands on her hips.

"I'm her best friend," Hope replied, pointing at me.

Belle gasped. "What?" She swung her gaze to me, her eyes wide. "I thought I was your best friend."

"You are," I told Belle, crouching down in front of her and lowering my voice, "I just let her think she is." I winked, causing Belle to grin and puff out her chest.

"Belle." Lola halted at my bedroom door, pulling in a breath. Her cheeks were red, and I had no doubt it was from trying to keep up with Belle. "I swear, if you run off one more—oh, sorry, I didn't know you had company."

I chuckled and took Belle's hand. "It's only Hope. She came to annoy me with her love life." I smiled at Lola.

"Hey!" Hope shouted, following me out of my room and down the stairs. We all moved through the living room and into the kitchen. "At least one of us has a love life. Yours exploded in your face—"

"You have a boyfriend?" Lola asked, leaning against the kitchen counter. Her dark-brown hair was pulled up into a messy bun on the top of her head, and her face was clean of makeup. "Why didn't I know this?"

"I—"

"Oh, yeah," Hope cut me off. "She totally had a boyfriend, but then his job—"

"Hope," I ground out. "I haven't even introduced you." I cleared my throat and widened my eyes, trying to silently tell her to stop. "This is Lola and her daughter, Belle. Lola is Mr. Easton's step-mom, and Belle is his little sister."

"Who's Mr. Easton?" Belle asked, her nose scrunching up.

"It's Cade, sweetheart," Lola told Belle and pushed off the counter.

Hope's mouth opened, forming an O as she finally understood what I was saying. "So…did someone say cookies?"

I rolled my eyes as she tried to change the subject. Thank god it worked when Belle told her, "You can be our assistant."

"I can?" Hope said, her hand landing on her chest. "Why, thank you."

Lola walked toward me and placed her hand on my arm. "You sure you don't have any plans? I can take the Cookie Monster home and bake with her."

"Nope." I shook my head. "I'm all good. I kind of need the distraction if I'm honest."

Lola bit down on her bottom lip, her gaze wandering to Belle and then to Hope. "You left so suddenly yesterday, are you okay? I didn't realize she was that girl's sister and—"

"I'm fine, really." I waved her off and tried to slow my heart as it beat faster. I didn't want to think about yesterday, not now. "I'll bring Belle back in a few hours."

Lola frowned, her eyes watching me intently, but I wouldn't tell her anything else. Not only because I didn't want her knowing everything, but the fact of the matter was, I didn't know if I was okay. My cutting had gotten so bad, I could barely go a day without it. It wasn't a relief anymore, but a ritual I felt the urge to do even while I was surrounded by three people who cared about me.

"Okay," Lola whispered and then stepped back. She crouched down in front of Belle and said good-bye, but I couldn't slow my heartbeat. It was pounding in my chest, begging me to do what I hadn't done yet today.

I'd been determined not to have to do it, but as Lola exited the house and left me alone with Hope and Belle, I knew I'd have to do something to calm myself down. I needed to resist for as long as I possibly could. I had to push everything down and not let it come out, but it was harder than anything I'd done before.

"Re—" My voice cracked, so I cleared my throat and tried again. "Ready?" I asked, shaking my head and concentrating on the task at hand.

"Yep!" Belle shouted, and Hope helped her up onto one of the barstools.

My shaking hands reached for the bowls, and then I gathered the ingredients, all the while telling myself everything was okay. All I had to do was concentrate on the task at hand, and then I'd forget all about my blades sitting in my case in my bedroom. I wouldn't think about the possibility of having to find a new area to cut my skin. All I needed to concentrate on was mixing the ingredients for the cookies.

I let Belle have the mixing spoon as I placed each ingredient into the bowl, and it wasn't until we were adding the chocolate chips, she asked, "Who taught you to bake cookies, Aria?"

My breath caught in my throat, my skin went red hot and then freezing cold, and I whispered, "My dad."

"That's it, sweetie, keep mixing," Dad's deep voice said. I stared up at him, grinning, and waiting for him to smile back. When he smiled, I knew we would have a good day. It was when he stared at me as if I wasn't really there that I worried.

He'd been having more bad days than good lately, and sometimes, he would only have a few good hours. I tried to tell Mom he was sad, but she told me he was fine and that sometimes daddies got sad.

I couldn't help thinking it was my fault, though. He only ever got sad when I did or said something wrong, which was why I was going to make him the best cookies ever.

"Like this?" I asked, mixing it as best as I could.

"Just like that." He grinned at me and then pulled some of the mixture out of the pan and rolled it into balls. "Now we need to do this, and then we can put them into the oven."

I nodded and started to form balls too, so excited for

having freshly baked cookies. Maybe Dad would let me watch some cartoons and sit with me while we ate them.

Once the tray was full, he put them into the oven, and we started to clean and put everything away. It wasn't until fifteen minutes later when the timer went off that things changed. Dad had started to pace the length of the living room, and it didn't matter how much I tried to get his attention and make him happy again, he just wasn't listening to me.

"Aria!" he shouted, and I stared at the oven door. The cookies needed to come out; otherwise, they'd burn. "Come here, quick!"

I took one last look at the oven, and then raced into the living room. My stomach dropped when I saw his pale face, but it was the way his gaze kept darting around the room that had me even more scared. Something had happened and—

"You need to go and hide."

"What? But, Dad, the cookies—"

"Now, Aria! Go and hide in your closet, and don't come out until I tell you to. They're coming for us, sweetie. They're coming to get us, and I need to protect you."

"But—"

"Now!" he roared, and I squealed. I spun around, ran to my bedroom, and hid in my small closet. I brought my knees up to my chest and counted as high as I could and then started from one again. I wasn't sure how many numbers I counted, but the smell of burning cookies drifted into my room.

The smoke alarm went off, and I jumped at how loud it was. I couldn't hear Dad mumbling anymore, not until the sound stopped, and then some crashing echoed from the kitchen.

I lay down on my side and stared at my closed closet doors, watching and waiting for him to come and get me. I waited and waited and waited, but he never came. It wasn't until Mom got home from her shift at the diner that I was allowed out of my closet.

"Oh, hon, I'm sorry about Dad. He's just having a bad day." Mom wrapped her arms around me and kissed me on top of the head, but nothing she said made a difference. The day had started out so good, and now…

Now the cookies were burned.

"Hope, can you watch Belle for a couple of minutes?"

I didn't wait for Hope to answer, not that I was sure I'd be able to hear her from the pounding in my ears. I raced up the stairs and into my bedroom. The room spun as I entered it, but I managed to make it to my desk drawer and to my case. I grabbed it and then twirled on the spot, trying to find the best place to hide and—

I crossed my room and opened up my closet door. It wasn't the same one I'd had to hide in all those years ago, but it was enough for the memories to come flying back to the forefront of my mind. I lost count of the number of times Dad had told me to hide, but almost always it was in my closet.

Stepping inside didn't calm me, nor when I shut the door, basking myself in darkness. But it was the feel of the case in the palm of my hand that centered me. I grabbed my cell and turned on the flashlight. The light hit off the blades, and I plucked out the third one. My thumb rubbed over it, feeling the smooth surface and sharp edges. I blinked at it as my other hand reached for the bottom of my sweater. I pulled it up enough to show the bottom of my belly and then tore the blade over the smooth, unmarked skin.

My head fell back as the trickle of blood flowed down, gathering at the waistband of my leggings. The high I'd been having was starting to dissipate, so I made another mark, crisscrossing them as to cause more pain.

And then my heartbeat slowed down. The room stopped spinning, my pulse wasn't thumping as fast, and the buzzing in my ears stopped. I'd successfully brought myself back into the here and now, and everything was okay again.

"Aria?" Hope shouted, and I squealed, the blade dropping from my fingers and onto the floor of my closet. I searched for it frantically. "My ride is here." My fingers landed on the cool metal, and I scrambled to put the blade away, wiping the blood on my black leggings.

"I'm coming! Two seconds!" I pushed my closet door open and gulped a huge breath then hid my case between a stack of jeans. I raced out of my room and down the stairs, wincing more than usual from the cuts. I had to get used to the new place, but I had no doubt it would satisfy my needs…for the time being.

"The cookies are ready to go in the oven," Hope said as she pulled the front door open. She frowned at me. "You okay? You look a little red."

I waved her off. "I'm good. I better head in there and finish the cookies."

Hope nodded. "I can stay if you—"

"Nope. Go have fun with your boyfriend. I'll see you tomorrow." I grinned and tried to school my features as I watched her jog to the sidewalk and slip into the car which was waiting for her. I waved then shut the door and headed back into the kitchen. "Where were we?" I asked Belle.

"Cookies need to be baked," she said, smiling up at me, and I couldn't help but wonder if that was what I looked like to my dad. Why wasn't I enough for him?

"Let's do it."

I grabbed the tray Belle and Hope had put the cookies on and moved to the oven. I may have had burned cookies when I was a kid, but I was determined Belle would never have them.

———

CADE

I sat behind my desk in my office and looked out of the window onto the track and field. Aria had been out there for forty minutes, and I hadn't been able to stop staring as she tried to better her times with each additional lap she ran.

It was Wednesday, which meant Reagan wasn't here because she had a doctor's appointment. I knew I should have been out there with Aria, but that would mean we were alone, and hearing Willow's warning on a constant loop in my brain meant I couldn't risk going out there. All it would take was for Willow to walk out on the track like she had last week, and it would all be over.

Each day that passed since the cookout was even more suffocating than the last. I'd kept my side of the bargain by not talking to Aria, but Willow didn't think it was enough to warn me only once. Every single time we spoke, she reminded me exactly what she held in the palm of her hands, and she wasn't shy about telling me what she would do if I wasn't adhering to her demands.

A knock on my office door had my head swinging toward it. The handle turned, the door creaked open, and then my stomach dropped when Willow's face appeared. My jaw locked as she stepped inside, closing the door behind her. I should have known she'd come and check on me for a second time today.

"Hey, handsome," she purred, sauntering toward me.

"Hey." I stared down at the papers on my desk, pretending to read them. Her hand landed on them, stopping me from having an excuse not to look at her.

"I thought I'd come and check in on you." She pushed up onto the edge of my desk and crossed her legs. I knew what she was doing, but it would never work. She'd tried everything possible to get me to touch her over the last few days, but I'd refused each and every time. "Today is track practice, right?"

"Yeah," I ground out, my gaze flicking over to the window and catching sight of Aria cooling down in the middle of the field. "I had some…paperwork to do, so I stayed in here."

"Hmmm." Willow's finger trailed up my arm and to my shoulder. "Sounds boring." She leaned forward and whispered, "I can think of much more exciting things to do at this desk."

My nostrils flared at the memories of what I'd already done on this desk with Aria. I'd spread her over this desk and touched her in ways she'd never been touched before. Mine was the first hand to graze over her nipples, the first finger inside her…it was me who had claimed her as mine, and now she—

"You like the thought of that?" Willow asked, her voice even lower. I glanced up at her, realizing she was looking down at my lap and the obvious outline of my erection showing through my sweats. She had no idea it was for the seventeen-year-old who had me twisted up in ways you could only imagine.

"Willow," I ground out. "Not here."

"Why?" She moved closer to me and opened her legs, giving me a clear view of her black panties underneath her skirt. "You know you want me, Cade. Stop resisting and let yourself take it."

"I don't—"

Three sharp knocks rapped at my office door, and then it opened. "I've finished my—oh." Aria's eyes widened, her gaze tracking over me and then where Willow sat. "I…I finished practice. I thought I'd let you know."

The room was silent until Willow jumped down off my desk and walked toward Aria. "You can go now." She gripped the door in her hand, staring down at Aria. I moved my attention away from her, knowing I couldn't look at her from this close and not say anything to her.

"I…okay." I kept my gaze focused on the windows as Willow slammed the door shut. The click of her heels was muted on the carpet as she moved back toward me.

"I have work to finish, Willow."

"But—"

I sighed and turned to face her, needing her out of my space as quickly as possible. "The sooner I finish it, the sooner I can leave and then call you." Her eyes narrowed. "Maybe we can get some dinner later?"

"I don't know." She shrugged, acting indifferent, but it was all an act. Everything was with her.

"I'll pick you up at seven then?" I asked, lowering my voice.

"Fine." She sighed and exited my office, and I finally was able to take a breath. Whenever I was around her, she sucked the life out of the room and made me feel like I was a piece of meat for her to play with—a game. She didn't care about the feelings she was hurting with what she was doing. All she cared about was getting what she wanted, no matter the cost.

I slammed my fist down onto my desk, causing papers to fly across it and my laptop to shake. I wasn't sure how much more of this I could take before I surrendered and either gave her what she wanted or told her to fuck off and put up with the consequences. The latter wasn't an option, I knew that, but it didn't hurt to entertain the thought of it.

My laptop pinged with a new email, and I groaned. I really did have paperwork I needed to finish. At least that wasn't a lie. I clicked open the email and drummed my fingers on the desk as I waited for it to load. The building was so quiet you could hear a pin drop, and as I started to read the email, I heard a door closing which meant Aria was leaving. I stood, and as soon as I finished reading the email, I raced out of my office.

I pumped my arms and willed my legs to go faster so I could get to Aria, and as soon as I ran into the parking lot, I spotted her getting into her mom's car. "Aria!" I shouted, speeding up the last few feet. Gravel kicked up as I came to a complete stop suddenly, and tried to catch my breath.

"Cade?" Jan called, dipping down so she could see me out of the open passenger door Aria was about to close. "What are you doing?"

I held my finger up, signaling for her to give me a second, and then crouched down. My one hand rested on the inside of the passenger door and the other on the edge of Aria's seat. I was hyperaware how close my palm was to her thigh, and apparently so was she because she shuffled away an inch.

"I just got an email." I flicked my gaze from Jan to Aria. "There's a track meet next Saturday. Three of the competitors have pulled out, which means there are two open spots."

Aria's eyes widened. "Really?"

"Really." I grinned at her and drank in the smile

she gave to me. It had been too long since I'd seen that smile. "You and Reagan have been given two of the spots."

"No way!" Her hands covered her mouth as she whispered, "Oh my god."

"A track meet?" Jan asked.

I tore my attention off Aria and told Jan, "Yeah, and there'll be scouts there. Scouts who can offer scholarships and training. It's…" I trailed off and looked back at Aria. "It's an opportunity that could change everything."

"Oh my god!" Jan shouted and threw her hands up in the air. "My baby could get a scholarship?"

"Yep." I had no doubt Aria would be offered one. The more she trained, the better her form and times became. She was a natural on the track, there was no doubt about that.

"When did you say it was?" Aria asked, finally getting her bearings. She leaned closer to me, but I wasn't sure she was aware she was doing it.

"Next Saturday."

Her face dropped, all the spark leaving her eyes as she bowed her head. "I can't go."

"What?" I frowned and placed my hand on her leg, forgetting where I was and who was around. "Why?"

"I have the fitting for the dress for Mom's wedding and—"

"Psssh." Jan swiped her hand through the air.

"I'll go and get my last fitting done, and we'll rearrange yours. This opportunity won't come around again, Aria. You gotta grab it by the horns and take it."

Aria's smile was slow to form as she turned to face her mom. "Really?"

Jan placed both of her hands on either side of Aria's face and whispered, "Really."

"So that's a yes then?" I asked, my hand tightening on Aria's thigh.

"No," Jan said, pulling away from Aria and winking at me. "It's a hell yes." Jan placed her hands on the steering wheel. "I hope you're coming on Saturday, Cade. We now have two celebrations."

"Two?" I asked, moving my hand off Aria and feeling the loss against my palm.

"Yep. The track meet and Aria's birthday. She'll be eighteen in three days' time. My baby is all grown up." She sighed, but the smile on her face couldn't be ignored.

"You're…turning eighteen?" I asked Aria, shocked by what Jan had said. I shouldn't have been, though. I should have known it was coming up.

"Yeah." Her voice was small as she stared at me. "I'm having a party at the diner. You should come." She paused, her cheeks reddening the longer she kept her attention focused on me. "If you want to, that is."

"I want to," I told her, not second-guessing for even one moment. Her answering smile was precisely what I wanted, and I couldn't bring myself to care about Willow's warning, not when Aria was looking at me like that. I cleared my throat, realizing I was staring at her for a little too long and stood.

"I'll let you get going."

I didn't wait for an answer as I closed Aria's door and then watched them drive out of the lot.

Chapter Seven

ARIA

Mom had insisted I wore the dress she'd bought me for my birthday party, and I couldn't come up with a valid excuse as to why I shouldn't wear it. I'd tried it on to appease her, having every intention of telling her it didn't fit or it didn't look right, but I was wrong.

The straps were braids of the maroon material and dipped down into a sweetheart neckline. It gripped my waist and then flowed out gently into an A-line and stopped at my ankles. It was the split I was worried about, though. It only came up to my knee on the left side, but one wrong move and everyone would get a glimpse of some of my scars.

Mom's gasp had my head whipping around to face her. She stood in the doorway to my bedroom.

"That's just perfect," she said, crossing the room to me and handing me a pair of wedges. "These will match."

"Mom, you know I hate heels."

"These aren't heels, Aria." Her lips lifted into a grin. "They're wedges." She placed her hands on my shoulders and looked at me from head to toe. I'd braided my hair, not even realizing it would match the dress.

"Wow. So much difference," I snarked at Mom but took the wedges out of her hands anyway. Today wasn't the day for defying her. If anything, today was the day to go along with everything. It was already late afternoon, and I hadn't cut once, which was a huge win in my book.

My stomach now had seven marks, all in various stages of healing, but not a fresh one today. And I was proud of myself. I'd resisted doing it before we left for the diner, and if I managed to make it to tonight without having to cut again, I'd have achieved something.

I was happy, happier than I'd been in weeks, and it was all because today I turned eighteen. Mom had woken me up, and Sal had cooked pancakes. They'd both been home all day apart from when Sal left an hour ago to get the diner ready. Having them both here with smiles on all of our faces made a difference.

I just wished I could tell them I needed it more.

I needed to be reminded of the people who loved me instead of thinking about the person who hadn't. There hadn't been one mention of Dad throughout the day, a stark contrast to every year since he'd died. Mom had taken to telling me how proud my dad would be, but this year, she hadn't said it. Maybe she had listened to what I'd said when we moved out of the apartment. Maybe my words hadn't fallen on deaf ears after all.

"You nearly ready to go, birthday girl?" Mom asked, and with a smile on my face, I nodded.

I pushed my feet into the wedges and did the straps up, feeling like the world was a completely different place thanks to the extra height they'd given me. Following Mom down the stairs in them was a feat, but I managed it okay and then exited the house.

It was only a few minutes' drive until we were pulling up into the diner lot. Balloons and banners decorated the outside of the diner, and a huge eighteen balloon sat in the entryway. The place wasn't bursting with people, but the ones who I cared about most were here, along with Uncle Brody's team and the waitresses and cooks from the diner.

"Happy birthday!" they all shouted at the same time. Belle and Asher ran toward me with a gift bag between them.

"What's this?" I asked, crouching down and

nearly falling over from the way the wedges had me balancing.

"Your present," Belle said. "Open it!"

"It's a computer," Asher told me, his grin spreading on his face and causing his cheeks to puff out.

"Asher! You're not meant to tell her what it is! It's supposed to be a surprise." Belle shook her head in dismay.

Asher looked confused with his little brows pulling down into a frown. "Huh?"

"You're so stup—"

"Belle." I raised a brow, but I couldn't wipe the smile off my face. "How about we go and sit and open it together?"

"Fine." Belle huffed. "But I'm sitting next to you."

"Nu-uh! I want to sit next to her," Asher shouted back.

"What if I want to sit next to the birthday girl?" Lola asked, interrupting their bickering.

I stood and righted myself in time to feel her arms wrap around my shoulders. "Happy birthday, sweetheart."

"Thank you." I pulled back and smiled at her, but I didn't manage to get another word out before I was wrapped in another pair of arms and Uncle Brody was wishing me a happy birthday too.

"Give the girl some space!" Sal shouted, ushering them away from me. "She's barely in the door, and you're all accosting her." He grabbed my arm. "Come on, Ri. I have a special birthday shake just for you."

"Shakes?" Belle asked, her ears perking up. She grabbed hold of my other hand and followed us through the small crowd. "I want a shake."

"Sal? Can you—"

"Already made her one, Ri. I know what shakes my girls like." He pulled us to a stop at the tables all lined up in a square, the same way it would be when kids had their parties here, but I didn't care. I couldn't remember the last time I'd had a party. Maybe when I was Asher's age, but I'd only ever seen photographs of it.

Sal pulled out a chair for me, and I sat down with Belle on one side and Asher on the other. I placed the gift bag on the table next to the tray of shakes. They were all topped with cream, but there was also a small slice of cake balanced on the edge.

"A birthday shake?" I asked, my eyes widening as I looked from the shake back to Sal.

"Yep. Try it."

I leaned forward, took a sip of the shake, and then a bite of the cake, and groaned. "Heaven in my mouth."

Sal chuckled and grunted, "I'm gonna get the food."

I smiled at him as he walked away and then took another sip of the shake. It really was heaven in my mouth. "This is so good," I said to no one in particular. I looked down at Belle who had a whipped cream mustache, and then Asher, who had spilled some down his white shirt.

"Open the present!" Asher shouted at me, clapping his hands.

"Maybe we should wait until—"

"You can open them all now," Mom said, placing her hands on my shoulders. We hadn't done any presents this morning, just spent time together, and if I were honest, that was the only gift I had wanted.

Uncle Brody and Mom started to place a few gift bags and presents around me, ready to open. "I don't know where to start…"

"Can I open this one?" Belle asked, plucking one from the pile.

I leaned down to look at the tag and saw it was from one of the waitresses. "Yeah, you can open that one." I grabbed another one off the small pile, seeing Mom and Sal's name, and opened it up to reveal a light blue comforter set. They also got me some running clothes and a bracelet. All that was left from them was a card, so I opened it, not expecting something to fall out onto the table. I frowned at the piece of plastic and picked it up, staring at the shiny silver credit card with my name on it. "What's this?" I asked, confused.

"It's a credit card," Mom said. "You'll be off to college soon so we thought you could do with something to have in an emergency or if, you know, you want something." I opened my mouth, about to tell her it was too much, but Mom kept going. "I know you'll be careful with it. You're responsible. It's why we decided to give you one—so you have a little more freedom."

"But I…" I let out a breath and stared at the card in fascination. "Thank you."

Mom pressed a kiss to my cheek. "You're welcome."

I opened up my purse and placed it in there next to my cell. I looked up, seeing only one present left—the one Asher and Belle had given to me—and when I saw the unmistakable sign for apple and the words *MacBook* written on the side, I nearly leaped out of my chair.

"What the…" I gasped, standing. "I can't take this."

"You can, and you will, baby girl," Uncle Brody told me, brooking no room for an argument. "Like your mom said, you'll be off to one of them fancy colleges soon, and you'll need a decent computer."

"I can't even…"

"Just say thank you, baby girl."

I shook my head at the grin on his face. "Thank you."

"No problem."

I placed it down on the table and darted toward him and Lola, trying to wrap my arms around them both at the same time. "I don't deserve all of this," I whispered.

Lola pulled back and gripped my shoulders, staring into my eyes with a fierceness I'd never seen before. "Don't you ever say that," she warned me, her own eyes misting with tears. "You deserve everything you could ever possibly get, sweetheart. Never, for one second, think you don't deserve all the love you have. Do you understand me?" She pulled in a breath, and I hated when a tear sprung from her eye. "We love you just as much as we love Cade, Belle, and Asher. You'll always be our second daughter, no matter what happens. Okay?"

My breath stuttered out of my chest, and I nodded. "Okay." My own tears ran down my face, and my breaths became harder to catch. "I need to…" I backed away and let her hands flow off my shoulders. "I just need a minute."

Lola nodded as I moved back, everything blurring thanks to the tears. They loved me. I was surrounded by love, and yet, I didn't feel it. I knew how they all felt, but deep down inside, I'd always feel like the girl who needed to hide in her closet away from the bad people who would come and find her.

Mom shouted my name as I headed toward the back of the diner and into the staff room, but I ignored her. I needed a minute to gather myself. I sat in one of the chairs around the small table and stared at the collection of lockers lining the wall.

I wasn't sure how long I sat there and read each of the names stuck to the metal with paper and sticky tape, but it wasn't until I heard footsteps that I looked up.

Cade leaned against the door, his gaze tracking the room, a small smile on his face. "This is where Lola used to tutor me." His stare met mine briefly, and then he looked away as he stepped forward. "We'd come in here once a week, and she'd help me with my schoolwork." He chuckled. "I thought I was hot shit back then."

I snorted. "And you don't think that anymore?"

He raised a brow and pulled the chair out next to me. "Nah. I know it's true now."

Laughter burst out of me, the kind that couldn't be stopped, no matter how much you tried. Cade always had a way of bringing me out of my own head, and I didn't think he was aware of how much he did it.

"I love hearing you laugh," he whispered, leaning closer to me. "It's so…freeing."

My laughter waned into chuckles, but at his

words, I sobered up. "What are you doing back here, Cade?"

"I came to give you a present." He held out a small box to me, wrapped in light-purple paper, and I took it with shaky fingers.

"What is it?" I asked, looking down at it and then back to him.

He tilted his head to the side and ran his hand down the scruff lining his jaw. "Open it and see."

I bit down on my bottom lip and pulled at the corners of it slowly. Butterflies took flight in my stomach as I pulled all the paper off, revealing a dark-blue box with a ribbon tied around it. Glancing up, I spotted Cade watching me carefully. I opened the box and inhaled a breath at what I saw.

"Wow," I murmured. I placed the box on the table, gently pulled the necklace out, and brought it closer to my face. The white gold chain was delicate, being weighed down by a teardrop locket. "It's beautiful."

———

CADE

I wanted to tell her so was she, but I refrained, holding back as much as I could. Maybe I shouldn't have been here, but there was no chance I was going to miss seeing her on her eighteenth birthday.

She flipped the locket over and rubbed her thumb over it, and it was on the tip of my tongue to tell her to open it and see what was inside, but I stopped myself. It wasn't the time or place, not yet. You couldn't see the clasp on the outside, and that was one of the reasons I'd bought it. It wasn't your traditional locket, which was why I thought it suited her so much.

"Let me put it on you," I murmured, afraid to talk too loudly.

I gently took it from her and leaned forward. She lifted her hair, and I breathed in her flowery scent. I'd missed that almost as much as I missed hearing her voice, but not nearly as much as I missed looking into her eyes and touching her.

Swallowing as she turned her back to me, I laced the necklace around her neck and clasped it at the back. I lingered, my finger trailing over the soft sensitive skin of her neck and down to the strap of her dress. It would be so easy to yank it down and kiss her in the way I wanted to—almost too easy. But I wouldn't do that to her today, not on her birthday.

"Thank you, Cade," she whispered, turning back to face me, her hands clutched around the locket. "I love it."

I love you, I wanted to tell her. I wanted to explain

to her how I felt, but what good would it do? We couldn't be together in the way we wanted to be, which left us at a crossroads. We could either be friends, or nothing at all. She'd said we could be friends at the cookout, but I wasn't so sure if I could look at her and not touch her. I wasn't confident I could talk to her about nothing of relevance all the while mourning the fact I couldn't have her.

My cell buzzed in my pocket, and I pulled it out, breaking the spell we were under.

Willow: Where are you? My parents will be here in an hour!

I huffed out a breath and glanced at Aria as she stood. "Are you staying for food?" she asked, her light-brown eyes hopeful.

"I can stay for a little while longer," I told her, knowing I was pushing my limits, but I couldn't help it when it came to Aria.

Cade: I had to go and see my dad. I'll be there in a bit.

"I'll see you back out there then?" Aria asked.

I nodded and ground my teeth together as my cell buzzed again. "Yeah." She walked out of the room, and I couldn't help staring at her. She didn't put an extra swing into her hips the way Willow did because she didn't need to. Aria was alluring in her own beautiful way—the kind of beauty that drew you in and never let you go.

> **Willow**: I swear to god, Cade. If you stand me up, there'll be hell to pay for you and your little girl fetish you have.

I let my head dip back and growled. There wasn't much more I could take of this. She was blowing up my cell constantly with both veiled and outright threats. It was enough to drive a sane person crazy, but all it was doing was making me angrier and angrier by the day.

There wasn't anyone I could confide in, especially now that Ford was away on an undercover job. It meant the one person who managed to keep me calm when it came to Willow wasn't here. I was alone, scared of what I would do if she pushed the right button to have me explode.

> **Cade**: I said I'll be there.

I pushed my cell into my pocket and sauntered back into the main part of the diner. I decided to sit in a booth with a couple of the waitresses instead of in the main area they'd set up. I wanted to be able to watch Aria without having eyes on me. I needed a few minutes where there was only me and her, and no one else around.

My cell buzzed several times over the next thirty minutes, and when I knew I was cutting it close, I stood from the booth and exited without saying goodbye. They didn't need to know I'd left. Today was about Aria and only Aria.

I crossed the lot, got into my car, and huffed out a breath to try to calm myself. I shouldn't have had to leave. I should have been able to stay until the party was over, and then I should have been able to hold her and kiss her and tell her how much I loved her.

But I wasn't able to do any of that. Instead, I had to leave and sit through a dinner with Willow, her sister, and her parents. I moved my neck from side to side and cracked it, feeling some of the building tension break. My cell vibrated again, and I ignored it as I turned the engine on and reversed out of the spot toward the back of the lot.

Straightening my car, I was about to drive when another car came whizzing in. I recognized the passenger as Aria's friend, Hope, but I had no idea who the leather jacket-wearing guy driving the car was.

Frowning, I idled, watching as Hope rushed into the diner and exited with Aria a few minutes later. Aria was shaking her head, but she had a huge smile on her face, and then the driver revved his engine.

My heart started to pound harder in my chest, my pulse thrumming as I watched Aria get into the car. The driver sped off with both of them in tow. Panting, I stared at the empty space they'd been in, willing myself to calm the hell down, but it was no use, I was right back there, in the driver's seat, revving my own engine and thinking I was a badass nothing could possibly touch.

"What's the highest speed you've ever gotten to?" Annabelle asked me, leaning over the center console.

I raised a brow and glanced away from the road and straight at her cleavage. Her breasts were practically hanging out of the dress she was wearing. "I dunno," I said, shrugging as I looked back at the road. "Maybe one ten?"

"Yeah?" she purred. I could tell she'd already had a few drinks before we left the apartment. Annabelle wasn't an in-your-face kind of girl, but she wasn't shy either. It was why we'd started to date a couple of months back, but when she drank, she was hard fuckin' work. Like tonight.

Or maybe I was pissed because I wouldn't be able to drink. In this college town, all the parties were always in bumfuck nowhere which meant someone had to drive. We'd taken it in turns—me and my two roommates who were sitting in the back of the car, beer bottles open on their laps and a case between them—but it didn't mean I looked forward to being the only sober one.

"Do it," Annabelle insisted. "Do it. Cade, show me how fast you can go."

I pulled up at a stoplight and shook my head. "No. I can barely see with my headlights on. It's way too dark on the back roads."

"Just do it, bro. You know how wet she gets when you go fast," Barry shouted, causing Austin to laugh up a storm. They were both drunk, that much was obvious, and we hadn't even made it to the house party yet. It was going to be a long night.

I gritted my teeth as they all cheered, egging me on to go quicker. I'd only had the car for a couple of months. The truth was, I didn't know how fast she could go, and I was kind of intrigued to see what numbers I could get out of her.

I pushed my foot down on the gas pedal, revving the engine as I stared at the lights we were stopped at. The red still flashed back at me, and a couple of seconds later, it went off, and in its place was green. My leg bounced off the brake, and my tires squealed up a storm, and then we were off, and I was determined to get the highest number out of her I could. The laughter surrounded me, encouraging jeers from the two guys in the back, and a squeal from Annabelle.

I flicked my gaze to Annabelle and saw headlights heading right for us. I was going too fast, but he'd run a red light, and then metal was crunching, and Annabelle's excited squeals turned into terrified screams. The car rolled so many times I lost count, and then everything was gone.

No noise.

No lights.

Just…gone.

I gasped a breath, trying to get rid of the memories of that night. I'd been a fool, an immature fool. If I had crossed the section at the appropriate speed, maybe they'd still be here today. Maybe one of them would still be alive. But I'd been going too fast when the impact hit on the passenger side, and neither of the guys had worn a seatbelt.

It was a combination of fault, but I knew I would have been the one to get the blame, especially with the amount of alcohol in the car. The broken beer bottles and leaking gas were the first thing I could smell when I'd come to, and then I saw their lifeless faces.

My eyes squeezed shut as I shook my head, trying to get the images out of my brain, but all I could think about was Aria sitting in a car with someone who wanted to show off the way I had.

I pulled my cell out, scrolling past all of the messages from Willow, and opened Aria's name up.

Cade: Please be careful. And wear your seatbelt.

I pushed my cell back into my pocket and gripped my steering wheel. Even if she didn't understand why I'd said it, I was hoping she'd read it and listen to me. There was nothing I could do about it now, so I lifted my foot off the brake and gently pressed the gas, aware of how slow I was pulling out of the lot. But I didn't care. I'd never risk another person's life again, which was why I headed right to Willow's.

I'd already taken three lives, and I was determined there wouldn't be a fourth.

Chapter Eight

ARIA

The music pumped through the sound system in the car as Hope's boyfriend took a sharp turn. My seatbelt kept me in place, but I had to put my hand on the seat to keep me upright. I wanted to tell him to slow down, but something was whirring in my system, my adrenaline spiking at how fast he was going.

I hadn't expected Hope to turn up and drag me away from the party, but apparently, she'd arranged it all with my mom, and now we were heading to the mall for Hope to pick something up and then go to another party. This one most probably wouldn't be like mine, though. I was guessing there'd be alcohol involved, along with people my own age.

I was eighteen. I could vote. I could leave home if I wanted to. The possibilities seemed endless.

My cell vibrated from my purse, and I pulled it out, reading the message from Cade.

Cade: Please be careful. And wear your seatbelt.

I frowned at the message and looked up. We were on the highway now as we whizzed past other cars. How did Cade know—

He must have seen me leave.

My breath caught in my throat, and I clasped on to the necklace he'd gotten me as I stared out of the window. Was he worried about me being in this car? Was he—

A gasp left my lips as I remembered him telling me about the crash he'd been in, and I understood why he messaged me. He was worried.

Hope's boyfriend took the exit for the mall, and I wanted to ask them to turn the music off, it was thumping through my head now and making things blurry. But I didn't. I kept quiet the entire ride to the mall where he pulled into a parking spot and switched the engine off.

"Don't be long," he grunted at Hope.

"I'll be as long as I need to be," she told him, her brow raised. She turned in her seat and grinned. "Wanna come with me, birthday girl?"

I unclipped my belt and pushed the door open, giving her my silent answer. There was no way I was going to sit in a car with her boyfriend when all I knew was his name.

Shuffling on the spot, I moved my gaze off the car as Hope leaned over and kissed him. She opened up the door and said, "Don't get too bored without me, Olly." He murmured something back, but I couldn't hear him as she slammed the door shut and walked toward me. "Can you believe how hot he is?" she asked, hooking her arm through mine and pulling us through the lot.

I raised my brows and hummed, not committing to anything. Hope didn't stop talking about how great Olly was and how awesome of a drummer he was, not even when we walked through the doors to the mall and she had to let my arm go because of the number of people milling around.

The bright lights inside had me wincing, and I stumbled to the side. My gut churned, my shoulders bowing in, and my heart raced. I should have stayed at the diner. I should have put up more of a fight.

"I've got to go upstairs," Hope said, heading toward an escalator.

I followed her, keeping quiet and staring down at all the people as we moved up to the next level. At some point through the crowd, I lost sight of her, but then I spotted a sports shop. Drifting toward it, I found myself fascinated by the display and the running shoes in the window. The lights from underneath them almost made them sparkle. Gone was my racing heart, and in its place was a calm I'd never felt before.

My feet carried me into the shop and toward the wall of running shoes. There were so many, and I wasn't sure what any of them did.

"Can I help you?" a man's voice asked.

I spun around, my eyes wide as I pointed to the wall. "Which ones are the best ones?"

The guy who was only a few inches taller than me, and definitely not much older than eighteen, said, "Depends what you want them for."

"I run track," I told him.

"Ah, then you'll want something like this." He reached for a black pair with a stripe down the middle. He turned it over and pointed to the grooves on the sole. "These will help you grip the track better. And they're so light you don't even feel like you're wearing anything on your feet."

I held my hand out for it, and he placed it in my palm. "Oh wow, that's amazing."

"Right?"

My fingertips trailed over the smooth material and dipped with each groove of the sneaker. I had to have them. There was no other option but to buy them. "Size seven." I handed them back to him, and spotted another pair of the same, but these ones were pink and white. "And one of those too."

"Okay." He grinned at me. "I'll be right back." He strolled away and pushed through a door marked staff only.

I waited for a couple of seconds and twirled, glancing around the store and seeing what else—

A gasp left my lips again, this one louder than any of the others. Were they running leggings to match the running shoes? Darting across the store, I pulled a pair off the rack and saw the same strip down the side in the same color as the sneakers. They matched! I had to have a pair. Or two. Or maybe three. *Wait. I should get four*—one for each practice, and then one for the track meet. Yes. I should get a special pair for the track meet. Maybe something bright and—

"Did you want to try the running shoes on?" the guy asked me, and I spun around to face him.

"Yes." I folded the leggings over my arm before I moved back to where all the running shoes were. As I sat on the edge of the box and undid my wedges, I realized I didn't have socks on. I couldn't try them on without any socks. I glanced around, trying to see if they had any and then spotted some. "Could you get me those socks so I can try them on? I'll buy them with the running shoes and my leggings."

The guy nodded, and just as I was getting the laces undone on the running shoes, my cell vibrated in my purse. I ignored it, too busy staring at all the things. My gaze bounced from one thing to another, and I willed the guy to move faster. Finally, he passed me the package of socks, and I pulled out a pair. I slipped them onto my feet and then pulled the running shoes on and stood.

"Oh wow." I blinked down at my feet and walked three steps one way and then three back. "They feel so different."

"It may take some getting used to, but you'll feel a difference for sure. And they'll help improve your times."

"Really?" I grinned. "I need my times to be the best they can be, especially as I have a meet next weekend."

"You do?" The guy stepped forward. "My cousin is going to a meet too. Says she's gonna get herself a scholarship."

I nodded and pulled the running shoes off my feet then handed them to him. "She can totally do that. My coach told me there's going to be loads of colleges there."

"Cool." He took the running shoes off me. "So you'll have these?"

"Yep." I grabbed my leggings. "Both pairs."

"I'll put them behind the counter for you."

"Thanks," I said, already drifting back to the clothes section. I needed a T-shirt or tank to go with the leggings. The sports bras were too revealing, but maybe I needed those so I could wear them as an extra layer.

I picked several up off the rack, reading the labels and deciding which one was best for me. The tank tops I got to match the leggings, and by the time I was at the counter, my arms were so full I could only just see over the top of them.

The grin on my face couldn't be wiped off as the guy rang me up, and I didn't even look at the total, I simply fished my brand-new credit card out and handed it to him. He swiped it, the computer pinged, and then he handed it back to me and passed me my bag full of goodies.

I wasn't sure how long it took me to find the next sports shop, but my wedges were hanging from my fingers, my feet too sore to be able to walk around in them all night. My cell buzzed again, but I ignored it and headed into the fourth sports shop. I'd already bought a special bag to put all of my supplies in, another pair of leggings and some more socks, and now I was heading toward the water bottles and jackets.

I didn't have a jacket yet, and the first one I spotted said it was night-proof. What did night-proof mean? I frowned at the label and read the little card, realizing it had material stitched onto the fabric that reflected back when headlights hit in. It was a genius idea, so I plucked one up from the rack and then found the same one in the men's section.

Cade was a runner, and I remembered him telling me once that he mainly ran early in a morning or late at night, which meant he needed one of these too. Grabbing him one to match mine, I then headed to the checkout when I spotted a men's dark-blue T-shirt that would be perfect for him too. I was thankful I'd worn one of his T-shirts before; otherwise, I'd have had no idea what size to get him.

The cashier of this store rang me up and added another collection to the bags I was already struggling to hold on to.

"This is a customer announcement. The building will be closing in ten minutes. Please complete your last purchases of the day and make your way to the exits."

I looked left and right, panic building up and causing my heart to race. I hadn't finished shopping yet. I still needed a water bottle to add to my collection. Darting toward the exit, I was hopeful I'd spot a store with one in the window, and just as I could see the doors, I spotted a school supply store.

Racing inside, I headed right for the water bottles and plucked a black one off the shelf, but on the way to the checkout, I got distracted by all the notebooks and pens. I could use one of those to keep track of my times. I plucked three notepads and a packet of pens off the shelf and ran to the checkout. The announcement said we only had a couple of minutes left to exit the mall, and I bounced on the spot as the girl rang me up.

I threw the items into one of my bags and ran toward the exit, not stopping until I was outside in the pitch black. There were no cars in the lot, only streetlights leading the way, but it didn't matter because I'd had the best few hours of my life and I felt freaking great. My feet carried me down the sidewalk, and I started to mumble to myself.

"I'm going to get the best times now. There's no way I can be anything but in the top three. And then I can get a scholarship and—"

I stumbled to the side, the bags weighing me down, and a branch hit me in the face. I wasn't sure how far I'd walked, but the soles of my feet were hurting, and my face stung from where the branch had scratched me. Spinning around, I tried to take stock of where I was, but I had no idea. I pulled my cell out, ignoring all the missed calls and messages, and clicked on the app to request a cab then sat on the edge of the curb while I waited for it.

The light from my cell allowed me to peek into the bags, and I did a little jig where I was sitting. I was so freaking excited to try all of this stuff on and see what difference it made. I wanted to go and try it out on the track now, but I knew I wouldn't be able to get onto the school grounds on a Saturday night.

Headlights flashed my way, and my app pinged

to let me know my driver was here. I hauled myself up into a standing position and grabbed my bags and wedges then opened the back door. "Hey!" I greeted him, pushing my bags in first and then getting in myself.

"Evening," the driver grunted, and as soon as I shut the door, he pulled out onto the road.

I watched out of the window for a couple of minutes and started to realize how close to home I had already been, but when we passed Cade's street, I held my hand up and shouted, "You can drop me here!"

"You sure? The app said—"

"Yeah, yeah." I waved him off and grabbed my bags as he pulled over to the side. "It's fine, you can still charge me the same." I pushed the door open and hauled myself out. "Have a great night!"

I dipped my head back as he pulled away from the curb and stared up at the clear night sky. The stars were shining bright, and half of the moon was visible. I wasn't sure how long I stared at it until I started to walk toward Cade's house.

Small stones dug into the bottom of my feet, but I was so close to his house now. His car was in the driveway, and all of his lights were off, but I was certain he wouldn't mind me waking him up, not once I showed him everything I had.

———

CADE

I groaned and rolled over, sure I'd only just fallen asleep. It couldn't be morning yet. I'd had the worse night possible, and it was all because of Willow. I'd been late by five minutes, and she'd let me know if it happened again, things were over, which meant I had to be extra nice to her stuck-up parents and resist stabbing myself in the eye to get away from the dinner table.

I'd made it back home around eleven and crashed on my bed, needing sleep to take me away into a land where I wasn't being blackmailed into doing anything.

A bang had one of my eyes opening, and I frowned, wondering what it was, but then I heard, "Cade!" It wasn't a shout, but not quite a whisper either, and then another bang echoed throughout the house.

What the hell?

I jumped out of bed and yanked a pair of sweats up my legs, then ran down the stairs. The banging didn't stop until I opened the door to Aria, whose fist was raised, ready to knock on the door again.

"Aria? What are you—"

"Hey!" Her smile was wide as she pushed past me and into the living room. She turned the light on as she went, and I frowned. What the hell was going on? I dipped my head out of the door, looking left and right and not spotting anything but darkness. Why was she here at——

"Cade! Come on, I need to show you what I got!" Her voice sounded higher-pitched and on edge.

Closing the door, I ran my hand over my face to wake myself up more before ambling into the living room. Aria was hunched over several bags she'd placed on the sofa, pulling things out and throwing them to the side.

"Aha! Found them." She spun around with two boxes in her arms, and I stepped toward her. A scratch on her face was dripping blood down her cheek, but it looked like it was dried. And that was when I took a good look at her. She was still wearing the same dress she had on at the party with no jacket and no shoes. What the hell had she done?

"Aria, what are you doing?"

She rolled her eyes, but her grin didn't drop from her face. "I'm showing you all my goodies, duh." She balanced the boxes in her arms and pulled something out of one of them. "I got new running shoes. They're going to help me with my times—and oh my god, Cade, they're so light." She lunged forward and passed me one. "Feel how light they are!"

I held it in my hand, already knowing how light they would be.

"Oh, I got matching leggings too." She dropped the boxes at my feet and spun around, causing her dress to whip around her because of the split. The bottoms of her feet were dirty—almost black. "And sports bras, and tank tops." She threw clothes as she pulled them out of the bags. "And a jacket!" She twirled and held the jacket up. "I got you a matching one, too. They're night-proof, and I thought because you go running in the dark, it would help you—"

"Aria—"

"—be seen by drivers."

I stepped forward and placed the running shoe on the arm of the sofa. "Aria—"

"Because you need to be safe, Cade. And running at night can be dangerous. The lady in the store told me the statistics of the number of runners who get knocked over by cars—"

"How did you buy all this stuff?" I asked, stopping a couple of feet in front of her. Her pupils were dilated, her gaze unable to focus on any one thing, and her chest was moving up and down rapidly.

"Mom and Sal gave me a credit card for my…" The grin dropped, replaced by downturned lips, and she blinked several times, almost as if she was coming out of a trance. The jacket she was holding tumbled to the floor, and she slowly turned, staring at all of the mess she'd made with the things she'd bought. "Oh my god, what have I done?" She backed away a step, her hand covering her mouth as her eyes welled with tears. "I don't know what happened, I was with Hope one minute and then… what happened?"

"Aria." I placed my hands on her shoulders, trying to get her to focus at me, but it was no use. She was off somewhere inside her own head. "Baby, look at me."

"I don't understand what happened. I don't…" Her fingers rubbed on her cheek, and she winced when they connected with the scratch. "Cade?"

I bent my knees so our faces were level and smiled gently. "Yeah, baby. It's me." My heart thumped in my chest, my pulse whirring through my ears as I realized something else was going on. The Aria who had banged on my door and whooshed into my house wasn't the Aria I knew. "What's going on?"

"I…" A tear fell down her cheek, and I couldn't resist swiping it away and keeping my hand against her face. "I don't know." She heaved a breath. "I don't know, Cade."

My stomach dipped the longer I stared at her and tried to piece everything together, but I couldn't come up with a logical answer. Something was happening to her, and there was no way I would stand by and let her lose herself more and more.

"We need to get you help," I told her.

She yanked herself away from me and paced

the length of the living room. "Because I went shopping?" She laughed, but the sound was manic. "I don't need help because I bought a few—"

"You didn't buy a few things, Aria," I ground out. "Look at the amount of stuff you got." I waved my hand to the sofa. "Something is going on with you—"

"There's nothing going on with me." She pulled her shoulders back and schooled her features into the mask I'd been so used to seeing her wear lately. And that was when I realized she'd been lying by omission this whole time. Since we'd been caught in my classroom by Willow, I thought she was fine, but I should have known better. You didn't go from cutting yourself at school to everything being perfect in the blink of an eye.

"Have you been cutting?" I blurted out, and at my words, she came to a dead stop. Her eyes were downcast, her gaze not meeting mine. Moving toward her slowly, I repeated, "Have you been cutting?"

"I—"

"Don't lie to me, Aria. Look at me when you answer."

She huffed out a breath, but I wouldn't let her get away without telling me. I'd been so stupid thinking she was okay. She wasn't okay. She was the furthest from okay possible, and I'd sat back and gone along with everything Willow said so nothing would change.

"Yes," she whispered, finally turning to look at me.

My shoulders slumped, and I tried to swallow past the lump in my throat. "How often?"

She'd told me months ago that she didn't cut more than once a week, so when she said, "Every day," I stumbled back a step. "Sometimes twice." My shoulders drooped, and I knew I shouldn't have shown her every emotion I was feeling, but the thought of her hurting herself over and over again was enough to knock me off-balance. "I had to," she said in a rush and darted forward. "You don't understand, Cade. I needed to be strong, I had to do it. Otherwise…" She trailed off, and I heard her unspoken words loud and clear.

"You wouldn't be able to survive?"

She closed her eyes and nodded. "Yeah."

"You need help, Aria."

"No." Her eyes sprung open, and she backed away. "Please, Cade. Please. I don't want anyone knowing I cut. Please."

I stared at her, really stared at her, and had no idea where to go from here. She was adamant about not wanting help with her cutting, but her turning up at my house in the middle of the night with bags full of clothes she'd bought had nothing to do with her self-harming.

Maybe if I got her to see a doctor about what happened tonight, she'd be willing to open up about her cutting in the future. She needed to take baby steps, and I was okay with that because there was no way I could sit by and watch the woman I loved disappear before my very eyes.

"Okay." I huffed out a breath and held my hands up. "You don't have to see anyone about your cutting, but"—I stepped toward her and grasped her hand—"I want you to go and see someone about what happened tonight." She opened her mouth, but I shook my head. "You know what happened isn't normal. *You know that*." Her limp fingers now gripped me tighter, almost as if her body was waking up.

"I know," she whispered. "But I'm scared."

I moved closer and wrapped my arm around her waist. "Why?"

"I'm scared they'll say I'm like my dad." She hiccupped a sob, and I held her tighter. "I'm not like him, Cade. I swear, I'm not. I'd never do the things he did. Never."

"I know you wouldn't." I placed my hand on the side of her neck, my thumb rubbing back and forth against the dip in her throat. "You're not him, baby. I promise you're not."

She nodded, tears flowing down her face as fast as rain hitting the ground during a storm. "I just want to feel normal again. I just…I want it all to stop."

Leaning my forehead against hers, I asked, "What do you want to stop, baby?"

"The pain," she croaked out. "The agony." She gripped my arms. "I need it all to go away."

"We'll do it," I told her, pulling away a little so I could stare into her eyes and drive my point home. "But the first step is to see someone, yeah?"

Her exhale of breath hit my face. "Will you take me?"

I pulled her against my chest and rocked her side to side. "Of course I will." I wasn't sure how long I stood there holding her, but once she stopped shaking, I pulled back and said, "Let's get you showered and in bed."

Her throat bobbed as she swallowed, and I led her to my bedroom. I let her hand go when we were in my bathroom and turned the shower on. The water crashed against the bottom of the shower floor, and when it was the right temperature, I stepped back and smiled at her. "Get washed, and I'll go find you something to sleep in."

"Okay," she whispered, and I hesitated to leave, but I had no choice. I couldn't stay in here with her, not when she was this vulnerable.

I left the door open ajar, enough to hear her if she needed me, and pulled a T-shirt and some sweats out of my closet. Swiping through my cell, I resisted googling about mental health. I knew all it would do was send me down a rabbit hole, so I opened up my messages and clicked on Lola's name.

Taking a deep breath, I glanced at the door, hearing the shower still running, then typed out a message.

> **Cade**: If you had a student presenting with mental health problems, and their parents asked you who they could go to for help, what would you say?

I knew she wouldn't message me back until the morning, but hopefully, she'd come back with an answer because whatever Aria was dealing with, her primary care doctor wasn't going to be able to help. With Lola being a teacher too, I often asked her opinion on certain situations to do with students, so I knew she wouldn't be surprised by the random message.

The water stopped, and I stood, pocketing my cell, and moving toward the bathroom door. "I found you some clothes." I opened the door a little but kept my eyes averted as I passed them through to her.

"Thanks."

I moved back while I waited for her to come

out, and a couple of minutes later, she exited with her wet hair hanging over her one shoulder.

"You can sleep in here," I told her, pointing at the bed. "I'm gonna sleep on the sofa."

"You don't have to do that, Cade."

I smiled gently, a small quirk of my lips. "Yeah, I do. Get some rest." I pulled my bedroom door open. "I'll see you in the morning." I waited until she had slipped into the bed, and even though I wished I could climb in with her and hold her all night, I couldn't.

She rolled over, putting her back to me, and I waited until I could hear her soft snores, then went downstairs to the mess she'd created. I placed all of the items back in the bags, intent on returning them all for her tomorrow, and then lay down on the sofa. I kept the light on, just in case, and stared at the ceiling, once again wondering if I was doing the right thing by not telling anyone.

I hoped for Aria's sake I was.

Chapter Nine

ARIA

I wasn't sure what woke me up, but as I rolled over and felt the soft mattress under my back, I knew I wasn't at home. The last time I'd woken up in this bed was the morning after Cade and I had slept together, and the day that followed was one of the worst in my life.

But today I had hope.

My body was frozen as I stared at the blinds on Cade's bedroom window and remembered everything from last night. It was as if time had moved in blocks, and there were chunks I couldn't quite remember and others that felt like a dream. It was a weird sensation, one I'd never experienced before, but I knew deep down it wasn't normal.

Cade was right, I did need help, but only for

this. I wasn't willing to tell anyone about my self-harming. That was still too fresh, too raw, but this… this scared me. This made me second-guess everything that had ever happened in my life.

The murmuring of Cade's voice vibrated through the bedroom floor, and I tried to listen to what he was saying, but couldn't quite hear him. I had no idea what time it was, only that the sun was high in the sky, and I was drained. My body didn't want to move, my brain didn't want to think. I just wanted to lie here for days and never leave.

Footsteps pounded up the stairs, and then the creak of Cade's bedroom door rang out. "Aria? Are you awake?"

"Yeah," I croaked out, turning my head to face him. He was dressed in a T-shirt and jeans, his sneakers on his feet and hair done, and if I hadn't known better, I'd have said he'd left the house already. "What time is it?"

"Just after one in the afternoon."

I shot up in the bed. "What? You let me sleep this long?"

"You needed it." He stepped forward and sat on the edge of the bed. "I went back to the mall this morning and returned all the clothes, so your mom and Sal don't know anything happened."

A lump formed in my throat and I glanced away from him, unable to bear looking into his eyes. "You did?"

"Yeah." His hand reached for me and landed on top of mine. I stared down at his fingers as they curled around my palm. "And I made you an emergency appointment with a psychiatrist."

"What? Why?" I shuffled away from him and climbed off the bed. I gripped my hair in my hands and stared at him. Why would he do that? Why would— "Do you think I'm crazy? Is that why you want me to go?"

"No, Aria, just listen."

"No." I pointed at him and backed away, hating the tears flowing down my face. "You think I'm crazy like my dad."

"I don't," he growled out, darting across the room to me. He grasped my arms enough to keep me in place but not so it would hurt. "I don't think you're crazy. I think there's something happening with you, and last night I witnessed it. You can't keep pushing it down and not expect anything to boil over. This is serious, Aria. You need to see a psychiatrist."

"What if I don't want to?" I asked, raising a brow. "What if I say no?"

He let out a puff of breath and stared right into my eyes. "Then I'm going to have to be forced to tell people what happened…and what you've been doing to yourself."

"You wouldn't." I ground my teeth together, hearing his threat loud and clear.

"I would." He pressed closer to me, his eyes showing me just how much he meant the words. "If it means I have to tell everyone to protect you from yourself, I'll shout it from the rooftops. Don't doubt how much I care about you, Aria, even if you don't like the way I show it."

"I hate you," I whispered, but from the pull of his lips, he knew I didn't mean it. Hate was the polar opposite when it came to what emotion I felt for him. My shoulders drooped as I asked, "When? When is the appointment?"

Cade let me go, took a step back, and checked his cell. "In an hour, so you need to get dressed." He walked across the bedroom and into the hallway, then came back a couple of seconds later with a bag. "I bought back some of the items I returned for you. Call it another birthday gift."

I glanced at the bag he placed on the bed and then at his back as he exited. Just as he was closing the door, I said, "Thank you."

He paused and turned his head to look at me. "You never have to thank me for anything, Aria. I'll always be there for you. *Always*." He clicked the door closed and left me alone in his bedroom with only my thoughts as company.

Why was he making me do this? But then I remembered the look on his face as he stared at me last night, the terror shining in his eyes; I'd scared him. And he wasn't the only one. If I were honest with myself, I frightened myself too. I had no idea what had happened, so maybe going and seeing this psychiatrist would help. It definitely wouldn't make anything worse.

I shuffled over to the bed and opened up the bag to pull everything out of it. There was a pair of the black running leggings with the purple strip, a matching sports bra, and tank top, as well as two boxes. I tried to keep my breathing under control as I stared at them all, hating the thought of Cade going back and returning everything I'd bought last night.

The first box held the running shoes I'd tried on in the shop, and the second box contained a pair of sneakers. I puffed out a breath and pulled the last item out—the open package of socks—and stared down at it all.

I'd lost sense of who I was last night, and even though I felt fine now, I was scared it would happen again. What if I didn't go to Cade next time? What if I didn't seek anyone out. The idea of that had me standing up and walking to the bathroom. I'd go and see the psychiatrist and get help. It was the only way forward; I could see that now.

It didn't take me long to brush my teeth and have a wash then get dressed. The running clothes fit perfectly, and the second pair of black sneakers Cade had bought looked good with the outfit. I wasn't sure whether this outfit would be my downfall or the start of a new chapter in my life. Either way, I was prepared to find out.

I headed down the stairs, spotting Cade waiting in the hallway, his thumbs flying across his cell screen. He looked up as soon as I was at the bottom, his gaze tracking over me and the bag I held in my hand.

"I need to get my purse," I told him, moving into the living room. It sat on the arm of the sofa, and even though I wanted to open it up and pull my cell out, I resisted. Now wasn't the time to get caught up with any messages I had. Instead, I needed to keep my focus. "Ready," I told Cade, my voice a little shaky.

He smiled and followed me out of the house. He pulled the passenger door open for me, and I slid inside his car, placing my hands in my lap over my purse while he got in the other side.

"It's about a thirty-minute drive," Cade said, pulling out of his driveway. "We'll get you something to eat on the way."

I nodded, unable to speak. My stomach rolled with each minute that went by, and when he pulled through a drive-through and ordered a burger and fries, I could barely eat them. I wasn't sure if time was going by at a snail's pace or as fast as lightning, but we were there before I knew it.

It looked like any other building, a sign outside and buildings either side of it. It definitely wasn't a mental hospital. "I'm scared," I whispered and bit down on my bottom lip. My shaky hands reached up and pushed some hair behind my ear as I stared at the building. "What if she says there's something seriously wrong with me? What if—"

"What if she helps you?" Cade cut me off, taking my hand in his and gaining my attention. "Let's go inside. You can talk to her, and then we can go from there. Baby steps, right?"

"Baby steps."

His answering smile was enough to have me take a calming breath and push open the car door. My pulse thrummed in my ears as I walked to where Cade waited in front of the hood. He held his hand out to me, and I didn't hesitate to take it. Together, we walked into the building, through a small entryway, and then into a waiting area. There wasn't anyone behind the receptionist area, but there was a button with a sign saying to ring it.

Cade reached forward and pressed down on it, causing a bell to ring out, and a couple of seconds later, another door opened, and a woman appeared.

"You must be Aria." Her smile was wide, her blond hair pulled back into a bun at the base of her neck, and her dark-brown eyes were inviting. She held her hand out for me, and I reached forward, gritting my teeth at how much they were shaking.

"I am," I whispered, placing my hand in hers and then pulling back.

"I'm Dr. Bay."

She greeted Cade in the same way, and from the way they talked, it sounded like they'd already spoken. "Would you like anything to drink?" she asked me, and when I shook my head, she waved her arm toward the door she'd just walked out of. "Shall we head into my office then?"

I glanced up at Cade and squeezed his hand harder. I didn't want him to come in with me, but I also didn't want to be alone. Alone was a scary place to be right then.

"I'll wait right here, and if you need me, I'll come to you, okay?"

"Okay." I let his hand go, wincing when our fingers disconnected. He had been anchoring me, and now I was drowning. I felt like I couldn't quite catch my breath as I followed Dr. Bay down the hallway and past two doors. She went into the third one, and although my steps were slow, I didn't stop.

It would have been so easy to sit in her office and give her some bullshit story about what happened, but I wouldn't do it. I'd tell her the truth about last night. I'd tell her how I felt because, at this stage, if I didn't accept the help I was offered, I wasn't sure I'd survive the next year.

———

CADE

My leg shook as I bobbed my foot up and down, my gaze fixated on the clock on the wall. Forty minutes had gone by in the blink of an eye, and now we were about to hit the sixty-minute mark. I wasn't sure if it was a good or bad thing she'd been in there for so long.

The longer she was in there, the more she talked, but the longer it took Dr. Bay to come to a conclusion. I was scared to death that Dr. Bay would say she had no idea what was happening. After I'd called her this morning and talked to her, she was confident she could help. I just hoped it was true.

My cell buzzed in my pocket, signaling a call, and I pulled it out, hitting the answer call button without looking at the screen.

"Yeah?"

"Where are you?" Willow screeched. "Where are you right now?"

My nostrils flared, and I ground my teeth together at her demanding tone. She had no fuckin' right talking to me like that, and right then, all I wanted to do was tell her to go and fuck herself and end the call.

"Out," I grunted, staring at the door Aria and Dr. Bay had walked through an hour ago.

"With who?" When I didn't answer her right

away, she continued, "My mom said she saw you with a girl a couple of hours ago. Is that true?"

I ran my hand over my face and my hair, then let my head drop forward. "I have no idea what you're talking about."

"Tell me where you are, I'm coming to you right now. And I swear to god, if you're with *her*, we're over. Which means *you're* over. You'll be done, Cade. Do you hear me? *Done.*"

The creak of a door sounded out, and I whipped my head up to see Dr. Bay smiling over at me. "She'd like you to come and see her now."

I stood and darted across the waiting room.

"Who was that? What the hell is going on, Cade?" Willow shouted down the line.

"I'll be there in a second," I told Dr. Bay, holding the door open and then watching as she walked away and into a door on the right. "Look, I'm visiting a friend who is in the hospital, okay? I've got to go, they're letting me in now."

"What?"

"I said I've got to go, I shouldn't even be using my cell."

"What's your friend's name? What happened to them?" Willow asked, talking a mile a minute.

"I gotta go," I grunted and ended the call. I couldn't worry about what she would or wouldn't do, not when Aria needed me. I pocketed my cell, ambled down the hallway, and knocked on the door Dr. Bay had gone through.

"Come in!" she shouted. Inhaling a deep breath, I pushed the door open and stepped into the room. I didn't know what I expected, but it wasn't the modern warmth the office was decorated in. The gray walls held paintings, and a desk sat in the far corner. But it was Aria sitting on a dark-gray sofa that pulled my attention. "Take a seat," the doctor said, indicating next to Aria.

I closed the door behind me and stepped forward, nearly stumbling when Aria's turned to me, and I saw the tears streaming down her face. "Baby," I croaked out, reaching for her as I sat on the sofa. "What happened?"

"I…" She shook her head. "I'm just…it's hard."

I grasped her hand in mine and nodded as if I understood, but I didn't. I'd never be able to understand how she felt.

"I asked you to come in here, Cade, so I can get a rounder picture of everything," Dr. Bay started. "Usually, in cases like this, it's better to get both the patient's feelings and understandings of what is going on, but also those who are around them regularly." She smiled at me. "Would it be okay if I asked you some questions?"

"Yeah, of course." I leaned back on the sofa but didn't let go of Aria's hand.

"Have you noticed any changes in mood with Aria? High one minute and then down the next?"

I thought back over the last few months and all of the times she would push everything down and act like it was all okay. "There have been times where she's"—I turned to face Aria and swallowed—"almost depressed or having an…episode? I don't know what you'd call it. But she'd be shouting and upset and then it's as if she clicks her fingers and pushes it all down. In the blink of an eye, she'll be back to normal."

Dr. Bay wrote on a pad as she nodded. "Okay. And I've already spoken to you about the incident that caused you to call me this morning, which indicated to me what may be happening." She leaned back in her seat and glanced at me, then focused on Aria. "I need you to know, Aria, it's very important you are completely honest with me. I won't be able to help you if you're not. I know it's hard, especially after some of the things we've talked about—your dad in particular—but I need to ask you one more time, is there anything else you're not telling me?"

The air in the room swirled, and I stared at the side of Aria's face. She'd told me she wouldn't tell the doctor about her cutting, and I had a feeling the doctor was sensing there was something she was holding back.

"No," Aria whispered, and my eyes fluttered closed. I hoped she would have— "Yes." Her hand tightened in mine, and I flung my eyes open. Aria flicked her gaze to mine, the pain and sorrow shining through her eyes almost gutting me. "I haven't been completely honest."

"You can do it," I whispered. "I know you can."

Aria bit down on her bottom lip, her chest expanding as she tried to calm her breathing, and then she blurted out, "I self-harm." Her shoulders sagged as soon as the words were out of her mouth. "The first time was when I was thirteen."

"Thank you for being honest with me, Aria," the doctor said, the tone of her voice that of a proud mother's. "Can I ask how you self-harm?"

"I cut," Aria responded right away, but her eyes were squeezed closed, her hand gripping mine so tight I was starting to lose feeling.

"And how often do you cut?"

"Once a week, maybe?" She paused and opened her eyes, but she stared at the wall. "This last month I've been doing it daily."

"So your low mood has been worse in the last month?" Dr. Bay asked, and I glanced at her, seeing her shoulders pull back. I wasn't an expert by any means, but the way she was sitting now told me she knew what was happening.

"Yes," Aria whispered. "Until last night. Last night I felt free. Like I was on top of the world, and nothing could bring me down."

Dr. Bay closed her notebook and shuffled

forward on her seat. "I think that's enough for today," she said. "Would you like Cade to be present while I tell you what happens from here?"

Aria squeezed my hand again. "Yes."

The doctor nodded, her gaze flicking to me very briefly and then landing back on Aria. "I want to do some blood tests to rule out anything else. I have a nurse here who can take those today, and we will get the results in the next day or two." I gritted my teeth as the doctor kept talking. "But I'm fairly certain they'll all come back negative. In which case, we will start you on some medication."

"Medication?" I frowned. "Why does she need medication?"

"Aria?" Dr. Bay called, waiting until she looked at her. "I think you have bipolar disorder." Aria's hand went limp in mine. "With the correct course of treatment, you can try and keep it under control, but the most important thing for you to do is see me once a week. Pills can help, but regular visits here will be the backbone of your treatment."

"So I'm crazy like my dad?" Aria asked, her tone full of heartbreak.

"No." The doctor leaned forward, almost as if she wanted to touch her and reassure her. "You're not crazy, Aria. You have a mental disorder. It's not your fault you have it, it's just the biology and the way you were made. Events during your childhood would have triggered it, and now that you've had a manic episode, we can determine exactly what is happening."

"Manic episode?" Aria asked, whipping her head around to face me. "I don't understand, Cade. I don't—"

"A manic episode is where you experience an extreme high, usually after a significant event," Dr. Bay interrupted. "I think your low mood and depression over the last month contributed toward it, as well as you turning eighteen."

Aria stared at me with wide eyes, and I could see this was too much for her to take in on her own. She needed me now more than ever, and I had no intention of letting her down. This wasn't just someone I cared about. This was the woman I was in love with.

"Baby steps, remember?" I told her, moving closer to her. "One step at a time. First, you get the blood tests."

"Yes," Dr. Bay said and ripped a piece of paper out of her notebook. She stood and walked toward us then perched on the edge of the table separating the sofa and her chair. "Write it down. One step at a time." She handed Aria the paper and a pen. "This way, whenever you feel like it's all too much, you can look at the list and know what the next step is."

We both watched as Aria wrote. "Step two is getting the results," Dr. Bay said. "I think if we schedule an appointment for Wednesday, then we can discuss the results?"

"Wednesday could work. Aria has track practice, but I can bring her afterward," I said.

"Perfect. Those are the only two steps you have right now. When I see you on Wednesday, we can talk it all through and go from there, how does that sound?"

"It sounds…" Aria trailed off, but I could sense the resolve building in her. With a clear direction, it would be easier for her to move forward. "Doable."

"Good." The doctor stood and moved to her desk. "I'll write you in for five p.m. on Wednesday, is that okay?"

"Yeah." Aria nodded and moved to the edge of the sofa. "And I need to go and get the blood taken now?"

"Yes." The doctor grabbed a card off her desk and scribbled something down on it then walked over to us. "This is my number—office and cell. If you need to talk, don't hesitate to call me. I'd rather you call me over nothing than not call me over something."

I stood and held my hand out to Aria. She didn't hesitate taking it, and together we followed the doctor out and into another room two doors down.

"Elizabeth will take your blood and see you out." Dr. Bay smiled at the nurse in the room and handed her a piece of paper. "I'll see you on Wednesday, and we'll go from there, okay?"

"Okay," Aria whispered, sitting down on the chair the nurse patted.

I leaned against the doorframe as she got her blood taken, not really listening to the conversation they were having. And once she had a Band-Aid on her arm and we were back in the car, I turned to her, grasped her face in my hands and whispered, "I'm so proud of you."

Aria's eyes welled with tears, but she didn't let them fall. "I'm so tired, Cade. So tired."

"I'm gonna take you back to my place and let you sleep the evening away. No cell, no one else around to disturb you. How does that sound?"

She sighed. "Sounds like perfection."

I flashed her a small smile and pulled out of the parking spot. My cell buzzed in my pocket, but I ignored it. It hadn't stopped while we were inside. I knew who it would be, and right now, I didn't have time to placate her. Focusing on Aria was my only priority.

Neither of us talked as I drove home, and as I took the turn into my street, I looked over at Aria. She was focused at looking out of the passenger window and didn't glance at me until I pulled into my driveway and turned the engine off.

I knew she didn't need me to talk, she didn't need my words to be flung at her. All she needed was support, and I'd always give her that. The dark circles under her eyes, coupled with the slumping of her shoulders, told me how tired she really was.

"Ready?" I asked, and she nodded in reply. I opened up my door, intent on going around to open hers, but she was out of the car before I got the chance. Her slow footsteps moved toward me, and I couldn't resist placing my arm around her shoulders and leading her into my house.

I locked the door behind us and led Aria up the stairs. I wouldn't sleep in my own bed again tonight, but it didn't bother me. Aria needed me more than she ever had, and I wouldn't let her down—not this time.

"I'm going to tell Mom I'm staying the night at Hope's," Aria said as she sat on the edge of my bed. She pulled her cell out, and her thumb flew across the screen as she let out a breath. "Hope was worried about me." She glanced up at me. "I wandered off and didn't even care that she was waiting somewhere for me." Her face crumbled, and I hated the way she looked right then. Every fiber of my being wanted to cocoon her in my arms and tell her it would all be okay, but I still had to keep some distance.

"It wasn't your fault," I told her, my voice firm. I crouched down in front of her and placed my hand over her cell. "Forget about everyone else"—she let me pull it out of her grip—"you need rest. And that's exactly what you're going to get, okay?"

Her light-brown eyes shone as she stared at me. "Okay." She shuffled up the bed away from me, and once she was settled and her eyes were closed, I pulled my cell out and swiped past all of the messages and missed calls from Willow. She didn't know when to give up. I knew I was treading a thin line with her, but I couldn't bring myself to care.

My cell buzzed in my hand, and Willow's message popped up on the locked screen.

Willow: Where are you?

I blew out a tired breath and took one last look at Aria. Her brows were pulled down into a frown, her hair covering half of her face. Even in slumber, she wasn't fully relaxed.

Willow: I can see your car outside your house!

A second later, banging thumped on my front door, and Willow's voice shouted, "Open the door, Cade! I know you're in there!"

My stomach dropped, but I didn't move my gaze off Aria. She needed the sleep, but I couldn't go down and talk to Willow right now. She had to wait because she was not a priority. I was choosing Aria over her, and I knew it would probably end things the way I knew them, but it didn't matter, not when it came to Aria. She was worth it. She would always be worth it.

Willow: I know you're in there, Cade! I swear to god. Open the damn door.

I stared down at the message on my locked screen and my teeth ground together. I couldn't do this anymore. I couldn't keep this pretense up. I needed a way out of what Willow had trapped me in. I needed a plan, one that wouldn't mean more pain for Aria.

Chapter Ten

CADE

I dropped Aria off at the end of her street on Monday morning. The bags under her eyes had lessened, and the smile on her face wasn't as forced. She needed peace and quiet, but most importantly rest, which was precisely what she'd gotten. She slept for fourteen hours and woke up extra early this morning so we could get some breakfast before I dropped her off.

But now I was heading to the school knowing I had a shitstorm coming my way after ignoring Willow last night. She'd stayed outside my door for nearly an hour while I stood in the same spot, waiting for her to leave. And once she did, I crashed on my sofa, not wanting to think about what would happen today.

I pulled into the lot and hadn't even exited my car before Willow was on me. "What the hell, Cade?" She threw her hands up in the air, and I raised a brow at her. Her hair wasn't its normal sleekness. Instead, it was messy and thrown on top of her head. Her usual makeup wasn't on her face, and the tight skirts and shirts she liked to wear were replaced with pants and a loose-fitting shirt. "I've been calling you all night. I came over to your house! Where the hell have you been?"

"None of your business," I ground out, slamming my car door closed. I stalked past her and groaned when she kept up with my pace.

"I know you were home last night. Your car was there," Willow continued, oblivious to the way I was acting. "Can't you see how worried I've been? Look at me, Cade. Just see the way I look!"

I took the steps to the entrance of the school two at a time, and just as I opened up the doors, students started to file off one of the school buses in the lot. "Are you serious?" I halted and shook my head at her. "It's an act, just like everything else. You want attention, and I'm not giving it to you."

"But you'll give it to your little whore, huh?" She spread her arms wide. "Why don't I just tell everyone—"

I grabbed her arm and yanked her inside the building, then pushed her against the wall. "I'm warning you, Willow. One more word from you and I won't be held responsible for what will happen."

"Are you threatening me, Cade?" Her eyes widened, but she wasn't scared. She was one of the best actresses I knew, and I couldn't help think she'd entered the wrong career.

"No." I let go of her and stepped back. "That's a warning. I've had a stressful weekend, so just let me get in the fuckin' building before you jump on me, yeah?"

"Oh." She pushed her bottom lip out, just like a child would. "I thought you were avoiding me."

It was on the tip of my tongue to tell her I was, but it wouldn't do me any good. I still had to tread carefully with her, even more so with everything else going on. I wouldn't allow her to add any more stress on Aria's plate, which meant I had to take it until I found a way out.

"No, I told you, I was in the hospital visiting a friend."

"What friend?" Willow threw back at me.

"A college friend. They got into a car wreck." The lie fell so easily from my lips as I glanced around, seeing students starting to enter the hallway. "I need to head to my classroom. Can we talk about this later?" I placed a kiss on her cheek, hating I had to do it but knowing it would soften her fall.

"Fine. But I want to know everything that

happened," she warned, and I nodded as I stepped away from her.

My teeth ground together, and I spun around, darting toward my classroom and needing to be away from her. She was pushing every button imaginable, and I knew I wasn't far from blowing up. It was a matter of time, and when it happened, I needed a plan in place. I needed something to protect Aria.

I closed my classroom door and pulled my cell out to type a message to Ford. He wouldn't get it until he was back from his undercover job, but that was perfect timing because it meant he wouldn't be around right now to ask any questions.

Cade: If you get this message and I'm not around, I need you to watch out for Aria. There's more going on than people realize. She needs support and help, and I think you're the only one she'll let do that right now—not that she'll have a choice. If something happens to me, I need you to tell her you know about Dr. Bay. Tell her you'll take her to her appointments, and do it because she needs it. She needs me, but I'm not sure I'm going to be able to be there for her. I'll explain it all the next time I see you, just please, do this for me.

I locked my cell and let out a breath. I'd given him just enough to be able to help Aria, but not too much as to where I would break my promise to her. With the plan now in place, I knew everything would be okay. If I didn't keep my cool, and Willow ended up telling everyone what she saw, at least Aria would be protected.

The day flew by, and before I knew it, it was lunchtime, and I hadn't heard from Aria at all. I'd seen her at her locker between lessons, but she hadn't looked at me. I craved going up to her and asking how she was feeling, but I knew it wouldn't help. All it would do was draw attention to us, and that was the last thing we needed.

Strolling down the hallway, I headed toward my office in the athletics building but halted when I heard voices. *There shouldn't be anyone in here.*

"No one ever comes in here at this time," I heard a male voice say, one I recognized as Harry the football player—the same student Ford had slammed against the lockers after Aria had gotten in a fight with Jasmine.

"You sure?" I tilted my head to the side, also recognizing that particular voice.

"Yeah, babe. I'm sure." Some movement echoed, and I drifted closer, looking through the gap in the door to the boys locker rooms. I could see them both clearly, and as soon as I realized what they were doing, I moved my hand to open the door wider, but something stopped me at the last second.

I pulled my cell out and clicked record, knowing this could be the answer to everything. I'd been searching and searching for a way out but hadn't come up with anything. And now…

Now I could call an end to it all with one little video.

"I'll show you how to do it, babe," Harry said, dipping down and snorting a line of white powder off a workbook. "Ahhh, that feels so good."

"Give it to me," Jasmine demanded, and snatched the rolled-up bill from him. Her face came fully into view, and then she bent her head and snorted a line too.

My grin was wider than it had ever been before as Jasmine leaned back and stared up at the ceiling. There was no denying their faces in the recording, so I clicked it off and pocketed my cell.

They said good things came to those who wait, and there was no doubt I'd waited long enough for this. My stomach fluttered as I made my way into my office and watched the recording again. I should have gone in there and taken them both to the principal—that was what I was meant to do—but Willow hadn't been playing fair since the moment she stepped into my classroom and caught Aria and me kissing.

You had to fight fire with fire, and mine was

roaring to life, promising to burn everything in its path.

My mood for the rest of the day was better than it had been in weeks, and when the school day was finally over, I leaned back in my desk chair and waited. I knew it wouldn't take her long to come and find me—it never did. Only this time, I had a surprise in store for her.

She had no idea what was about to come her way. She thought she was a master manipulator, but I'd grown up around men who manipulated people on a daily basis for their jobs. I'd learned more than she could ever know about, and now it was time. Time for me to give the final strike.

"There you are!" Willow waltzed into my classroom, her makeup and hair now done to perfection. The act hadn't worked this morning so she'd obviously decided to drop it. "You didn't come to the teachers' lounge at lunch."

I hummed in response and leaned forward, steepling my fingers on my desk. "I didn't want to."

"What?" She raised her brow and sat on the edge of my desk, reaching out her hand for me. I grasped it before she could touch me and stood.

"Don't touch me."

Her eyes sparked at being told no. "I think you should take that back."

"Nah." I let her hand go and sidestepped her. "I don't think I will." I smiled, the same kind of smile she gave me when she got what she wanted every single time over the last few months. The ball was in my court now. She just wasn't aware how much.

She stood slowly, the mask slipping off her face and revealing who she truly was. "All it will take is one visit to the principal's office," she warned. Her threats had become more brazen over the last couple of weeks and were no longer veiled. "Your life would explode around you, Cade. Is that what you want?" She shrugged and took a step toward the door. "It's your funeral."

"Wait." The smile on her face lifted to heights I wouldn't have imagined possible. She thought she'd won. She thought she had me right where she wanted me. She was wrong. "Let me show you something first."

I pulled my cell out and clicked on the video, pausing it at the start. I kept my features neutral as to not show her too soon, and then passed her the cell.

"What's this?" she asked, clicking play. She didn't have to wait long to find out what it was. Her mouth dropped open, and a small gasp left her lips.

"Maybe I should come to the principal's office with you?" I said, my brow raised. "I'm sure he'd be interested to know what his students are getting up to on their lunch breaks."

"No, no, no, no." Willow darted away from me,

her chest lifting on a sharp breath. "I deleted it. You have no evidence now."

I laughed. The kind of laugh I couldn't control, no matter how much I wanted to. "For a teacher who has such high ambitions, you really are stupid." I dropped all pretenses from my face and sauntered toward her. I kept just enough distance so we weren't touching. "You remember the cookout you invited yourself too?" She opened her mouth to answer, but I didn't let her. "There were seven men around that table. One was me, the other was Aria's stepdad, and the other five?" My lips slowly lifted into a smirk. "The other five are DEA agents. Agents I grew up with. Agents who taught me things you could only dream about."

"I…I don't understand…"

"I'm telling you that wasn't the only copy. Just because you deleted it, doesn't mean it doesn't exist."

"I…what do you want, Cade?"

I held my hand out. "My cell for starters." She placed it in my palm, and I stepped back. "This is what is going to happen. You're going to forget all about what you saw in my classroom." She stepped forward, but I continued, "You see, I let you get the better of me. I let your threats work their way into my brain without realizing one thing." I closed my laptop and slid it into my bag, acting like I was having a normal conversation. "You have no evidence. It's your word against mine. And I'm sure once I showed people my actual evidence, and what your sister has been doing, they'll be inclined to believe me and not you."

"You son of a bitch." She stomped her foot. "I won't let you get away with this."

"Oh, sweetheart." I chuckled and shouldered my bag, feeling lighter than I had in months. "You have no choice. One sniff of me thinking you're coming for Aria or me, and I'll pass that tape along to my dad and let his team deal with it." I pulled the classroom door open and looked at her one final time. "Ball is in your court."

I winked and strolled out of the room with a shit-eating grin on my face.

———

ARIA

"Your blood results came back normal," Dr. Bay told me as soon as I sat on the sofa in her office. "Which confirms you have bipolar disorder."

My stomach sank, and my eyes started to mist over. I was hoping something would show in my blood because at least if it was something physical then I could explain it away, but instead, I was becoming just like my dad. I was crazy, and now she was confirming it.

"I want to start you on a few different medications. Each one should stabilize your moods and…"

She kept talking, but I wasn't really listening to her. I was focused on what this all meant and how it all could have started. Was I born like this? Or did events in my life make me this way?

Cade's hand touched my thigh, and I flicked my gaze down to it, but I couldn't quite make it out past all the blurriness. I swayed to the right, feeling myself becoming off-kilter and tried to push everything out of my brain, but it was all too much. Everything was too much.

"What have you done?" Mom screamed.

I pulled the covers over my head, trying to block out all of the noise coming from the living room, but it was no use. I could still hear every word.

"I didn't do anything," Dad told her, talking way too fast. "She needs a bike, Jan. She needs to be able to ride a bike. So I went and bought her one."

"You used the rent money!" Mom shouted, and I could just imagine how angry her face looked. "And you didn't just buy her a bike. You got yourself one, and then you went and spent five hundred dollars on clothes and accessories. What the hell were you thinking?"

"I want to set you up with a regular appointment as

well, Aria. We'll start with once a week and see how you feel. If you need it more than that, we can do it, but we won't know until we start." Dr. Bay's voice broke through my nightmare, and I whipped my head up to face her, feeling tears streaming down my cheeks from the change of direction. "I can see this is a lot to take in." Dr. Bay paused, and Cade's hand squeezed my thigh. "Is there anything you'd like to talk about today? Any questions you have?"

"Stop asking me questions!" Dad roared, holding his head in his hands and pacing back and forth. "All you do is ask me questions."

I wasn't sure who he was talking to, but I stared at him with wide eyes and brought my knees up to my chest. "Daddy?"

"It can't happen. I can't do it." He shook his head and ran toward the wall, not stopping until his body collided with it. "Get out of my head!"

My bottom lip wobbled, and all I wanted to do was get up and help him, but I was scared, so I stayed curled into the corner of the sofa.

He groaned and rolled over, his gaze connecting with mine right away. "Aria, they're coming for you, sweetie. You need to hide again, okay?" His voice was different now, softer, more like the daddy I knew. "No! Stay where you are!" He shook his head and stood. "Don't move, Aria."

I didn't know what to do or how to act. I had no idea—

A lock clicked in the front door, and hope rose within me. Mommy was home, she'd make it all better. The door swung open, and Mommy stepped inside. Her face was tired and sad, but I knew she'd protect me from Daddy when he was like this.

She stared at each of us, and Daddy started to pace again, shouting things I didn't understand.

"Aria." Mom darted toward me and picked me up. "Don't come out of your room, no matter what you hear, okay?"

"Aria?" Cade's deep voice shocked me out of my memory, and I shook my head. "Baby?" He lowered his voice. "What's going on?"

"Am I like my dad?" I asked, but I wasn't sure who I was asking as I stared at Cade. "Will I end up like him?" Cade's dark-blue eyes swirled with emotion, but I wasn't sure what it meant. Was he sad I was going through this, or sad he was stuck with me?

"I requested access to your dad's medical records, Aria," Dr. Bay said, and I turned to face her. My breath stalled in my chest, afraid of what she was going to say next. "Your dad had a lot of mental health issues. Bipolar disorder, yes, but he also had schizophrenia and borderline personality disorder." Her brows pulled down into a frown. "Your dad stopped getting treatment and wasn't taking his medication."

"He wasn't?" I asked. "Is that why he was so…" I took a breath and closed my eyes, trying to push all my thoughts away. "So…"

"Aria." Dr. Bay waited until I had my eyes open to continue. "Your dad didn't stick to his treatment plan, but had he, he would have lived a semi-normal life." She shuffled forward on her seat. "With the combination of medication I want to start you on, and regular visits with me, I have no doubt you will conquer everything in front of you. But the trick is to stick to the treatment plan."

"So I can get better?" I asked.

"Better isn't a word I would use." Dr. Bay flicked her gaze down to her notepad on her lap and then back to me. "Under control. You can get it under control. But it won't happen overnight. It's going to take time for everything to kick in and work."

"And in the meantime?" Cade asked.

"In the meantime, you keep things as normal as before. Keep to your regular schedule, and don't make allowances. If you feel sad, let yourself feel it. Don't think you have to push it aside. Be in the moment with your sadness."

"Okay." I let out a breath, the first one that felt like I didn't have an elephant sitting on my chest for. "And the medication?"

She explained what medication I would be

taking and how often to take it, and then booked me in for a regular visit every Tuesday evening. Cade said he'd bring me to them until I told my mom what was happening, but I refrained from informing him that I wouldn't tell her. I was afraid she'd think I was like my dad, just like I had.

Cade took the prescription for my medication from her as we exited, and once we had picked them up from the pharmacy and were on our way back home, I eventually managed to say, "Thank you."

"For what?" Cade asked, glancing at me briefly and then looking back out the windshield.

"For helping me." A small smile curved on my lips as I stared at him. "For believing in me and not letting me drown."

He pulled up at the curb in front of my house and turned to face me. His gaze flicked down to the locket I wore around my neck, causing his own lips to lift up into a smile. "I promised, remember?" I did remember. I remembered each and every one of his promises. "Is it okay if I call you later?"

Butterflies took flight in my stomach as I nodded. "I'd like that."

———

ARIA

"I wish we could be there," Mom said, wrapping her arms around me and squeezing me as tight as she could. "You're gonna do so well, I just know it." She pulled back and turned to face Cade. "I want a recording of every time she runs, got it?"

Cade saluted her and grinned. "Got it."

It was Friday lunchtime, and we were leaving early because it would take us four hours to get to the center where the meet was being held. Reagan's dad was driving her there because they had family near the track, so it was just Cade and me in a car for four hours—alone. I wasn't sure if I was nervous or excited, most probably a combination of both.

"You go get 'em, Ri, you hear?" Sal grunted and wrapped his arms around me too. He didn't do this often, but when he did, it made me realize just how much he cared. It was hard to get that feeling from Sal, but lately, he'd been showing me more and more.

I'd started to take my medication, and although Dr. Bay told me it would take some time to get them into my system, I already felt better. I was actually seeking treatment and not doing it alone like I'd always done.

Sal let go of me and stepped back, a huge grin on his face as he wrapped his arm around Mom's shoulder. Maybe it was time to tell them what had been going on, but their smiling faces made me doubt it. It was only two weeks until their wedding, and then they'd be off on their honeymoon.

I pushed my shoulders back and told myself I'd wait until they got back. At least that way I wouldn't spoil their wedding with all my fucked-up-ness. "I'll message when we get there," I told them both, watching Cade close his trunk which held our suitcases. We'd only be gone for two nights, but it was enough to fill the carry-on suitcase I'd borrowed from Lola.

Cade opened up the passenger door for me, but I didn't look at him, afraid I'd give too much away in front of Mom and Sal. I waved at them as we exited the lot, and once we were on the highway, I relaxed a little.

"I can't believe this is happening."

"Why?" Cade asked, his attention focused on the highway. "Your times have been getting better and better, and you're dedicated." He paused and flicked his gaze to me briefly. "You're built for running track, Aria. It's just natural for you."

I bit down on my bottom lip and stared at the tattoos dancing on his arm with each of his movements. "You think?"

"Nope." I could spot his grin from his side profile. "I know."

I rolled my eyes and chuckled. "You're gonna make my head huge." I leaned my head back on the headrest but didn't take my gaze off him. Things had become more comfortable between us over the last week.

"Nah." His right hand moved off the steering wheel and reached for mine. This wasn't the kind of thing friends did, I knew that, but I couldn't help lacing my fingers with his and loving the way my hand got lost in the size of his. "That's impossible. You already have a big head."

I slapped his shoulder and laughed. "Shut up." I yawned, feeling everything from the last week catching up with me. So much had happened in such a small space of time, and my brain was still trying to process it all.

His hand squeezed mine. "You should get some sleep. We have a busy weekend."

"Maybe just for a little while," I said, turning toward him and bringing our linked hands to my chest.

I closed my eyes, and before I knew it, Cade's voice was waking me. "We're here, baby."

Groaning, I let go of his hand and stretched my arms above my head, smacking my knuckles off the roof of his car. "Ow." Opening my eyes, I tried to take stock of where we were, and when the name of the athletic building came into view, I sat upright. "Oh my god, we're here!"

"That's what I just said." Cade chuckled and pushed out of his car at the same time I did. My sleepiness left me in an instant as I followed him into the building.

He kept his distance from me, his hand not reaching for mine, but I was okay with that. I tried not to overthink it, not when I had to focus on the race tomorrow.

The building inside was huge, and we found the locker rooms pretty quickly, then headed out onto the main track and field. There were so many different things happening on the field. People practicing long jump and javelin throwing as well as shot put. I was fascinated, but it was the track that drew most of my attention.

I crouched down and pressed my fingers to it, in awe at how rough but smooth it was. "Wow. It's so much better than the one at school."

"Yep." Cade tilted his head toward a board attached near the entrance of the track. "Let's go check when our practice time is."

"We get a practice time?"

"Yeah." We halted in front of the board. "Each school gets time to practice on the track tomorrow morning. The races start at four p.m." He placed his finger on the board and dragged it down until he saw Reagan's and my name. "Twelve until twelve thirty." He blinked several times and turned to face me. "Early breakfast, then lunch after practice and some warm-ups after that." I raised my brows at him, having no idea why he was staring at me as he was working out the schedule. "What are you grinning at?" he asked, his own lips spreading.

"Nothing." I shrugged but couldn't wipe the happiness off my face. "You just look excited."

"I am excited." He stepped closer to me, but shook his head and moved back. "Come on, let's go and check in to the hotel."

I spun around, seeing a few people staring at us, but unlike before, where I would have wondered why they were staring, I couldn't bring myself to care. I was happy beyond belief, I just wasn't sure if it was because I was hours away from taking part in my first track meet, or because I got to spend so much time with Cade. Either way, I wasn't going to think about it too much.

It was only a ten-minute drive to the hotel we were staying in, and from the looks of the check-in desk, we weren't the only ones staying here from the track meet.

"Name," the woman behind the desk asked when we got to the front of the line.

"Easton," Cade said, pulling his wallet out and handing the woman a card.

She didn't look up from her computer screen as she asked, "Would you like to add breakfast to your room?"

"No, thanks," Cade said, and finally the woman looked up and took the card from him.

She swiped it and handed it back, then spun

around to collect some papers from the printer. "You're on the fifth floor, room five-twenty-seven." She handed Cade the papers and then two keycards. "Enjoy your stay."

I kept quiet as I pulled on the handle of my suitcase and followed Cade toward the elevators. His bag was slung over his shoulder along with mine that had all my running gear. He clicked the button next to the door, and a couple of seconds later, they opened up, and we stepped inside.

"So…" I stared at the doors, not willing to look up at Cade. "We're staying in the same room?"

"Yeah," Cade answered right away. "I got us two beds, though. It was the only room left unless we wanted to travel thirty minutes each way."

I nodded, understanding why. We could totally share a room together with different beds. It was no different to when I'd stayed over at his house last weekend. He'd slept on the sofa, and I'd had his bed, and we'd managed just fine with no *incidents*.

The door whooshed open, and we both stepped out, then walked down the hallway. We passed every number but ours until the end, and then Cade swiped the card on the door handle. He opened it up and waved at me to go in first.

"Wow." The decor was modern, the room nice and cool from the AC. A door to the left housed a bathroom with a standing shower, and then the room opened up to a bed. A singular bed. "Erm…Cade?"

"Yeah?" he called, his footsteps coming closer. "Ah, shit." We both stared at the king-sized bed, silence stretching between us. "I'll go back down and see if they can switch our rooms."

"Okay," I whispered, not looking away from the bed as he left the room. I drifted toward the window and pulled the curtain aside to look out of it. The skyline was beautiful, the late afternoon sun casting a glow over the top of the buildings.

The door swung open not long after, and I turned to face Cade whose features were etched with anger. "They don't have any more rooms. Fuck." He spun around and stared at the section of the room between the bathroom and bed. "I can make a pallet on the floor—"

"No." I stepped away from the window. "It's fine. We can share a bed—"

"I don't think that's a good idea," Cade interrupted, his intense gaze focused on the bed now.

I blew out a breath, my stomach sinking. Of course it wasn't a good idea. "Because of Miss Simmons?" I asked.

"What?" He frowned as he stared at me. "No. Willow and I…well, let's just say she has nothing to hold over me now."

"Huh?"

Cade sat on the edge of the bed, his hand

rubbing over his face as he did. "She was threatening me, Aria. She said she'd tell everyone about us."

"But I took the blame in the classroom. I don't understand."

"She asked me if we'd been more than that, and I didn't answer her."

I let my head drop back and groaned. "Dammit, Cade. Did no one ever teach you silence speaks a thousand words?"

"Well, what did you expect me to do, Aria?" He stood and spread his arms wide. "I couldn't fuckin' lie and tell her you meant nothing to me. I couldn't fuckin' do that."

My heart hammered in my chest at his words. "So what does this mean now?"

"It's done. I dealt with it, and now she has no leverage."

"So she's not going to come after us?"

"No." He let his arms drop to his sides. "But that doesn't mean we can sleep in the same bed." He backed away and opened up the closet. "There are things in here for a pallet. It'll be fine. We'll make do."

"But—"

"No buts." He shook his head and pasted a smile on his face. "Get unpacked, and then we can go meet with Reagan and her dad. You need an early night tonight."

Chapter Eleven

ARIA

I moved my arms above my head and stretched my entire body out. There was nothing like having a huge bed to yourself all night, although it had taken me a while to get to sleep with Cade on the floor next to me.

Cade hadn't been kidding when he said I needed an early night. He had me back in the room by eight, and I hated to admit I'd fallen asleep not long after. But today was the day. Today I could potentially be offered a scholarship and start fresh.

Soft snores sounded from the side of me, so I rolled over and stared down at Cade. He'd used a sheet as his mattress and collected two pillows and a blanket to create his bed. I'd insisted over and over again that there was enough room for both of us in the bed, but he'd refused to get in here with me. He was probably right to keep refusing, but I didn't feel right with him on the floor while I had this giant bed all to myself.

I tilted my head and stared at his peaceful face. His lips were in a straight line, parted slightly, and I couldn't help but remember the last time they'd been fused against mine. So much had happened since then, and yet, I still felt the same way.

He'd pushed his way into my heart and soul, and nothing I did seemed to get rid of him. He was there, not willing to leave, and if I were honest, I didn't *want* him to leave. I propped my hand on the side of my head and continued to stare down at him. Last night, he'd told me a little about what happened with Miss Simmons, but my gut was telling me there was more to it.

What had she said to him? And more importantly, what had he done to get her off his back? Did this mean he didn't have to keep up pretenses with her anymore? Was it really all an act?

Cade's lashes fluttered, and he rolled over onto his side, slowly opening his eyes. His gaze landed on my face, and I smiled brightly. "Holy shit!" He jumped up into a sitting position causing the sheet to fall from his chest, and I'd be lying if I said I didn't look. "What the hell, Aria?"

"What?" I asked, my voice soft and innocent. "What did I do?"

"You were staring at me." He let out a breath and shook his head. "Fuck. You scared the life out of me." He ran his hand over his face and through his hair several times, and then looked back at me. "Why are you smiling so wide?"

He raised a brow in suspicion, and I shrugged. "No reason." He pushed himself up off the floor and stood, but I couldn't take my eyes off him. All he was wearing was a pair of sweats low at his hips, and I was utterly enthralled.

"Aria, stop," he warned.

I raised my brows and flicked my gaze to his face. "What?"

"Stop looking at me like that." He took two steps away from me. "Stop it."

"I have no idea what you're talking about." I pulled the covers up to my shoulders and lay back down in my bed. I really had no desire to move from my spot, not yet anyway.

He darted toward me, placed his hands on either side of me, and whispered, "You know exactly what I'm talking about, baby." His gruff voice so close to me was making me squirm, and I glanced at his lips. "That right there, I know what you're doing. I've only got so much willpower, Aria."

My chest lifted on a breath as I said, "I can't help it." It was an admission. Something he wasn't expecting if the tic of a muscle in his jaw was anything to go by.

Neither of us moved, locked in a stare I never wanted to end. We were alone, in a room, with nothing and no one to stop us, and yet he was resisting it. I'd backed away from him so much the last couple of months, but with his confession about Miss Simmons last night, I couldn't come up with a reason why I shouldn't kiss him.

I leaned forward, just enough to let him know what I wanted, but he yanked himself away and spun around. "Fuck!" He slapped his hand on the wall as his shoulders bunched up. "I can't do this. Fuck. I can't—"

"Cade?"

"Just…just wait, Aria. I'm trying real fuckin' hard right now to do the right thing." I swallowed past the lump building in my throat, and when he turned back to face me, I couldn't quite meet his eyes. "I'm trying to be the good guy. I'm trying to give you space. Fuck…I'm trying, Aria, but you're not making it any easier."

"I don't understand," I whispered, really not understanding what he was saying. I didn't get it. Why was he trying to be a good guy? That hadn't stopped him months ago when he'd first kissed me. It hadn't stopped him when I gave him my virginity, so why now? Why—

"Oh my god." I threw the covers aside and darted off the bed. "This is because of my diagnosis, isn't it?" I could feel the blood draining from my face. "Is that it? You don't want to get too close because I'm crazy?"

"You're not fuckin' crazy, Aria," he growled out, and the way his eyes sparked with fierceness made me believe his words. "This is to do with that, but it's also not." He let his head dip back, exposing his throat and making his muscles tense even more. "You've just been through a shit storm. You've got so much going on with your medication and then school, and now this meet, and I don't want to add more shit to your plate. It's as simple as that. I'm not willing to sacrifice your health just for what I want."

"I—"

"I'm not talking about it again, Aria. Get ready. We need to go and have some breakfast, and then we'll head to the track."

I stared at him, really stared at him, but he'd pushed his shoulders back, resolved in what he was saying. I understood it now, I really did, but that didn't mean I had to like it. I had a plate full of things to cope with, but there was always room for Cade. *Always*.

Instead of saying anything and trying to tell him that, I spun around, then entered the bathroom. It didn't take me long to have a shower and brush my teeth, and once we changed places and he was in the bathroom, I got dressed in my track clothes. I pushed my feet into my sneakers and packed my track shoes and water bottle in my bag.

Just as Cade was exiting the bathroom, completely dressed, I tied my hair into a high pony-tail and declared, "I'm ready to go."

"Give me a minute," Cade grunted, rifling through his bag for something. He pushed his feet into his sneakers and grabbed his wallet and keys, and then we were both out of the door. Neither of us spoke as we exited the hotel and got into the car. He didn't ask me what I wanted for breakfast, but when he stopped at a drive-through and got us pancakes and bacon to go, I was glad.

"I'm so hungry," I groaned as Cade passed me the food to put on my lap. We ate in the lot before heading to the track. The lot was already packed with cars, and I could hear cheers inside the center as I pushed out of the car. "Oh, god." I put my hand on my stomach as it rolled.

"Aria, you okay?" Cade asked, opening his trunk and pulling a bag out.

My muscles locked as I stared at the center doors, my breaths starting to come faster. "I don't think I can do it." I backed away a step, my nerves getting the better of me. No one had ever watched me run, and now I'd be surrounded by people staring at me and commenting on how fast or slow I was.

"You can." Cade halted in front of me and bent so his face was level with mine. "I know you can do it. After everything that has happened over the last week, this should be smooth sailing."

"But what if I fall? What if the track is too different from what we practice on? What if—"

"What if you do great?" Cade counteracted. "What if your nerves are a good thing?"

"How the heck can they be a good thing?"

Cade shrugged and stood to his full height. "Means you care. Come on." He took a step back, but he didn't take his gaze off me. "Let's go boss this."

"Boss this?" I raised a brow, glad he'd distracted me. "Who are you right now?"

He pushed his hand through his hair and pulled his lips up on one side. "Cade Easton, baby, and don't you forget it." He ended with a wink and pointed at me.

A laugh burst from my chest and freed all of the tension that had been building up since I'd opened my eyes this morning. "Fine, okay, let's boss this." I straightened up, pushed my shoulders back, and made a beeline for the center.

———

CADE

I'd tried to not show any nerves as both Aria and

Reagan had been practicing, but the closer to the races they were taking part in came, the harder I was finding it to hide them. I'd kept off to the side and tried to keep both of them calm, but now they were warming up, and I wasn't allowed on the field to help them.

They knew what they were doing, but it didn't make it any easier. It was all in their hands, and win or lose, they were the masters of their own destinies.

I turned my head toward the left, spotting all the scouts in the first couple of rows of seats. They were taking notes and photos of which runners they were interested in, and I'd already had several come and talk to me about Reagan. She was a known name on the circuit and had already been offered four scholarships, but her dad thought she could do better than the schools she'd already been offered.

"Cade Easton?" a gruff voice asked from behind me.

I turned around, trying to keep half of my attention on the field. "That's me."

"Good." He held his hand out to me, and I shook it. "I'm Harold Lefinter, the head coach for the athletics department at Shire Oaks College."

"Nice to meet you." If either one of the girls were offered a scholarship from him, they'd be set for life. The college was only thirty minutes away from where I lived, and they had one of the best programs in the country. I'd applied to go there myself when I was in high school, but I hadn't stood a chance against the athletes that they turned into household names. "I've heard amazing things about your program."

Harold's stony face didn't move an inch, and it was only then I noticed he wasn't holding a clipboard in his hands. "Enough amazing things to come and join it, son?"

I backed away a step, sure I'd heard him wrong, but as I repeated his words in my head, I realized I hadn't. "I…why?" It was a stupid question, but I'd been caught off guard. Why would someone like this approach me while we were at a meet to offer high school kids scholarships?

"We were handed your name about four years back when you graduated from college. I've been keeping an eye on your career, and I see you have two students in the track races now."

"I do." I smiled wide and turned so I could see them. "Reagan is taking part in the four hundred and twelve hundred, and Aria is doing the eight hundred and sixteen hundred."

Harold came to stand next to me and crossed his arms over his chest as he looked out onto the field. "Aria the tall one?"

"No. That's Reagan." I turned to face him, feeling my chest puff out. "You wouldn't think Aria is a runner, not with her gait, but wait and see what we've been working on."

"Hmmm. Interesting choice taking a chance on

someone who doesn't fit the usual standards."

I raised a brow and turned to face him fully. "See, here is where I don't agree with the 'standards.' If you have a student athlete that you take at face value of what they can do right then, you're already losing. It's the potential you need to seek out. That's what I'm looking for."

Harold's gaze met mine, and his lips started to pull up into a smile. He looked like an entirely different person with his smile. "Yeah. You're exactly what we're looking for." He pulled something out of his pocket. "I have a position opening up—it's not in track, though." He paused to let that sink in. "But I have a feeling you could coach anything we threw at you." I nodded, agreeing with him. I had never loved one sport more than another, not when it came to athletics. If I could help a student achieve what they wanted to, then that was more than enough for me. "Give me a call in a couple of weeks so we can talk."

I took the card from him and stared down at it as he walked away. I'd just been handed an opportunity of a lifetime, but I wasn't sure what I would do with it. Things were so up in the air, and right then, I needed to concentrate on the races ahead and not what could come from the conversation with Harold.

Pocketing the card, I concentrated back on the girls and the board as they started to call the races.

Reagan's race was up first, and I waited with bated breath as she took the start line. It only took minutes for her to come in second on the four hundred, and then after a small break, the eight hundred started.

My stomach dropped as Aria took her starting position. She was on the inside track, but all of those runners would dart for the inside line once the race had started. She'd never had to run with this many people before, so it was a new experience for her.

The loud sound went off, and she shot out of her position. It would only be twice around the track, but this wasn't the one we'd been practicing the most. Her favorite was the sixteen hundred, and this one was just a bonus. She pulled ahead during the first lap, but lost a couple of places on the second lap and finally came in fourth.

I wasn't sure what she was thinking because I couldn't see her face from here. But Reagan went over to her, and I stared as they talked while they waited for the next race to be called up.

"Come on, Reagan!" I heard her dad shouting from behind me in the front row of seats as she took her start position.

Reagan's start in the twelve hundred was amazing, and she kept a good pace up until the second lap, and then she flew. She pulled ahead without much effort and crossed the line in first place. She ran over to me, and I high-fived her.

"Well done, Reagan."

"Thanks, Coach." Her smile was wider than I'd ever seen before, and I could tell she lived for races like these. She turned around and stood next to me as they called the next race up. "She got caught off guard by the other runners," Reagan said.

"Shit," I whispered under my breath.

"It's all good, Coach," Reagan commented, and I glanced at her briefly. "I told her what to do and to just run her race. She's got this."

She had this, I knew she had, but it didn't mean I wasn't worried for her. I inhaled a deep breath and watched with narrowed eyes as she took her start position. This time she was in the middle, but there was something different in the way she held herself while she waited for the starting gun to shoot off.

Her head lifted, her gaze focused on the track in front of her, and then the sound blasted out. She kept a good pace in the first lap, keeping with the middle of the pack, but then sped up a little on the second lap. I was on tenterhooks as she went into the third lap with two other students ahead of her. Both of them had much longer gaits than she did, but I didn't doubt her for one second.

As soon as she hit the last lap, she darted forward, picking up her pace and going faster than I'd ever seen her go before. She weaved past the person directly in front of her and didn't let up until she was first place. There were only fifty meters left, and the student behind was catching up to her.

"Come on, Aria!" Reagan screamed, but I couldn't say a word. I was frozen, unable to do anything but watch as she crossed the line. "Damn, that was close. I didn't see who crossed the line first."

"Me neither," I told Reagan, staring at the board which would announce the winners. Aria slowed down to a walk, her hands on her hips and her attention half on the board and half on us as she moved closer to us.

The name of the third-place student came up first, and Aria halted on the track about twenty meters away from us. We all waited, our breaths held as the second-place name came up, and then Aria's name flashed on the screen next to first place.

"Oh my god!" Aria shouted, spinning around and staring at me. "I won?" she asked, and I nodded. "I won!"

"You won!" I shouted back, unable to stop my feet from moving forward. She ran toward me, threw herself at me and her arms around my shoulders. "You won," I repeated, spinning her around and then depositing her back on the ground. I was hyperaware of where we were, and although there were so many other things I wanted to do, I knew I couldn't. I had to hold back—for now, at least.

"I can't believe it." She shook her head, and

then spotted Reagan and ran toward her too. "We both won!"

I stared at both of them, proud of what they'd achieved. They'd both won the race they had trained heavily for. This was what I wanted to do. I wanted to help people achieve what they set out to, and help them realize goals they never even knew they had.

My gaze slid into the bleachers and met Harold's, and I had no doubt I'd call him. We'd come here to get Reagan and Aria more options for college, but now I also had another option. Something fate had sent my way.

"Let's go celebrate!" Reagan said as her dad came down onto the side of the track. "I vote burgers and anything junk food related. I'm so hungry." She turned to face her dad. "What do you say, Dad?"

He looked down at his watch and sighed. "We have to get on the road in two hours."

"So enough time for food then?" she asked, a grin spreading on her face.

"Yes, enough time for food."

Reagan fist-bumped the air and grabbed Aria's arm. "Come on, let's go get changed quickly before he changes his mind."

Aria's gaze settled on mine, a silent question showcased in them, and I nodded. They deserved a treat, even if it was only a burger.

———

ARIA

"I swear, I'm not even sure I can move right now," I moaned as the elevator doors whooshed closed. I had no idea the amount of food Reagan could put away. For someone so food-conscious, she went all out after a race. Burgers, fries, shakes, onion rings, you name it, and the table was full of it.

The doors opened, and Cade stepped out, but I was comfortable where I was leaning, and feeling kind of sleepy too.

"Come on." He held his hand out for me. "Let's get in the room, and you can have a shower then an early night."

"A shower sounds amazing right now." I placed my hand in his and let him pull me out of the elevator before the doors closed, and then down the hallway. "Can you believe Reagan wouldn't let me shower there? They even had individual stalls."

"She was desperate for a burger." Cade laughed and halted in front of our room door. "I've never seen a girl eat the way she does."

I walked past him into the room, glad Cade was carrying my bag for me. "Right? I swear she ate enough for all four of us." My feet dragged across the floor toward the bathroom, and I groaned as I pulled the door open. "Everything hurts."

Cade chuckled, but his ringing cell cut him off. "It's Dad, video calling." I wasn't sure what he was waiting for, but he clicked to answer the call at the last second. "Hey, Dad."

"Cade! Finally." Cade sat on the edge of the bed while I leaned against the bathroom door. "Is Aria there?"

"Yeah, she's here."

Cade flicked his wrist at me, and I groaned as I moved closer to him near the bed. I dipped my head to the right and stared at the screen, seeing Uncle Brody's face. "Hey!"

"Baby girl!" He turned his face away and looked at someone. "Hold on, they all want to see you." He pulled the cell farther away from his face, letting me see all the people around him. Mom and Sal were there, along with Lola, Belle, and Asher.

"So, tell us!" Mom shouted, jumping in her seat. "What happened?"

I flicked my gaze to Cade, a small smile starting to pull at my lips. "I came in fourth on the eight hundred."

"Fourth is good, Ri," Sal said, grinning at me. "Proud of you."

"Thank you." I paused, and then shouted, "And I came in first in the sixteen hundred!"

There was a second of silence, and then they all cheered. The sound was so loud I winced, but I couldn't help laugh at the way they were reacting.

They may not have been here with me, but they were always there in spirit.

"Oh my god, Aria! That's so amazing!" Lola shouted, plucking the cell out of Uncle Brody's hand. Mom's face appeared next to her, and they hugged.

"I can't believe I actually won," I told them, still not quite able to believe it. I'd zoned in like I never had before.

"Believe it," Mom said. "I knew you could do it."

I yawned and started to sit on the end of the bed, but Cade's hand stopped me. "She's about to fall asleep, guys," Cade said. "And she stinks of sweat."

"Hey!" I couldn't really be offended because he was right.

"We'll let you go," Lola said, her smile wide. "Get some rest. We all love you!"

Cade clicked the red button to end the video call and stood. "Get showered before you fall asleep standing up," he told me. I nodded and headed into the bathroom. "I'm just gonna head down to grab some water and a few snacks for later. Do you want anything?"

"Some water and maybe some chocolate," I shouted from the other side of the bathroom door. I switched the shower on and sat on top of the toilet seat, letting the steam fill the air.

"Okay, I'll be back in a few."

My muscles were aching, and I was hoping the hot spray would loosen them up a little. I stepped inside the cubicle and a moan escaped my lips as the hot water hit my skin. I didn't move for several minutes, just letting it wash over me.

Dipping my head back, I wet my hair, washed it, then moved on to my body. By the time I turned the water off and stepped out, I felt even more sleepy than I had before. I wrapped a towel around me and unlocked the door.

"Cade?" I waited to see if he answered, and when he didn't, I stepped out and pulled my suitcase up onto the bed. My hair was dripping down my back, my towel tied at my chest as I pulled out a pair of panties and my pj's.

I placed the suitcase back on the floor, and the clothes next to me then lay back. I'd only allow myself a couple of seconds and then get dressed. That was what I told myself anyway, because I didn't know how long later, but the hotel door slammed shut, and Cade appeared in my line of vision.

"Crap." I shot up into a sitting position, grasping my towel to make sure it didn't fall down. "Sorry, I was just…" I trailed off, my stomach bottoming out as I stared up at Cade.

His gaze was focused on my face then dipped down to my exposed collarbone and then past the towel and to my legs. "You should get dressed," he gritted out, his knuckles turning white as he gripped the bottle of water he held.

"I...I am." My cheeks started to burn from his attention, and my hands started to shake. He always had a way of making me feel alive. I stood and grabbed my clothes, but as I started to walk past him, his hand curling around my wrist stopped me.

My chest heaved on a breath, and I glanced up at him. We were side by side, neither of us looking away from each other. The air swirled in the room, causing the hairs on my body to stand on end.

"Aria." It was one word from him, but the way he said it meant so much more than any other time he'd said it. His gaze flicked down to my necklace, the one he'd given me for my birthday. "I'm still trying real fuckin' hard, baby."

My lips parted, and I couldn't help but glance down at his hips. His erection was obvious through his sweatpants, and I moved an inch closer to him. "What if I don't want you to try?" I whispered, afraid to talk too loud. "What if I want you to give in and do what you want?"

He pulled away from me, walked over to the small table near the bed, and placed the bottle of water and snacks he had in his arms down. "I can't. We can't."

"Why?" I asked, not moving from the spot I was

standing in. We were only six feet apart, and yet it felt like miles.

"Because…" His stare met mine. "Because it's wrong."

My shoulders sagged at his words. I wanted to fight, I wanted to know why it was wrong. "Why is it wrong? Because you're my teacher? Is that all there is standing in your way right now?" I waited a beat, and when he didn't reply, I nodded. "I get it. You're scared." I laughed sadly. I knew I'd lost. "You're scared of what might happen if you give in."

I spun around, my clothes in my hand, and took a step toward the bathroom. "You're right." His deep voice echoed around the room, but I didn't stop. "I am scared." I placed my hand on the door handle to the bathroom and turned my head, staring at him as he took steps closer to me. "I'm scared of what will happen if I let go and just be with you."

Fate had set us on this path. We just had to choose whether we would defy it, or obey it. "I'm scared too," I whispered. "But nothing good ever comes without taking a chance, Cade. You pushed me away, I pushed you away, but now…now there's no reason for us to do that anymore, so why? Why are we dancing around and—"

"Fuck it." He darted toward me and grasped my arm to spin me around. My chest collided with his a second before he wrapped his arm around my waist and pulled me up so our faces were level. "I can't anymore. I can't keep being so close to you and not touch you." His large hand stroked down my arm and back up again, stopping at the necklace. "Fuck, baby, I've waited what feels like a lifetime to do this." I opened my mouth, about to ask him what he'd waited to do, but his lips closing over mine gave me the answer.

My hands gripped his shoulders as he pressed his lips so hard against mine, I was sure they'd bruise. His tongue dipped into my mouth at the same time he lowered down onto the bed, and I placed my legs on either side of his thighs causing my towel to open and leaving only the thin material of his sweatpants separating us.

Fast and needy, we craved each other, and as soon as he pulled away and yanked off his T-shirt, I was back on his lips, not caring my towel was falling off me. My nipples scraped against his tan skin, and I gasped from the sensation.

"God, I missed these lips," Cade growled, followed by a groan as I rocked my hips against him. "I need you so bad right now."

I pressed light kisses to his cheek and down his neck then worked my way to his ear where I whispered, "Take me. Show me how much you've missed me."

His hands gripped my waist harder, his fingers

digging into the skin. "Fuck, I love when you talk like that."

It was on the tip of my tongue to tell him I loved him, but it was too soon. Too many things had happened over the last six months, and I didn't want a few words to break what we were rebuilding right now.

He lifted us up, just enough for him to pull his sweats down, and then he was right at my entrance. One push and he'd be inside. I pulled back, staring him right in the face, enthralled with the way his dark-blue eyes captured my attention, refusing to let go.

Slowly, I pushed down, feeling the head of his cock inside, and inch by slow inch, I took nearly all of him. He stretched me, more than he had the first time, but this was different. Him refusing to look away, and me holding all the power on top of him.

"Baby," he murmured, his gruff whisper causing goose bumps to spread over my skin. "I don't know what I did to deserve you, but I'm never letting you go again."

"Promise?" I asked, lifting my hips and then thrusting them back down, causing his body to jerk.

"Promise." He pressed his forehead to mine and moved his hands to my hips. "You and me, always."

I gasped as he lifted me up and yanked me back down, controlling the rhythm. "Always."

Chapter Twelve

ARIA

A smile curved on my lips as I stared at Cade's side profile. His attention was focused out the windshield as he drove on the highway, and even though I was sad we were heading home, it didn't encompass the way I felt after the last twelve hours.

We'd spent the night touching each other and talking. He'd seen the new scars on my stomach, and even though I was afraid of what he'd think, all he did was kiss each one of them and remark about how there wasn't a fresh one.

Because there wasn't.

I hadn't cut since I had what Dr. Bay liked to call my manic episode. It had scared me, more than I liked to admit, and I'd told Cade as much. He'd informed me of everything that had happened between him and Miss Simmons—Willow as he called her—and I hated what he had to do just to keep her quiet. But now that we were here, and nothing stood in our way other than the fact he was still my teacher and coach.

"I can feel you staring at me," Cade murmured, his brow raised as he glanced at me briefly. "Stop being a creeper."

"Who? Me?" I pointed at my chest and widened my eyes, acting completely innocent. "I'm not being a creeper."

His chuckle made goose bumps spread over my skin. "You totally are being a creeper. A hot, sexy creeper, but still a creeper."

I gasped. "You think I'm hot and sexy."

He shook his head, his chuckle now moving into full-blown laughter. "I swear, I'll never get tired of listening to you." His hand reached over and settled on my thigh over my jeans, his fingertips resting above the scars hidden underneath the denim.

"Good." I placed my hand over his, moving my fingertip up and down his long fingers. "What's going to—"

Cade's cell ringing cut me off, and then his mom's name flashed on the screen above the center console.

"Shit." Cade glanced at me, his nose screwing up. "I'm gonna have to answer this, that okay?"

I shrugged. "Fine by me."

He clicked a button on his steering wheel and cleared his throat. "Hey, Mom."

"Finally!" Her voice surrounded us through the speakers. "I've been calling you for hours."

"Sorry." His fingers tapped on the steering wheel, and his other hand gripped my thigh tighter. "I've been away at a school event. I'm just driving home now."

"Ah yes, you said you were at an event. I must have forgotten." I raised my brows at the way her voice sounded, both bored and interested all at the same time. How the heck did she manage to achieve that? "Anyway, I'm calling to tell you I booked your flights."

Cade groaned. "I told you I'd book them, Mom. You know I can only come on certain days."

"I know that. Honestly, Cade, do you think I never listen to you?" she tutted, and I turned to face Cade. I thought my mom was bad, but his…I'd only heard her talk for a couple of minutes, and already I could see how tense Cade was. "Your flight leaves on the Thursday night, and you return Sunday evening. All good, yes?"

"Mom—"

"Good. See you then!"

The line went dead, and Cade slammed his hand on his steering wheel. "Fuck's sake!" A muscle in his jaw ticked, and he let go of my thigh and moved his hand into his hair. "I swear, the woman is a walking, talking, stress creator. How does she expect me to fly to France on a Thursday evening when I have classes to teach the next day?"

"I'm sure——"

"And all because she's getting married for a fourth time. Why can't she just live her life without the whole wedding all over again?"

"Cade." I waited for him to glance at me, then took his hand in both of mine. "Breathe. I'm sure the principal will let you take the day off. And it's not like it's real soon, right?"

"Three weeks." Cade groaned and took the exit off the highway. "The week after your mom and Sal get married."

"I…" I bit down on my bottom lip, trying to keep my emotions at bay. It wasn't fair for me to be sad that he was leaving for a long weekend, but yet, I was. It wasn't something I'd been prepared for, and I was being selfish. "I'll be staying with your dad and Lola that week," I said instead of what I really wanted to say which was for him to stay home.

Cade pulled the car to a stop at a set of lights and turned to look at me. "You will?" He frowned. "Why?"

"Mom and Sal are leaving for their honeymoon the night they get married, right after the party. They're going to be gone two weeks."

"Yeah?" His lips started to spread into a grin but

stopped when he turned to look out of the wind-shield. "And I'll be in France for a few of those days. Shit."

I held his hand tighter as he drove closer to my house. "They'll be gone for two weeks, you'll only be gone for three nights. Plus, you can bring me back a present."

"A present?" Cade asked, his lips now lifted and the tension evaporating from his body. "What kind of present?"

"I don't know." I shrugged, my stomach dipping as he entered my street. "Maybe a magnet or something?"

"I'm going to France, and you want a magnet as a present?"

"What can I say"—I turned in my seat as he pulled up in front of my house—"I'm easily pleased."

His eyes sparked, his hand gripping me tighter as his gaze dipped to my lips. "Very easily pleased," he said, his voice lower now. "Fuck, I wish I could take you back to my place right now."

"So do I," I whispered, spotting Mom opening up the front door. "I have an appointment with Dr. Bay on Tuesday. Are you still going to take me?"

"You know I am." He leaned forward, blocking the view with his body as he brought my hand up to his lips and pressed a soft kiss there. "I'll call you later. Go celebrate your win."

I swallowed and waited a second. I just needed to let his gaze wash through me and remember the way he stared at me. "I'll see you tomorrow at school?" I asked, spotting Sal now walking toward the car with Mom.

"See you tomorrow," he whispered, letting my hand go.

I floated out of the car and met Sal at the trunk as he got my suitcase and bag out. Mom said something to Cade, but I was too inside my own head to hear what they were talking about. I followed Sal onto the curb and watched Cade drive away, wishing I was still in the car with him.

———

ARIA

"So you win the race and don't even message me? I thought I was your best friend?"

I closed my eyes and counted to three before I turned to face Hope. "Sorry. The weekend was crazy and—"

"You won!" She threw her arms around my shoulders and squeezed the life out of me. "I need to know everything." Her hands gripped my shoulders as she pulled back. "What was it like? Where did you stay? Was Mr. Easto—"

"Hope," I interrupted her, widening my eyes

and looking around. "Lower your voice." We were surrounded by students in the hallway, and I had no doubt they weren't paying attention to us but on the off chance…

"What? Listen here, girly, you bailed on me on your birthday—which I still haven't forgiven you for, by the way—and now you win at your meet, and you don't even message me? I want details. It's the only way we can stay besties."

I groaned, hating that she'd brought up my birthday again. She'd used it at every opportunity she could over the last week to get what she wanted, even though I'd spun her the story of my mom needing me back home. But she hadn't let up.

"Fine," I ground out as the bell to the last class of the day rang out. "My mom is picking me up from school today. Meet me on the steps, and I'll fill you in before I leave for my dress fitting."

"Awesome!" She pulled away and flashed me a huge smile. "It's a date."

I shook my head as she danced down the hallway, weaving through the students rushing to their last class of the day.

"Will you be joining us today, Aria?" a deep voice asked. The same voice that had whispered how much he wished he could take all my clothes off last night. He hadn't been able to because I'd had to stay at home, but he'd made a promise for this weekend. One where it could just be the two of us, no interruptions or boundaries to get in our way.

Flicking my gaze over to him, I stepped forward. "Yes, Mr. Easton."

Cade stood in the doorway to his classroom, blocking most of it, but he didn't move an inch as I tried to enter. My hip connected with his thighs, grazing past him, and I let my hand drift over him too.

"Aria," he growled, only loud enough for me to hear. "You're playing with fire."

"Am I?" I asked innocently.

"You have three seconds to get to your seat. Otherwise, I won't be held accountable for what happens to you."

"Promises, promises," I sang, skirting away from him and to my seat.

I knew exactly what I was doing to him. I enjoyed watching him lose his cool, and I wondered if the thrill of being caught was the reason I was so obsessed, but as I watched him pace at the front of the class, discussing the current subject, I knew it wasn't.

I'd been in love with Cade before I even knew what love was, and everything that had happened over the last six months only made it so much stronger. It was unbreakable, impenetrable. He was all I could think about since we'd reconnected after the track meet. His hands were imprinted on my soul.

He told us to turn to a certain page in our books, but I couldn't move an inch to do what he'd said. I was enthralled, obsessed with watching the way he moved, and the curve of his lips as he quickly glanced at me told me he liked it. The weekend couldn't come soon enough, and as soon as the bell rang for end of class, and all the students filed out, I walked up to his desk.

"Great lesson," I remarked.

"Yeah?" He pushed his laptop into his bag and stared down at me. "What was it about?"

"Erm…" I blinked, not even able to remember any of what he'd said in the lesson. "I can't…remember."

"Too busy staring at a certain—"

"Mr. Easton, may I have a word with you?" We both turned to see Miss Simmons standing in the doorway, her narrowed eyes watching us. "You may leave, Aria. The adults need to talk."

Cade stepped in front of me, his gaze meeting mine as he inclined his head, signaling to follow him. "We have nothing to discuss, Miss Simmons," he said, his voice brooking no room for argument. "Excuse you."

She didn't move from the doorway as her stare slid to me. "You shouldn't be alone in a classroom with her. Imagine what people could think."

Cade leaned forward, his voice dropping dangerously low. "Imagine what people would think if they knew what Jasmine was doing. I somehow think that would be bigger news than a teacher talking to a student."

"A student he's fucked," Miss Simmons gritted out.

"Tell me, Willow." Cade dipped his head to the side, and I moved over so his body was fully shadowing mine. "Are you jealous because I didn't fuck you? Is that your problem? Or is it because you don't like the thought of me having the upper hand."

"You don't have the upper hand, Cade." I gripped the back of Cade's shirt. "You never will."

"Yeah?" His hand reached around and collided with my arm where he squeezed. "We'll see about that when I hand the evidence into my dad then, huh?"

"You wouldn't."

"I will if you don't get out of my goddamn face. I warned you what would happen if you didn't leave either of us alone. This is your final warning. One more time, and it's over." He paused, and I wasn't sure what he did, but then he demanded, "Now move."

I peeked around his body, blinking as she huffed and stomped away. Her heels clicked along the floor as she marched to her own beat.

"Jeez, Cade." I let out a breath and swiped some hair off my face. "You're scary."

He stepped out of the classroom, and I followed after him. "Only when it comes to protecting the people I care about." He kept his body inches away from mine as we walked down the hallway and around the lingering students. "Which is you, in case you were wondering."

His gaze slid to mine and I smiled up at him. "I think I got that impression loud and clear."

"Good." He halted outside the school office. "I gotta head in here. Remember to tell your mom you'll be gone all weekend."

"I know." I bit down on my bottom lip. "I'm gonna ask Hope to cover for me."

I'd told Cade last night that Hope knew some of our history, and even though he wasn't happy about it, he knew I couldn't go back on what I'd told her. Besides, her knowing would come in useful, like this weekend.

"Okay." He glanced around the hallway and whispered, "Imagine me kissing you goodbye right now."

My cheeks burned from the blush that was no doubt rising. "My imagination is never as good as the real thing." I stepped back. "I'll speak to you later?"

"Yeah, baby. Later."

I backed away another step, then spun around,

and headed outside. It wasn't until I exited the doors and saw Hope's face that I remembered what I'd promised her earlier.

"I thought you'd stood me up again." She planted her hands on her hips and pushed her bottom lip out.

"Sorry, I had to talk to…Mr. Easton." I jogged down the steps, not seeing Mom's car anywhere. "Come on." I grasped her arm and pulled her to the side. "I'll fill you in."

Once we were in a spot where no one could overhear, I gave her a rundown of the last weekend. Her facial expressions were a vast range of excitement, shock, awe, and lastly, something in between all three.

"So you're *together together* now?"

"Yeah. I think? I'm not one hundred percent sure, to be honest." I leaned against the wall and stared at the parking lot entrance. Mom was late, but at least it had given me time to tell Hope what had happened. "He's taking me away this weekend. Can I tell my mom I'm staying at your house?"

"You want me"—she pointed at her chest—"to cover for your romantic weekend away with a…" She glanced around and whispered, "Teacher?"

"Erm…yes?" I pushed up off the wall as Mom's red car peeled into the lot. "Is that…can you…"

"Hell yes!" She squealed and threw her arms around me. "Oh man, I've never been part of a plot like this. I got this covered. I'll plan the entire weekend out with fake things we're going to do. No one will ever know."

I chuckled. "You don't have to do that."

"Maybe we could go pretend ice skating. Or maybe see a pretend movie."

"My mom is here, I gotta go." She waved me off, not really looking at me as she continued to name things we could go and do on our pretend weekend. "See you tomorrow!" I shouted, running toward Mom's car and jumping inside. "Hey."

"Wow. What put that smile on your face?"

I shrugged, knowing exactly who put the smile on my face. "Just excited to go try the dress on."

Mom sighed as she pulled out of the lot. "I can't wait. I can't believe, this time next week, I'll only be days away from being married to Sal. And the diner is so close to being finished too. It's all coming together now."

"I can't wait to see when it's all done," I told her, leaning back in my seat. "Oh, before I forget, is it okay to stay at Hope's this weekend? Her sister is going away again, and she doesn't want to be on her own."

"Again?" She took a turn. "Yeah, that's fine. Sal and I won't be home much this weekend anyway, so it's kind of perfect."

My stomach fluttered at the lie I'd just told her, but it was nothing in the grand scheme of things.

There was so much more she didn't know about, and even though I knew I was going to tell her after she got home from her honeymoon, it didn't make it any easier.

For now, I'd bask in her happiness as well as my own, and take each day as it came.

Chapter Thirteen

CADE

"This is the key to the front door, and this is the one to the back door." Dad handed me two keys, each marked with fobs that said precisely what he'd just told me. "The housekeeper hasn't been for a couple of weeks, so you may need to dust or something."

"I got it," I told him, pocketing the keys.

"What are you going up there for anyway?" he asked, his dark-brown eyes telling me he already knew.

I shrugged, acting like it was no big deal. I was taking Aria away, and not just to any place, but to my great-grandparents' lake house. The house had been passed down to my dad, and he'd owned it for years. The first time I'd been there was the summer Lola was pregnant, and I'd fallen in love with the small town right away. "Just haven't been there in a while, so I wanted to go and spend the weekend."

"You know, the first time I went back there was with Lola. You taking a girl there, son?"

"I—"

"Because if you are, know that it's a special kind of place. You don't take just anyone to see that kind of beauty."

"What kind of beauty?" PB asked, running into the kitchen and colliding with my legs.

"The lake house," I told her, bending down to pick her up. She may have been eight, about to turn nine, but she would never be too big for a hug from her big brother.

"We're going to the lake house?" she asked, clapping her hands in excitement. "I want to bring my pink swimsuit."

She wiggled in my hold, so I let her go, but stopped her as she tried to run out of the kitchen. "There's only me going," I told her.

"Awww." She pushed her bottom lip out. "I want to come. Please?" She dragged the last word out, and if it weren't for the fact Aria and I had to keep our relationship secret, I would have said yes.

My thoughts jarred me. *Relationship*. We were in a real relationship. Neither of us had confirmed what we were, but there wasn't a doubt in my mind what I wanted it to be. Me and her. Just us. Something fluttered in my chest, and I pressed my hand against it.

"Please, Cade? Pretty please with a juicy red cherry on top?"

"Sorry, PB. I can't bring you."

Her bottom lip wobbled, but within a second it was gone, anger taking over her little body. "This weekend is going to suck!"

"Belle," Dad warned. "Don't say suck."

"What do you want me to say then, Dad?" She planted her hands on her hips, looking so much like Lola it was scary.

"I…erm…I don't know. Maybe not good?"

"Fine." She swung her gaze to me. "This weekend is going to be not good. You're going to the lake house, and Aria is away this weekend too." My stomach dropped, and I was hyperaware of Dad's eyes burning through the side of my face. "I have no friends! Ugh. I hate this stupid life." She twirled around and stomped out of the kitchen, shouting about how unfair it was that she was still eight.

"Look what you caused now," Dad huffed, pushing his hand through his hair.

"Me?" I raised my brows. "That ain't nothing to do with me. That's Lola's and your genes creating a monster."

"Don't call your little sister a monster."

"What would you like me to call her?" I asked, waiting for his answer, but when he couldn't come up with anything, I shrugged as if I'd made my point. "I better get going."

I backed away a step, and just as I was about to turn around, he said, "Yeah, wouldn't want to keep Aria waiting, huh?"

My back straightened, the little hairs on the back of my neck standing on end. "What?"

"Nothing." Dad grinned, but I heard him loud and clear. He wasn't stupid, not by a long shot. There was a reason he was a DEA agent and had gone undercover so many times in my life. He was a master at figuring people out, just like Ford was.

Shaking my head, I turned around, partly on edge from what he'd said but also a little relieved. It wasn't easy keeping a secret for so long, especially when that secret was Aria. I wanted to shout from the rooftops how I felt about her. I wanted to tell all the people we loved how in love with her I was. But we couldn't. Not yet.

It didn't take me long to get back to my house where Aria was waiting outside with a small bag full of her clothes. I'd barely pulled up at the curb when she ran down the driveway and toward the car. I wanted to get out and open the door for her, but she beat me to it, her laugh tinkling around in the car as she slammed the door shut.

"Excited?" I asked.

"How could you tell?" She grinned so wide she could barely contain it. I waited until she had her belt on, and then pulled away from the curb. "How long will the drive be?"

"About two hours." I leaned back a little more in my seat and kept my attention on the road ahead. "I thought we could cook tonight and then maybe go out on the lake tomorrow?"

Aria spun in her seat, her hands grasping on to my arm closest to her. "Can we go fishing? You know how to fish, right?"

I chuckled and brought one of her hands to my lips. "I do."

"Will you teach me? I've always wanted one of those photos where you're holding a giant fish."

My grin was matching hers now. "Then, tomorrow, we shall fish."

She clapped her hands and sat back fully in her seat, humming under her breath. "I can't believe we're doing this."

"Me neither."

Aria clicked the radio channel over and sang along with the songs the whole way, and as soon as we pulled into the small town, she gasped. "Oh my god, it's like something off TV."

"Yep." I maneuvered the car through the central part of town which consisted of one street. "Everyone knows everybody—population is about four hundred."

"No way." Aria leaned forward, staring out the window at everything. I tried to see it through her eyes. The one restaurant and one diner, the small stores, the tackle store, and a boat store. It wasn't until we turned off Main Street that we came closer to the house my great-grandparents had owned.

I turned and drove up the driveway, then stopped in front of the house.

"This is…beautiful."

"Wait until you see the back." I opened my door and rushed around to Aria's side, grabbing her hand and jogging around to the back. Her laughter followed us, and I couldn't help join in with her. We were carefree, nothing and nobody to bother us. "This is one of my favorite places to be," I told her, slowing down as the lake came into view.

"Oh, wow…it's so peaceful, like a painting."

"I know, right?" I pushed my fingers between hers and held them against my chest, bringing her onto the dock which had several small boats attached to it. "Dad and Lola sit out here for hours when we come here on vacation. They always said there was something about this place that called to them, and I never understood, not until now."

Looking down at Aria, I waited for her to meet my stare, and when she did, she whispered, "Why only now?"

"Because of you." I stepped closer to her, letting her hand go and wrapping my arm around her waist. "You made me realize what I was missing."

Her throat bobbed as she swallowed. "I did?"

"Yeah, baby." I drifted my palm to the side of her face and dipped down. "You did." I pressed my lips against hers. I tried to control myself and not let things get too hot and heavy, but it was almost an impossible task when it came to Aria. She made me go insane, and I loved every second of it.

She shivered in my arms, and as much as I'd like to think it was because of me, I knew it was the temperature dropping. "Let's head inside." I wrapped my arm around her shoulders and walked us back around to my car. I handed her the front door key as I got our bags out, and just as she was pushing the door open, I was right behind her. "We'll sleep in my room," I told her. We could have stayed in the master, but knowing Dad and Lola always slept in there freaked me out.

"Whose house was this before your dad had it?"

"His grandparents." I pushed open my bedroom door. "He used to spend loads of time here as a kid. That's what he told us anyway." I stepped back so she could enter the room.

She pushed some of her dark-red hair behind her ear and smiled down at the bed. It wasn't a single, but it definitely wasn't as big as the one in my house she'd said she loved so much. "I love it." She sat on the edge of the bed. "Could you pass me my bag? I need to make sure I packed all my medication. I have a gut feeling I may have left a bottle behind."

My heart hammered in my chest as I passed her the bag, and I didn't move an inch as she pulled all the contents out and produced her orange pill bottles.

"Nope." Her shoulders sagged in relief. "I remembered them all."

A breath I hadn't realized I'd been holding burst out of me, and I sobered as I stood there, watching her hold her pills. Everything would be a constant battle for her. She'd always struggle with her moods and the craving to self-harm, and the question was whether I wanted to be by her side, supporting her the whole way.

I shook my head. It was never a question. I'd be there every step of the way.

———

ARIA

"Why is it so slippy?" I yelled, trying to keep the fish I'd caught in the palm of my hands. It wasn't even that big, not compared to the ones Cade had expertly caught, but I was damn proud, and I needed a photo to commemorate it.

"Because it's a fish?" Cade commented, and I glanced up at him. He held his cell up as he took a picture, but his lips were spread in a wide grin. He thought this was funny, me trying to wrestle this small fish long enough before we put it back into the lake.

"You're so funny." I rolled my eyes, but I couldn't keep the smile off my face. We'd had the best day, and even after being out on the lake for five hours and only now just catching my first fish, I didn't want it to end. I wanted to stay here forever, just me and him and the vast open space.

Cade moved closer to me on the boat, causing it to rock side to side, and me to squeal. "Come're," he said, his voice low and demanding, and dammit, it hit me in all the right places. I moved closer to him, like sails in the wind, my gaze not leaving his until the fish started to squirm again.

"Got it," he said.

"Got what?"

He took the fish out of my hand and handed his cell out to me. I stared down at the screen as he put the fish back into the lake, seeing a picture of me staring at him and him looking back at me. It was perfect.

"You didn't get the fish in it," I told him, trying to keep all of my emotions at bay. We'd never had a picture together, not like this one, not with us staring into each other's eyes with smiles on our faces and love in our eyes. It was almost too much to see.

"Swipe right." I did as I was told and saw a picture of me holding the squirming fish, my face all screwed up, but I didn't care. It was my first ever catch, and I had every intention of framing this image.

"I love it," I told him, handing him back his cell.

He pocketed it, and I sat down just as he turned the engine on, causing it to roar to life. "I have reservations for tonight."

I held on to the side of the boat, my stomach not used to being out on the water as he drove us across the lake and toward the house. "Reservations?" I asked, my eyes wide as he sped up more. I wanted to tell him to slow down, scared I'd puke all over the place, but it was only minutes before he was pulling to a stop at the edge of the dock.

"Yep." He turned the engine off and tied the boat up then got out. "We're going on a proper date." He held his hand out to me, and I took it without a second thought. "In public."

"We are?" I asked, my eyes wide. "But I didn't bring any clothes for a date."

Cade threw his arm over my shoulder, and we walked side by side toward the back of the house. It was so peaceful here, and part of me never wanted to leave. We'd watched the sunset from the dock last night, only the sounds of nature surrounding us, and it was one of the best nights I'd ever had.

"I'm sure Lola has something here you can borrow." He halted at the back door. "Head inside and get ready. I'm gonna clean up the boat and then grab a shower." He leaned down, his lips landing on mine briefly, leaving me wanting—needing—more. But he was gone all too soon, and all I could do was stare as he walked down the dock and back toward the boat.

My stomach fluttered, my breaths coming a little faster. He was taking me out on a real date. One where we could be in public with nobody to watch out for. Here, we could be who we wanted to be. We could be open in the way we felt about each other. We didn't have to hide.

I bit down on my bottom lip and stared at him cleaning out the boat. His T-shirt pulled taut against his defined chest, and his shorts rode up on his thighs. I hadn't been brave enough to wear shorts. Instead, I'd stuck to my jeans, making sure everything was covered.

I didn't want him to see the scars and concentrate on them, not while we were out here. He knew they were there; he knew why I was wearing jeans when it was too hot for them, but he didn't say anything about it. He let me be who I was and never tried to change me.

He was the one person in my life who knew me completely, and now he was taking me out on a date. I shook my head, then spun around to go inside. If Cade was taking me out, then there was no way I wanted to smell like lake and fish. I needed a shower and to find some clothes stat.

Instead of using the shower attached to Cade's

room, I used the one in the master bathroom, knowing I'd need to come in here anyway to look through Lola's clothes.

It didn't take long for me to shower, and I dried my hair so it was as straight as I could get it, then applied minimal makeup. I didn't feel the need to load it on my face, not for Cade. I tried to keep myself distracted because, every time I thought about what would happen tonight, I felt like I was going to collapse from nerves. I'd seen him in ways most people hadn't. He'd been there through everything bad and good, and yet, I was losing my shit over him taking me on a date.

I pushed my shoulders back and stared at myself in the mirror. It was just Cade. Cade who I was in love with. Cade who made me feel everything.

His footsteps banged on the stairs as I entered the walk-in closet to the master bedroom. "I'm getting in the shower!" he shouted to me.

"Okay! I'll meet you downstairs," I told him, my eyes wide at all the clothes in this closet. Why did Lola keep all of them here instead of at her house? I didn't think she had this many clothes at home, but I remembered Cade telling me this was Uncle Brody and Lola's favorite place to come.

I flicked past several short dresses and then finally came to a floor-length one. Its light-blue material was thin, and I was guessing this was some-thing she wore in the height of summer. The plunging neckline was a little daring, but it called to me in a way nothing else ever had. It was definitely first-date material.

Plucking it out, I remembered I'd packed the wedges Mom had given me for my birthday—*just in case*—and then darted out of the room. I could hear the shower running from outside our bedroom, so I shot inside and grabbed the wedges.

The dress fit perfectly, dipping in at my waist and then flowing down to my ankles. The strap that held it around my neck was a gunmetal gray, and there was a broach just underneath my chest to cinch in the waist. I'd already debated whether Lola would let me keep it, but then I remembered she didn't even know I was here in the first place. We were still a secret…for now.

I heard the shower turn off just as I exited the bathroom, but I was too nervous to go into the bedroom, so I headed back down the stairs and outside. The sun wasn't quite setting, but the sky was full of colors bleeding into each other. It was a work of art, one that captivated my attention. I couldn't stop staring at it as my feet carried me back out onto the dock.

Wrapping my arms around my waist, I kept my gaze focused on the sky. I wasn't sure how long I stood there, but I didn't hear Cade's footsteps until he was directly behind me, his hand flattening against the bottom of my back. "Beautiful," he whispered. "You're absolutely beautiful, Aria."

I turned slowly, my stomach dipping so much I wasn't sure I'd be able to stand upright much longer. Inhaling a breath, I was captivated by his cologne, and enthralled with the way his dark-blue eyes stared down at me.

"Cade," I whispered, not really sure what I was going to say.

His throat bobbed as he swallowed and pulled me closer to him. "You ready?" he asked, his voice breaking in the middle of his words, and I tilted my head, realizing he was as nervous as I was. This was our first date, one we would remember for the rest of our lives.

"I'm ready," I told him and placed my hand on the side of his face. His scruff scraped against my fingers, and I traced the outline of his lips. "I'm always ready when it comes to you."

He smiled down at me, and I wished we weren't going out. I wanted to stay in this little bubble we'd created and never leave.

"Come on." He wrapped his arm around my shoulder and turned so we could walk back toward the house. We moved around the side and then past his car. "It's only a few minutes' walk."

The closer we got to the restaurant, the more nerves took over my body, and by the time he was pulling open the door, I was a full-on mess. What if someone saw us and knew who we were? What if—

"Cade?" a deep voice asked from toward the back of the compact room. The restaurant was the smallest one I'd ever seen, but there was a vibe to it like nothing else. "Is that you?"

Glancing at Cade had me seeing his growing grin, and then he held his other hand out to the man coming toward us. "It is," Cade said, his hand on my waist squeezing a little in reassurance.

"Well, I'll be damned. Don't think I've seen you in about six years." The man paused and looked him up and down. "You've grown." I stared at the man, noting the wrinkles on his face and his white hair. He couldn't have been a day under seventy. "And who's this lovely lady?" His gaze swung to me, and I wiped my clammy hand on my dress.

"This is Aria." Cade pulled me even closer to him. "My girlfriend."

I wasn't sure what else the man had said. I hadn't even caught his name as he showed us to a table toward the back, because I was way too busy repeating what Cade had said over and over again.

Girlfriend. He'd called me his girlfriend. Did that make him my boyfriend? He'd just put a label on our relationship, and I couldn't have been happier. We were doing this. Really doing this.

"I'll take a beer. What about you, Aria?" Cade

asked, his voice finally breaking through all my thoughts.

"I'll take a water please," I replied, my voice low.

The man wandered off to get our drinks, and Cade took hold of my hand. We were opposite each other, but I wished I could sit next to him. "You okay?" he asked.

"Yeah." I blew out a breath. "Just nervous."

He nodded. "I get it. It's weird being able to do this." His lips quirked on one side. "But I love it. This is what it will be like as soon as the school year is over."

I gripped his hand tighter. "Will it?"

"Yeah." His eyes shone with happiness as he said, "I've been offered a job at Shire Oaks College to coach. I've accepted it, so I won't be working at the high school after this school year."

"Oh my god." I leaned forward, wanting to throw my arms around him, but the table was in the way. "You're going to coach at Shire Oaks?"

"Yep." His face nearly broke from the way he was grinning. "Which means as soon as school is out, so are we. I'm not keeping you a secret for much longer. I need everyone to know exactly how I feel about you."

I couldn't believe the words coming out of his mouth. He was telling me we'd be out in the open for everyone to see. It scared me, and I wondered what everyone would think, but I was ecstatic over what he'd said. We'd been a secret for what felt like so long that it seemed strange to have people know about us, but I was ready for us to be out in the open. More than ready.

"No more hiding?" I whispered.

He placed his legs either side of mine, making me feel more secure than I ever had. He lifted my hand to his lips and placed a kiss on my knuckles, all the while not looking away. "No more hiding, baby."

Chapter Fourteen

ARIA

Things had been different between us since we'd come back from the lake. I was more secure in what we were, and I didn't doubt for one second how Cade felt about me. He'd promised me it would only be a matter of time until we could be out in the open, and I was counting down the days like my life depended on it.

We'd spent all our free time together since we'd come back from our "romantic getaway" as Hope liked to call it. I stayed at home enough to not look suspicious, but when I was in my bed alone, all I craved was having Cade next to me.

Tonight Mom thought I was staying over at Hope's again, and Hope's sister thought she was staying at my house. We were both lying to be with the people we loved, and neither of us thought twice about it.

A knock sounded on the door, and I stared as Cade walked out of the kitchen and into the hall-way. I was fascinated with the way he strolled around his house in only sweatpants and his bare feet. It was orgasm worthy, and it would never get old seeing him like that.

I tried to listen to the murmurings in the hallway but couldn't understand what they were saying, and a couple of minutes later, Cade appeared with a bag of takeout. He always made sure I had a full stomach so I could take my meds.

"Chinese okay?" he asked. I didn't know why he asked because he knew I'd eat anything, *especially* Chinese food.

"Hell yes." I groaned as he stepped closer, but I wasn't sure whether it was the smell of the food or the way his abs tensed with each of his steps that caused it. He seriously needed to put a shirt on if he was going to sit next to me because all he would do was distract me.

I pulled my feet up onto the sofa and leaned forward as he dragged the coffee table closer. We'd found ourselves in a routine over the last week, one we'd easily slipped into, and one I never wanted to change. I wondered what it would be like once school was finished? Would we still have nights like this in his house? Or would he take me out and not care who saw us in public?

Even though I wanted the latter, I loved the former. I loved having him all to myself.

Cade opened up all of the boxes and passed me some chopsticks, and I grinned at him. "What?" he asked, his own lips pulling up into a grin. I shook my head and snapped the paper off the chopsticks to separate them.

"No." His hand landed on my wrist to stop me, his long fingers wrapping around the soft skin, and my breath hitched. "What are you grinning at?"

I shrugged. "Just you." I bit down on my bottom lip, my gaze connecting with his. "You ever going to put a T-shirt on, or are you just going to sit there half-naked all night to torture me."

His nostrils flared as he glanced down at my lips and then back to my eyes. "Do you want me to put a shirt on?"

I swallowed, trying to cool my body down, but it was damn near impossible when he was sitting so close and touching me. "Yes. No." His laughter had goose bumps spreading over my skin, and I wanted nothing more than to crawl over to him and press myself against his chest.

"Don't seem very sure there," he said, his voice deeper now. "Maybe we should make it equal." His hand whispered up my arm and to my shoulder, pulling on the strap of my pajama top. "Maybe you should be half-naked too."

My breath caught in my throat at the way he was staring at me. He never failed to make me forget about everything around me, and that was part of what had led us down the twisted path we'd been on. We were out on the other side now, and in the safety of his home, so I decided to throw caution to the wind.

I placed my chopsticks on the arm of the sofa and slowly leaned forward, making sure not one part of me was touching him as I whispered, "Maybe I should." My hands flowed down to the edge of my pajama top, and I slowly lifted it. A week ago, I never would have been so bold, knowing he'd see the scars marring the skin on my stomach, but I felt safe with Cade. I always felt safe with him.

"The food will go cold," he murmured, his dark-blue eyes hooding the longer he stared at me. He may have voiced his concern over the food, but his hand reaching for my waist told me his body wanted this more than the takeout.

"We can warm it up," I said, lifting my top over my head and baring my chest to him. His gaze flicked down to my breasts, the sound of his sharp breath making it known how much he wanted me. I leaned over him and placed my legs on either side of his thighs. Since the hotel at the meet, this was my favorite position, and I had a feeling it was his too.

His large hands gripped my back and drifted down to my ass where he squeezed and yanked me forward. "How do you never fail to make me lose my mind?" he asked, but I wasn't sure he wanted an answer.

I leaned closer to him, my lips now only a hairs-breadth away from his. "I have no idea, but you have the same effect." I pressed my lips down onto his, groaning at how soft they were, and pushed even closer to him. He encompassed his arms around me, banding me to him, and threatening to never let me go.

He pulled back a fraction of an inch, his gaze connecting with mine. "I think we should take this upstairs."

I placed my hand on the side of his face and smiled at him. "Why wait?" I asked, and slammed my lips back onto his. The smell of the food drifted around us, but I didn't care. The food could be warmed up, but the fire sizzling between us could never be put out.

———

ARIA

Mom stood in front of the mirror in the honeymoon suite, her gaze trailing over her off-the-shoulder ivory dress. Tears sprung to my eyes. She looked beautiful in every way possible. Her hair was in an elaborate twisted bun at the base of her neck, and her makeup was minimal but just enough to accentuate her features.

"I can't believe in an hour I'll be married." Her voice was low and soft as she met my gaze in the mirror.

I smiled wide at her and stood. We'd both slept in the honeymoon suite last night, and because Mom and Sal were leaving for their actual honeymoon later this evening, I'd have the room all to myself tonight. Although, part of me hoped Cade would turn up.

"You look stunning, Mom." I took three steps toward her and stood beside her as I glanced at the mirror. My dress was a golden color, the straps thin and leading down to a beaded bodice. At least with this dress, I didn't have to fight Mom over the length because she wanted it to hit the floor when I wasn't wearing the heels she'd chosen for me.

"So do you." She turned to face me. Her hands gripped my shoulders as she blew out a big breath. "How long do we have until we have to go down?"

I flicked my gaze to the clock on the wall, my

stomach dipping at how fast time was flinging by. "Five minutes. Do you want me to come down with you, or go down now and make sure Belle is ready?"

Mom's hands gripped me harder for a fraction of a second, and then she let go. "Head down now. I need a minute to gather myself."

"Okay," I whispered. I turned to walk away, but stopped at the last second and placed a kiss on her cheek. It had been years since I'd shown Mom any affection without her pulling it out of me, but things were changing now.

I was happier than I'd ever been. Cade and I were in an amazing place, especially after last weekend. My meds were starting to balance me out, most importantly, I hadn't cut for nearly three weeks. My therapy with Dr. Bay was hard, but I always felt better when I walked out of her office and to Cade in the waiting room.

Things were going good, which made me realize just how broken Mom's and my relationship was. We needed to work on it, but the only way we could do that was if I were honest with her—something I hadn't been in years. It was on the tip of my tongue to tell her everything but now wasn't the time or place. I had to wait.

"I'll see you down there," I murmured, and walked away from her. The suite was huge, and by the time I got to the door, I was feeling a little more steady in my heels.

My heart was hammering in my chest as I took the elevator down to the ground level. The room they rented for the ceremony and then the party afterward had been decorated by the staff. We'd gone to look at it early this morning, and as I got closer, I noticed how different it was with all the white wooden chairs occupied by people.

"Aria!" I heard Belle shout, and I whipped my head around. "Over here!"

I grinned as she poked her head around a wall. They'd set up a little spot for us to wait until we walked down the aisle. "Hey!" I crouched down in front of her, my eyes welling with tears. "You look so pretty!"

She twirled around in her gold dress, so similar to mine but with a poofy skirt. "We're the same!" She wrapped her hands around my neck and lowered her voice. "Are you scared of all the people?"

"A little," I admitted, seeing Lola out of the corner of my eye. "But I'll be right behind you, so I know I'll be okay."

"You will." She smiled wide and let me go. "Where's Auntie Jan?"

"She's coming," I said, at the same time the elevator doors whooshed open, and she appeared. "There she is." I stood and pointed at Mom as she made a beeline for us.

"Auntie Jan!" Belle shouted, waving her hand wildly in the air.

Mom smiled over at Belle and gasped. "Oh my god! You look beautiful," she told Belle, which made Belle beam even more.

"Okay, guys," Lola said, clapping her hands. "Here's your flowers." She handed each of us a bouquet, Mom's being the biggest, and stepped away from us. "I'm going to tell them you're ready." Her chest moved as she took a big inhale. "Let's do this."

"Let's do this," Mom repeated, her nerves obvious.

Lola left us behind the cornered-off area, and a couple of minutes later, the music started. We all took our places, Belle in front, then me, and Mom behind the both of us. The doors opened, and Belle began to walk down the aisle. Once she was halfway down, I followed her, and my heart beat crazily out of my chest.

I didn't recognize most of the people standing and watching us come down the aisle, but the closer I got to the front, the better I felt. Uncle Brody's and Lola's faces came into view first, and then Ford and Uncle Brody's team, and finally, Cade.

My breath left me as my gaze met his, and even though my feet wanted to carry me to him, I continued walking down the aisle and to my spot on the left. The music changed, and I had to break my stare with Cade to look at my mom as she came down the aisle.

It was only seconds until she was at the altar with Sal and they were saying their vows. It all went by quickly, and before I knew what was happening, the officiant was telling Sal he could kiss the bride, and everyone was cheering.

Asher broke free in the commotion and ran right to me. "Aria!" he shouted, but I could barely hear him over all the applause. I bent down as he got closer and didn't hesitate to pick him up. It was a balancing act with my bouquet of flowers too, but he was the perfect gentleman and took them from my hands as he planted his face in them to sniff. "Ew." He screwed up his nose, and I laughed, so carefree I would have scared myself if I really thought about it.

Mom and Sal walked back down the aisle, and I followed them out with Asher holding on to me tightly and Belle beside me. The plan was to have drinks outside while they turned the room around for the evening party, so I followed the crowd out there.

"When I get married, I'm going to wear the bestest dress," Belle told me, twirling around and making the skirt of her dress come up. "It's going to be amazing, and everyone will be super jealous of how beautiful I look."

"Is that right?" I asked, unable to wipe the smile

off my face as we finally made it outside. "And who will you be marrying?" I moved to the right, staying toward the back of the crowd, and pulled Belle with me. I couldn't see Uncle Brody or Lola.

"Duh." Belle rolled her eyes as if I was stupid. "Ford, of course."

"And I'll be coming to this wedding, right?"

"Yes! You can help me plan it."

"It's a deal," I told her as a hand connected with my back.

"You look so fuckin' beautiful right now," Cade whispered in my ear, only loud enough for me to hear. He placed a kiss on the side of my neck, and I couldn't bring myself to care if anybody saw him do it.

"There you are!" I heard Lola say, and I spun to see her heading toward us. "We need to do pictures —" She halted, her eyes widening, and then she demanded, "Do. Not. Move. A. Single. Inch." She held her hand up. "I mean it, stay exactly like that." She yanked her cell out and snapped several pictures. "You can move now," she told us, a grin on her face.

"What was that about?" I asked, boosting Asher higher on my hip. He was getting heavier and heavier by the second.

Lola stepped forward and showed me her cell, and my smile widened even more. The four of us were standing together, all with grins on our faces and happiness shining in our eyes. "I'm framing that one," Lola said. "It's perfect."

"What's perfect?" Uncle Brody asked, wrapping his arms around her waist from behind.

"This picture." She showed him her cell and his gaze flicked over to me and then to Cade who was still standing behind me, his hand lingering on the bottom of my back.

"Looks good," Uncle Brody said, but there was something else shining in his eyes as he stared at me. Something I couldn't place but had me at ease.

I boosted Asher again, feeling my arm go dead, and Cade said, "Let me take him." He plucked him out of my arms before I had a chance to tell him I was okay, and Asher took my flowers with him. He didn't seem to want to give them up, so I let him have them.

"Come on, you two." Lola grabbed mine and Belle's arms. "Picture time!" She pulled us away from Uncle Brody and Cade, but I couldn't resist taking one last look at Cade. He winked at me, and I needed his touch like I needed my last breath.

The end of the school year could not come soon enough.

Chapter Fifteen

ARIA

Sal grunted as he was led onto the dance floor by Mom for the obligatory first dance. It was a tradition Mom wouldn't pass up on, and she'd made it known since they'd been engaged. I even saw them practicing a few times in the living room.

The music flowed from the band on the stage, and they swayed left to right, all the while I tried to keep my gaze on them. Our table with me, Mom, Sal, Belle, and Uncle Brody was separated from everyone else's, and I tried my hardest not to keep veering my attention to Cade. I didn't want to be too obvious, not in front of all these people.

The song changed to a different one, and people started to walk out onto the dance floor. Lola came over to Uncle Brody and raised her brow, and it was all he needed to stand up and take her onto the dance floor. Ford came and kneeled in front of Belle to hold his hand out for her, and I shook my head. He had no idea she'd already planned out their wedding. I didn't want to be him when she found out it would never happen.

I leaned back in my chair and watched everyone dance, keeping my attention fixed onto them. There was only one more song until Mom and Sal were announcing they were leaving.

"You be good," Mom told me as she pulled me in for a hug. "I'm going to miss you so much."

"I'll miss you too," I told her because I would. She may not have been home most of the time, but she was always around. We'd never spent time apart, not like this, but I knew she'd have the time of her life.

She let me go, and Sal wrapped his arms around me, grunting, "Don't get arrested while I'm gone." I couldn't help but laugh at his words. I pulled away from him and stood back as they said their goodbyes to everyone else and exited the room.

"They'll be back before you know it," Lola said from beside me.

I turned to look at her. "I know." I was sad they were going, but I was also happy. Mom deserved to have this time with Sal. They both worked so hard and needed a break. "Plus, I hear the people I'm staying with are pretty cool."

"Pretty cool?" Lola raised her brows and planted her hands on her hips. "I hear they're the coolest people of all."

"Oh, really?" I laughed. "That's some high expectations right there."

"I think they can live up to them," she said with a shrug of her shoulders. "Oh, this is my jam!" She rocked her hips side to side as she made her way back to the dance floor, and I stood off to the side, watching the floor fill up with people again.

"You just gonna stare at people dancing all night, or get out there?" a gruff voice said from behind me.

I twirled around to see Ford's face, his lips quirked the smallest amount. "Got no one to dance with," I told him. It wasn't the truth, not really, but the one person I wanted to dance with hadn't asked me so…

"Come on." Ford grabbed my wrist and weaved us through the chairs. "Let's dance."

It was on the tip of my tongue to tell him no, but as soon as he wrapped his arm around my waist and pulled me close to him, I was already dancing. The song slowed down, and Ford dipped me lower, causing a shocked laugh to escape my lips.

"That's what I wanted to hear," Ford said, his lips turning up even more. "It won't be long now," he said, and I frowned up at him as I clasped his biceps.

"What won't be long?"

He winked and spun me under his arm then brought me back to his chest. "You'll se——"

"Mind if I cut in?" a deep voice I'd been craving to hear ground out from beside us.

"Told you." Ford let me go. "You're welcome."

I stared after him as he sauntered across the dance floor and to one of the tables, but it was only seconds until I was in the arms of the man who I desperately wanted.

"He did that on purpose," Cade growled out, placing his one hand on the bottom of my back and closing my hand with his other.

I flicked my gaze up to him at the same time he looked down, his dark-blue eyes sparkling. "I think he did." I pressed a little closer to him, wishing we weren't surrounded by people. "I wish we were alone."

His chest expanded on a breath, and he dipped down to whisper, "One hour. Meet me in your room in one hour."

I pulled back, hearing the crescendo of the song end, and stared up at him. "Cade?" I frowned when he wouldn't look at me, my stomach dipping with nerves. "What's going on?"

He let go of me, bringing my knuckles up to his lips where he planted a kiss. "One hour," he demanded and then walked away. He disappeared into the crowd, and just as I was about to follow him to ask him what was happening, Asher gripped on to my hand.

"Dance!" Asher shouted, and I couldn't turn him down. His little face was beaming as he threw his body into dance moves I had no idea existed, but it didn't matter how long I stayed on that dance floor, I still couldn't get Cade's words and facial expression out of my head.

He'd looked almost angry as he'd told me to meet him in my room, and I couldn't help wonder if my life was about to be turned upside down. Things had been so great between us this last couple of weeks, but maybe I'd been living in a dream world. What if things weren't that good? What if he couldn't handle all the baggage I came with?

"I'm heading up to put the kids to bed." I whipped my head around to face Lola who was now struggling to hold Asher on her hip.

"I'll come up with you," I said and took hold of Belle's hand. "We were up really early this morning, so I think I may go to my room too."

We made it out of the main room and toward the elevators, the sound of the band dissipating with each step farther away we took.

"Can you read to me, Aria?" Belle asked as we stepped inside the elevator. Lola clicked the button for the fifth floor, and I clicked the seventh.

"No, missy, you're going straight to sleep. It's way past your bedtime," Lola told her, using her mom voice which meant there was no room for argument.

"But—"

"Nope." The elevator doors opened, and I moved to the side so they could exit. "We'll meet you downstairs in the morning, okay?" Lola said to me.

"Okay," I whispered back, tiredness setting in quickly, but as soon as the doors closed, the thought of seeing Cade any minute had it disappearing.

Butterflies swarmed crazily in my stomach as I made it to the seventh floor, and then I was stepping out of the elevator. I didn't know why I thought Cade would have been waiting for me, but he wasn't. The hallway was empty, so I pulled my heels off and walked toward my room.

The key unlocked the door, and I entered the darkened room. The full moon paved my way toward the balcony doors, and I wasn't able to resist standing out there and watching the clear sky. It had cooled down a lot since this afternoon, but not enough to need a jacket, so I let my heels drop to the carpeted floor and stepped onto the balcony.

My hair was held up with several pins, so I pulled them all out and massaged my scalp, letting the wind flow through the strands. I leaned my arms on the railing and stared out at the view. We were in the middle of the countryside, and all I could see were rolling fields. It was so peaceful out here, but it didn't compare to the lake. The lake had captured my heart, and I wasn't sure it would ever let it go.

"I'm not sure whether to stand and watch you, or come and touch you."

I jumped out of my skin and spun around, my hand flying over my heart to stop it racing so fast. "Cade," I breathed. "How did you get—"

He held a card in the air and grinned but didn't move from where he was leaning against the balcony doors. "I let myself in." He pocketed the card, and I pressed my back against the railing. "You're so fuckin' beautiful it hurts." My cheeks burned from his words and his undivided attention, and I gasped as he stepped forward, making the tiny balcony seem that much smaller. "I haven't been able to take my eyes off you since you walked down the aisle." His hand connected with my waist, his fingers gripping me.

"I wish we could have been together down there," I told him. I wasn't afraid of admitting I'd missed him today. I wanted him to be able to hold me and smile down at me without worrying about anyone seeing us.

"I do too, baby." His hand fluttered over my waist and over the side of my chest, finally landing on my collarbone. "It won't be long." His voice was lower now as he fingered the chain to the necklace he'd gotten me for my birthday. "Did you know this is a locket?"

I tilted my head to the side. "I thought it was, but I couldn't find the opening."

His eyes softened, his body pressing closer to mine as he fiddled with the teardrop of my necklace. "I had an inscription put in there," he whispered. I moved my head down, but I couldn't see what he was doing or what it said. "Want me to read it out to you?" he asked.

I placed my hands on his chest, feeling his thumping heart under my palm. Was he nervous? "Yes, please."

His breath fanned over my face, but he didn't look down at the necklace as he said, "Me and you, always." He paused, his hand moving to the side of my neck. "I love you."

I blinked, sure I'd heard him wrong.

"You…I…"

Cade pressed his forehead against mine. "I love you, Aria. I'm not sure how long I've loved you for, but it's been longer than I realized. I love you more and more each and every day."

Tears sprung to my eyes, and I couldn't do a thing to stop them trickling down my cheeks. "I love you too." I closed my eyes, almost as if it was too much to stare at him. "I love you so much."

I wasn't sure what I did to deserve someone like Cade, but I knew I would never let him go. I'd found the kind of love you only ever experienced once in a lifetime.

"Let me show you just how much I love you," he said, his voice deeper now as he picked me up and walked into the bedroom. He was gentle, caring, loving.

This wouldn't be the frantic kind of night where we needed to touch each other as much as we could. No, this would be the kind of night I'd never forget.

He laid me down on the bed, coming down on top of me, and whispered, "I love you."

"I love you, too."

I'd never tire of saying those words, not to him.

———

CADE

Aria's hand was firmly encased in mine the whole drive from her Tuesday session with Dr. Bay, right up to the point I pulled into Dad's driveway. Since I'd told her three days ago how I really felt, I never wanted to stop touching her. I wanted to hear her voice every second of every day, but now that she was staying with Dad and Lola for the next two weeks, it would be harder than ever before.

At least when Jan and Sal were here, they worked so much, they didn't think twice about looking for Aria in her bed. Either that or Aria could get away with messaging her mom and telling her she was staying at Hope's.

We couldn't do that now, though. Lola and Dad were big on family, which meant she had to be home each evening for dinner. But today was Tuesday, and I wasn't sure if she'd told them where she was going and that she'd be late.

"Ready?" I asked Aria and turned to face her. She was biting down on her bottom lip, her gaze connected with mine.

"Yeah." She puffed out a breath and moved her hand from mine. I hated not being able to touch her with people around. I wanted to tell my dad and Lola so we wouldn't have to hide it from them over the next couple of weeks, but we'd discussed it at length and decided to tell everyone all at once, which meant we had to wait.

"I'm ready."

We both pushed out of the car, and we hadn't even made it to the front door before we heard Belle shouting, "Aria is here with Cade!" I closed my eyes and puffed out a breath. You couldn't get anything past Belle, not with her nosy nature. She flung the front door open and planted her hands on her hips. "You're in trouble."

I wasn't sure who she was talking to, but when I looked at her, I saw her attention was focused solely on Aria.

"Me?" Aria asked. "Why am I in trouble?"

"Because you're late for dinner. And I'm so

hungry." Belle moaned and placed her hand on her stomach. "I'm starving to death here, Aria!"

"You're so dramatic." I darted toward Belle and wrapped my arms around her, flinging her in the air. "You'd never starve, not with the amount of food you eat."

Belle gasped in my arms, and I heard the front door close as I entered the living room. "Are you calling me fat?"

"What?" I shook my head and let Belle down. "No. That's not what I said."

"Uh-huh, you did. You said I eat all the food. That's mean, Cade." I opened my mouth to tell her that wasn't what I meant, but she ran into the kitchen shouting, "Dad, Cade called me fat!"

"No, I didn't!" I followed her, feeling like a ten-year-old kid who was denying what his little sister said and not the twenty-five-year-old I was. Dad's brows flew high on his head as Belle looked up at him. "I didn't say you're fat, PB. I said you can't starve because you eat loads of food."

"See?" She pointed at me. "He just called me fat!"

"I didn't—"

"Belle Easton, sit your butt at this table right now," Lola demanded, her lips in a straight line. Well, shit, Lola really wasn't happy. Maybe Aria *was* in trouble after all.

"Ugh. Fine." Belle stomped over to the table and sat next to Asher, and it was only then I noticed Aria lingering in the doorway, gnawing on her bottom lip.

"Aria?" I asked, trying to gain her attention, but she was too focused on Lola.

"I'm sorry I'm late," Aria whispered. "I…erm…I have a standing appointment on Tuesdays and forgot to tell you about it."

"No worries, baby girl," Dad said, moving over to the table.

"I really am sorry," Aria said again.

Lola stepped toward her, her head tilted to the side. "You okay, sweetheart?" She placed her hand on Aria's arm, and even I could see her jump from the contact all the way from here.

"Yeah, I just…" She flicked her gaze over to me and then away. "I normally just…I…" She was finding it hard to talk, and I understood why. The sessions with Dr. Bay were never easy on her, and usually she would come back to my place and sleep the evening away. She wasn't used to having to interact with other people after them.

"She's tired," I interjected, unable to stop myself. "Come and eat, then you can go to sleep," I told her, doing my best to convey to her I knew what she was trying to say.

Lola rubbed her hand up and down Aria's arm and nodded. "What Cade said. You look really tired, but you need to eat first." She pulled her into the kitchen and toward the table.

"You staying for dinner, son?" Dad asked.

I shook my head and leaned against the counter. "Can't, I need to start packing."

"Packing?" Belle asked, perking up at my words. "Where are you going?"

"France."

Belle's eyes widened, her mouth opening in shock. "No way!"

"Yep." I pushed off the counter and moved toward the table. "I'm leaving on Thursday."

"Can I come?" PB asked, and I should have known it was coming. She always wanted to go on trips with everyone.

"No can do, PB. My mom is getting married—again." I placed a kiss on the top of her head at the same time reaching for Aria's back. Aria turned to look at me, her eyes shadowed in sadness. She always had that look after seeing Dr. Bay, and I hated I couldn't hold her like I had last week. "You still okay to take me to the airport, Dad?"

Lola placed some food in the middle of the table and then walked back toward the counter to get another tray. "Yeah, what time you leaving?" Dad asked, scooping some potatoes onto his plate and then onto Belle's and Asher's plates.

"Right after school. I'm going to leave my car at home." I paused and let my hand drift over Aria's back, then stood upright. "Could you pick me up from there?"

Lola sat down next to Dad and started to cut up Asher's food. I remained standing behind Aria. I wouldn't be able to stay, but I needed her to know I was here no matter what.

"Yeah, I can do that. I'd have to pick Aria up anyway," Dad said.

My shoulders drooped and a relieved breath rushed out of me. I had time to drop my car home and come over here for him to take me, but that way, I wouldn't be able to see Aria just before I left. I wanted all the time I could get with her. I was greedy, and I wasn't afraid to admit it.

———

CADE

I stared out of the window of my office, my gaze tracking the field and the track. I'd taken Aria and Reagan's practices back down to twice a week but I worked them just as hard. Just because they'd been to a meet and won races, didn't mean we could get complacent.

A knock sounded on my office door a second before it opened, and I knew who it was without having to turn and face her.

"I can't believe I'm not going to see you for

three days," her soft voice said, and I finally spun on my chair. Her lips were pulled up into a sad smile, one that told me she didn't want me to leave, and I wanted to tell her I felt exactly the same way. I wished I didn't have to go to another one of Mom's weddings, but I didn't have a say in the matter. I'd be the only family she had there.

"I know." I planted my feet on the floor and pushed my chair farther back then opened my arms for her. She came willingly, not an ounce of hesitation, and cuddled up against my chest.

We could have done countless things for the next ten minutes until my dad would be here, but all I wanted to do was hold her. We hadn't had a night together since Jan and Sal's wedding, and as much as I wanted a repeat of the night, this was exactly what I needed.

I needed to feel her against my chest.

I needed her to know I was here, even if I would be thousands of miles away.

I needed her to know it was her and me against the world, always.

She dipped her head back, and I looked down at her. "I'm going to miss you," she whispered.

"Me too." I placed a soft, gentle kiss on her lips. "It'll fly by, just like the next few months." We were counting the days down until her graduation, and when we would tell everyone how in love we were, but until then, we had to keep quiet. We had to keep our secret. The danger wasn't gone simply because Willow had left us alone. All it would take was one person to find out and go to the authorities. Although we weren't breaking any laws now, it would put a stop to my teaching, which would mean I couldn't coach.

My cell beeped with a message, and I looked down at it. I let out a breath, holding her tighter. "We need to leave."

"Just ten more seconds," she pleaded, and I gave them to her. I'd give her anything she asked for without a doubt.

She pressed a kiss to my lips, her eyes firmly closed, and then she opened them, showing me every emotion she possibly could. Her light-brown orbs never failed to pull me in, but since we'd confessed how we felt, something was different between us. We were more secure in each other and the knowledge where we were going.

Aria had started to tell me some of the things she talked about in her sessions with Dr. Bay, and no matter how angry it made me of what she had to grow up in, I always kept my feelings to myself.

She didn't want me to form an opinion about what had happened to her over the years and all the shitty things she'd seen, but I couldn't help blame Jan a little. She always made out their relationship was solid, but it was all surface level. She must have known the pain Aria was in, but she'd swept it under the rug, just like everything else.

I could feel myself starting to tense the longer I thought about it, so I shook my head to try and dissipate the thoughts. I didn't want to think about it, not in front of Aria.

"I love you," I whispered, pressing one last kiss to her lips.

"I love you too." She sighed and placed her head against my chest as my cell went off again.

Just ten more seconds.

Ten more seconds of bliss, and then we'd leave.

Chapter Sixteen

ARIA

Cade had been right. The days had flown by. From the time we dropped him off at the airport, I'd thought I'd be counting down the minutes, but I hadn't. He'd told me to keep busy, and that was precisely what I'd done. I'd played with Belle and Asher. I ran on the track Friday after school. I helped Lola around the house on Saturday and even helped Uncle Brody while he was tinkering with his Mustang.

I did anything I could to keep my brain occupied. Anything so I wasn't thinking. But my thoughts were starting to stir by Saturday evening, and when I woke up Sunday morning, they were in full effect. All I could think about was what would happen over the next week. Cade would be home in a few hours, and then I only had six days until Mom and Sal would be back too.

Six days until I had to tell them the truth.

Six days until I had to confess what I'd been doing to my body.

Six days until they found out my diagnosis.

"Aria?" Lola shouted outside Cade's bedroom door. That was another thing. I'd had to sleep in his bed—alone—while I stayed here. I'd been so used to staying at his house and falling asleep with him next to me, that I found it almost impossible without him. "I'm heading out to the store with the kids to get some groceries. I'll be back in a couple of hours."

"Okay!" I shouted back, glancing down at my chemistry workbook. I'd been staring at it for the last hour and not taken in a single word. "I'm going to finish my homework."

I heard her retreating footsteps, and soon after the sound of her car engine, and then she was gone, and I was alone. I hadn't been alone in the house all week, and although they'd managed to keep my thoughts busy, I was grateful for the silence. I needed some space—space I was used to having when I was at home. I wasn't used to being surrounded by people at all times of the day, not like this.

I tried to focus on my homework, and finally, with some peace and quiet, I managed to do a couple of hours. I finished up my chemistry and half of my world history assignment, but then the words all started to blur together, and nothing was making sense.

Slamming my workbook closed, I decided to take a break. I'd been holed up in Cade's room most of the afternoon, counting down the minutes until he would be home and going over and over all the outcomes of what would happen when I told Mom and Sal everything. But I needed a rest from it all—from my thoughts.

My head dropped back, and I groaned. I couldn't keep sitting here overthinking everything that would happen over the next week. Cade was gone. Mom and Sal were gone. I had time—time to just be me. And that was exactly what I was going to do.

I pushed off the bed and headed downstairs. The house was kind of eerie with no one else in it, but I shook off the feeling and went into the kitchen. I pulled the refrigerator door open and grabbed a yogurt, but as I was closing it, I frowned.

I'd been counting the days down, marking them off my imaginary calendar in my head…

But I'd forgotten.

I'd forgotten what day was coming up.

I'd failed to remember the date.

I'd woken up this morning and not thought twice about it. But as I stared at the calendar pinned to the refrigerator, it all came flinging back at me with so much force I stumbled.

The yogurt slipped from my fingers, colliding with the floor, and splashing everywhere, but I didn't move from the spot I was in. My gaze was only focused on the date, the numbers two and seven staring back at me, threatening to knock me over.

My shaking fingers reached for the calendar, and I yanked at it, ripping half of the month in the process, but I didn't care. It was all there for me to see, and I'd forgotten. *I'd forgotten.*

"Daddy?" I didn't shout because he never liked me to raise my voice. He said the loud noises scared him, but I wasn't sure he'd be able to hear me from here. "Daddy?" I said a second time, hearing another bang coming from the living room. He'd sent me to my room while he was pacing, but there was something different about the way he had been talking—something that had me on edge.

I pushed the handle down on my bedroom door and stepped out of my room and into the hallway. I needed to be as quiet as I could, so I tiptoed toward the living room.

I gasped, the calendar falling from my hands. Today. It was ten years today, and I'd forgotten. My heart raced in my chest, making it hard for me to catch my breath. I couldn't breathe. The air was stuck in my lungs, not willing to come out.

My hand collided with the wall as I tried to move out of the kitchen, but it was too much. The world started to spin and wouldn't stop. I needed out of here, I needed to be alone. I pushed my shoulders back, telling myself all I needed was to make it back to Cade's bedroom then it would all be okay, because when I was in there, I could make it all better.

I managed to get halfway up the stairs and had to close my eyes to try and right myself, but it was a mistake.

His mumbling was getting louder, and as I peeked into the living room, I could see him sitting in his chair, holding something in his hand. What was he holding?

"Daddy?" I whispered, but when he didn't answer me, I took a step inside the room. He didn't hear me call him. He never seemed to hear me when he needed to the most.

My eyes flung open and I crawled up the rest of the stairs. It was too much. Everything was too much. I knew what I needed—what I always needed when this happened. I had to try and push the memories aside until then. Finally, I stumbled inside Cade's bedroom and slammed the door behind me. My eyes widened as I stared around, spotting my bag on the floor.

My case. I needed my case.

I flicked the lock on the door, needing to be alone, and then darted for the case. It held my salvation—a salvation I hadn't needed in what felt like forever. In reality, it hadn't been long at all.

"I can't do it anymore," Daddy whispered, his voice so broken I could feel it in every inch of my body. A tear slid down his cheek, and I moved closer to him. All he needed was a hug. It would make him not so sad. When Mommy hugged me, I always felt better.

"It's okay, Daddy," I said, my voice low. I glanced down to his lap and what he was holding, then halted. I knew exactly what it was because he'd made me hold it to his head a couple of months ago. I'd pulled on it several times, but nothing had happened.

I sat on the edge of the bed and unzipped the case, finally able to take a full breath as the blades came into view. My fingertips dragged over the cool metal, and my pulse started to slow, the whirring in my ears not as bad.

"I'm sorry," Daddy said, and finally he looked up at me. His

sad eyes were filled with tears, and he didn't stop them as he lifted his head.

"Daddy?"

"I'm sorry, sweetie." His words were broken, his hand shaking, but I didn't understand. Why was he saying sorry? He hadn't done anything wrong.

I plucked one of the blades out and pressed it against my ankle. It was the first piece of skin I could see, so I pushed it against the soft skin on the inside. The scratch of the blade had a gasp escaping my lips, but it wasn't enough—not today.

The lights glinted off the metal as he raised it to his head, but it would be okay. Nothing would happen, just like last time.

A second ticked by, and then another one, the third one was met with a bang so loud I covered my ears from the sound. But I wished I hadn't. I wished I would have covered my eyes as the bullet tore through his head. Blood splattered behind him, and over the wall, the red a stark contrast to the light color Mommy had painted it.

My heart beat fast as his head slumped, his hand dropping to his lap with his gun still attached to his palm.

"Daddy?" I stepped forward, feeling the tears sliding down my cheeks. "Daddy!"

. . .

Tears flowed down my cheeks, a waterfall which couldn't be stopped as I dug the blade in harder. I gritted my teeth as the red flowed out of the cut, fascinated with how fast it was spurting out, but finally, it was enough.

Finally, the images of my dad dissipated.

Finally, I could breathe.

Finally, I could close my eyes and not see his pale face and lifeless eyes.

———

CADE

I rolled my head to the side, my tired eyes still firmly closed, but the roar of Dad's engine was keeping me awake. I'd spent the last ten hours on a flight home from France, and although I'd lost six hours of my life flying there, I'd gained it back today. Jet lag was a bitch—a bitch which was laying me on my ass. I felt like I could sleep for a week, and the only thing keeping me awake was the thought of seeing Aria.

"Tired?" Dad asked.

"Yeah." I rubbed at my sore eyes and sat up straighter as he turned into his street. "The weekend was nonstop."

"I can imagine." Dad chuckled. "Your mom doesn't do things by halves."

"She doesn't," I grunted. From the time I'd landed in France, there had been parties and dinners, and then the wedding. I hadn't had a second to think, much less call home or message with Aria. We'd barely talked, and I wasn't afraid to say I missed her. The image of her face perked me up, and my stomach fluttered as Dad pulled into the driveway next to Lola's car. Another couple of cars were littered outside the house, and I had no doubt it was Ford and Dad's team.

My body was sluggish as I pushed out of the car, and it took all my strength to lift my suitcase out of his trunk. "I could sleep for a week," I groaned out, following Dad into the house.

"Aw, does Cade need a nap?" Dad asked, his lips quirked up into a grin.

"Shut up." I barged past him as he opened the front door and I hadn't even made it into the living room when I was greeted by two terrors, otherwise known as Belle and Asher.

"You're home!" Belle shouted, throwing herself at me. I had no idea how I managed to catch her without falling over, but all I did was stumble a little. She wrapped her arms around my neck. "I missed you so much. Next time you go to France, you have to take me with you."

I chuckled and squeezed her tighter. "It's a deal," I told her. I almost wished she had been there with me. At least then I would have had an excuse not to have to attend all the events Mom and her new husband hosted.

Dad walked past me and grabbed Asher on the way, throwing him in the air and catching him, but he halted when Ford stepped out of the kitchen, blocking the entrance.

"Something is—" He was cut off by banging upstairs, and he flicked his gaze up to the ceiling.

Dad placed Asher on the floor. "What the…"

"Think you're having some teenage trouble," Ford said, glancing at me and then back to Dad. "Aria won't come out of her room."

"What?" I frowned and put Belle down. "What do you mean?"

Ford shrugged and backed away into the kitchen, his features telling us he needed to talk in private.

"Stay in here," Dad told Belle and Asher, who were already climbing back on the sofas and watching TV. We both moved into the kitchen where Ford was leaning against the counter, and the team was sitting around the dining table. A container of yogurt was splashed on the floor, but it was the calendar Ford held up that held my attention.

"Lola said she came back from the store to this," Ford told us. I stepped forward, realizing the calendar was ripped in half. "She said something about today being an anniversary and then shot upstairs, but she's been up there for about five minutes, and Aria won't come out."

"Anniversary?" I asked, not understanding what the hell was going on. Why would Aria rip the calendar?

"Sounds like she's just being a teenager to me," Dad grunted. "Probably needs some space."

I tended to agree. Aria did need space—she needed time to get her mind around things. Some would call it hiding, but I knew she was making sure she didn't crack the mask she had to put on in front of everyone.

"Beats me." Ford shrugged and threw the calendar down onto the counter. "If her dad died ten years ago, then maybe she wants some peace and—"

"What did you say?" I growled out, my heart starting to race in my chest. My gut told me something wasn't right, not once he'd said those words.

"Huh?" Ford frowned.

"What did you just say?"

"I said her dad died ten years—"

My eyes widened. "It's the anniversary of her dad's death?" Ford nodded, and I didn't wait another second to dart out of the kitchen, through the living room, and up the stairs. Footsteps followed after me, but not at the rushed pace I was going.

"Aria! Open the door!" Lola banged her fist on it several times, her head turning so she could look at me. "She's not answering, Cade." Her hazel eyes were shadowed in sadness, but I knew mine would have shown fear.

"Aria!" I shouted, banging my fist twice and trying the door handle, but it was locked. When she still didn't answer, I backed up a few steps, the worst images possible entering my head, and all I wanted was to scrub them clean. The tiredness that had been wearing at my body disappeared as I ran at the door, trying to get it open.

"Cade!" Dad shouted. "What the hell do you think you're doing?"

I backed up again. "We need to get in there."

"She just needs some space," Ford said, and I glanced over at him. I tried to tell him silently she didn't need space because I couldn't tell them what had been going on. I couldn't break her trust and reveal her secret.

"No." I ran at it again, causing the hinges to shake a little. "We need in that room right now."

"What's going on, Cade?" Lola asked, her hand gripping at her T-shirt. "What's happening?"

"I don't know, but…" I couldn't say it. I couldn't say my gut was telling me she'd done something she shouldn't have, so instead, I ran at the door again, and finally, it opened. The wood splintered, and I managed to catch myself at the last second so I didn't go tumbling to the floor.

My gaze flicked around the room, but it only

took a fraction of a second for me to spot Aria. Her body was half on the bed and half off the bed, and I scanned it, looking for any signs she'd hurt herself. Her face was pale, but her stomach and thighs were clear of any—

"Fuck!"

Blood was trickling out of her ankle, but it was the pool on the carpet that had my pulse skyrocketing.

Lola's gasp sounded behind me, but I didn't have time to turn around and explain anything to her. I wrapped my hands around her ankle, trying to stem the flow, but it was no use. The red liquid seeped through my fingers, unstoppable on its path out of her body.

"Jesus," Ford gritted out, coming to kneel next to me. He whipped his head around and grabbed one of my T-shirts off the floor. I had no idea what it was doing there, but the white material turned red as soon as he started to wrap it around my hand and her ankle. "Let go," he told me, and I did as he said then pressed my hands back onto it as he tied it to her. "She needs a hospital, now!"

His words had me moving, and I didn't think twice about lifting her up off the bed and cradling her against my chest. Ford held on to her ankle, but the blood was already staining his hands, and we hadn't even made it out of the room.

Dad's eyes were wide, watching the scene from

the hallway with horror, his arms wrapped around Lola. I didn't have time to stop and explain things to him, so we ran past them, and Ford let go of her leg as we darted down the stairs and out the front door. We didn't close it behind us as we headed to Ford's car parked at the bottom of the driveway.

Ford yanked open the back door, and I slid inside with Aria's lifeless body on my lap. Her chest was still moving—barely—and it gave me hope she would be okay. But the blood...there was too much blood.

The sound of the engine starting had my head snapping up, and I took one last glance at the house where Dad and Lola were running to Dad's Mustang.

"There's too much blood," I told Ford, staring at it as it started to stain his back seats.

"Fuck!" He drove the car faster at my words, and within seconds we were out of the neighborhood. "We'll be there in four minutes. Hang in there, Tyson."

I pressed my hand to her cool, pale face, the blood on my fingers staining her cheeks. "Please, baby, please, wake up." My throat burned, a lump forming that I'd never be able to swallow past. "I can't lose you. Not now, not after everything."

"I got your message," Ford blurted out, taking a corner too fast but managing to keep all four tires on the road. I hadn't seen him since before I'd sent him the message, and I knew I'd told him I would explain what it meant. Only now I didn't have to, he was witnessing it firsthand. "Is this what you were talking about?"

"Yeah," I gritted out, placing my fingers underneath Aria's nose, thankful when I could feel her light breaths on them.

"And Dr. Bay? She knows—"

"Shit!" I yanked my cell out of my pocket at his words and held Aria tighter as I found the number and dialed it, balancing it on the seat next to me and willing someone to pick up.

"Dr. Bay's office—"

"Dr. Bay. Emergency three," I reeled off, remembering the code she'd given me when we first talked. I never thought I'd have to use it, not with Aria, but as I looked down at her lifeless face, I understood she hadn't hit rock bottom when she first met with Doctor Bay. This was her lowest point, and I hoped and prayed it wouldn't be her end point.

The line clicked, and then Dr. Bay's voice came over the line. "Hello?"

"It's Cade Easton," I blurted out. "We're on our way to the hospital with Aria."

"Okay, Cade. Tell me which hospital." There was some shuffling over the line as I told her. "We're one minute out. She's cut her ankle and is losing loads of blood. Today is the anniversary of her dad's death."

"Shit," Dr. Bay whispered. "I didn't know."

"Neither did I." I saw the signs for the emergency room. "We're at the hospital."

"I'll meet you there," she said, and I left my cell on the seat as Ford squealed to a stop and opened the back door. We rushed into the emergency room, not stopping until I was in the center and was shouting for help.

Several people rushed over to me with a bed, and someone in dark-blue scrubs told me to put her on it. They wheeled her away. My feet carried me forward, intent on going in there with her.

"You can't go in there," a soft voice said. I turned to look at the nurse, about to tell her I didn't care what she said. I wasn't leaving Aria's side, not again, but beeping machines had my attention back on Aria as they slammed doors to a room shut.

"No!" I shouted, running toward them as they started to pump at her chest. She couldn't be gone, not now, not after everything. She'd fought too hard, she'd gotten help, she was in a better place. She couldn't die. I refused to let her die.

"Cade." Ford grabbed my arms, but I wrestled to get out of his grip.

"Son!" Dad's voice shouted, and my chest started to cave in. I couldn't take my gaze off the room as she flatlined. I couldn't look away in fear that, if I did, I'd miss the moment her heart beat again.

Lola's gasp echoed next to me, and the fight left my body. I'd not been there. I'd left her, and now she'd left me, in the most permanent way possible.

The nurse touched my arm, but I didn't make a move to acknowledge her. "You can all wait in the waiting room. A doctor will update you as soon as we have information."

My feet were stuck to the white floor, unable to move. I couldn't leave until I saw the—

A beep sounded, and then another, and I took another step toward the room, seeing the beat of her heart on the monitor.

She was alive—for now.

Chapter Seventeen

CADE

It had been hours. Hours of me pacing the waiting room while they worked on Aria. Hours waiting for someone to come and tell us she was okay. Hours while I was left in limbo, feeling my heart cracking, threatening to shatter.

Dad had tried several times to get me to talk, but I wouldn't say a word, not until I knew she was okay. I needed to know she was still fighting—still breathing.

Lola sat huddled in the corner with Dad next to her, and Ford sat opposite them. Dad's team had been at the house when we'd left, so I assumed they were watching Belle and Asher. Lola said she'd called Jan and Sal on the way to the hospital, but they wouldn't be here until the morning. The clock on the wall read 3 a.m., and the more time went by without an update, the more I fretted what would happen.

Was she dying in there? Or had they brought her back completely and needed time to assess her. Had Dr. Bay turned up yet?

"Sit down, son," Dad said, his voice tired. "You're gonna wear a hole in the floor." I didn't stop pacing, not until he stood and entered the path I'd been walking for hours. "If you're not gonna tell us what's been going on, then at least try and get some sleep."

"Can't," I croaked out, my eyelids getting heavier and heavier by the minute. "I need to know she's okay." I pushed my fingers into my hair, gripping on the ends and feeling the burn along my scalp. "I get it now," I said, meeting Dad's stare.

"Get what?"

"When you told me you couldn't choose who you love." I slowly sat down in one of the wooden chairs, not moving my gaze off his. "I never understood what you meant when you said that, but I get it now." I paused. "I get it."

"You love her," Dad said. It was a statement, not a question, but I nodded anyway. "That kind of love only comes around once in a lifetime, son. You make sure you hold on to it and never let go no matter what." He sat next to me, his hand squeezing my shoulder. "She'll be okay."

"How do you know?" I asked, hoping he'd tell me something I desperately needed to hear. He patted his chest over his heart. "I know in here. This isn't how this ends. Fate wouldn't bring you together to rip you apart."

"I hope you're right." My voice wasn't my own. It was different—tired, heartbroken, hopeful. I let my eyes close for a second, feeling the utter tiredness set in.

"Get some sleep. I'll wake you up if anyone comes in."

I couldn't even open my eyes to tell him I needed to stay awake. My body shut down, and with it, my brain. I needed rest, but I didn't want it. I wanted to be here when someone came in to tell us how Aria was doing. She needed me to be there with her, holding her hand and promising I'd never let go. She needed me, but I needed her more. I needed her more than I'd ever realized.

"Lola?" The sound of Jan's voice had my eyes springing open and my body shooting out of my seat. Tears streamed down her face as she ran toward Lola. "What happened?"

"I…" Lola's gaze flicked over to Dad and me. "I went out to get groceries, and when I came back." Lola paused, and I could see she was trying to collect herself. "When I got back, I noticed my calendar was ripped and realized what the date was."

"The date?" Jan asked, her brows furrowing. "I don't—oh my god. Her dad."

"But then Aria wouldn't answer me and then… it all happened so fast. I don't…I don't know how it happened. She cut herself, and…" Lola hiccupped a sob, and although I knew how she felt, I couldn't help feeling anger toward Jan. She hadn't been there when Aria needed her most. She'd known what was happening in her house all those years and hadn't protected her from it.

"Cut herself?" Jan asked, her voice sounding far away.

I stepped forward, anger swirling through my veins at an unstoppable speed. "Yeah," I gritted out. "But you already knew about that, huh?"

Jan's stare swung to me, but it was Sal who said, "What the hell you talkin' about, Cade?"

My lips quirked at the corner, but it wasn't in happiness. I took another step forward, now only a couple of feet away from them. "Jan knows what I'm talking about." I paused to wait and see what she said, but her wide eyes were the only indication she'd heard me. These weren't my secrets to tell, but my anger was fueling me, and there was nothing I could do to stop it. "Did you know she never stopped?" I asked her, my hands clenching into fists at my sides. "She kept on cutting herself." I shook my head, able to see the images of her scarred body so clearly in my head. "She's covered in scars."

"No." Jan shook her head and stumbled back. "No, she's not."

"Yeah, she is." I banged my fist on my chest. "I've fuckin' seen them. I've seen every single mark marring her body. I've sat with her while she's been in an indescribable amount of pain. I've helped her. *Me.*" I banged my fist on my chest a second time. "It was me who was there, and you just fuckin' ignored it!"

"Watch your fuckin' tone, Cade," Sal warned, but the woman I loved was in this building, and I still had no idea if she was even breathing.

"No," I ground out. "I won't fuckin' watch it. I won't keep quiet any longer." I pointed at Jan, knowing I was on the verge of completely losing my shit. "You should have known. You should have been able to see the pain she was in. How could you think she'd be okay after everything she witnessed with her dad?"

"I…" Jan moved her hand to the base of her neck, glancing around at us all. "I thought she was okay. I was okay, I was—"

"She was a child!" I shouted, so loud I hurt my own ears. "She was a goddamn child who watched her dad kill himself, and you thought she would be okay?"

"I—"

The door creaking open cut her off, and I swung my head to face it. A breath whooshed out of me at the sight of Dr. Bay.

"Cade?" she asked, stepping inside the room and shutting the door behind her.

My breaths started to come faster as she ambled closer, her heels clicking on the floor. "How is she?"

Doctor Bay glanced around the room, her gaze landing on Jan last and then back on me. "Maybe we should talk in private."

"No," Jan ground out, and I looked over at her. Gone was the vulnerable woman I'd seen seconds ago, and in her place was the Jan we all knew. The Jan who liked to pretend everything was okay. "I'm Aria's mother, so *we* can talk in private."

Dr. Bay's throat bobbed. "I'm afraid I can't talk to you. Aria has Cade Easton as her emergency contact so—"

"What?" Jan sneered, turning her face to look at me. "Why does she have you as her contact?"

I opened my mouth to tell her why, but Dr. Bay cut me off, "I think this should be talked about another time." She had a point, but there was no way I'd allow Jan to call any of the shots. She'd had her chance to look after Aria, to make sure she was safe, even from herself, and she'd failed.

I shook my head and turned my attention back to Dr. Bay. "You can tell us all here. We're her family." I pulled in a breath. "How is she?"

"She lost a lot of blood." Dr. Bay took a breath. "She's currently resting after a transfusion, but I still need to asses her when she wakes up. Do you know if she's been taking her medication, Cade?"

"I—"

"Medication?" Jan asked. "Why would she be taking medication?"

"I don't know," I told Dr. Bay. "I've been away for the last three days and came back to…" My breath caught in my throat as I remembered the way she'd been lying on my bed, blood flowing out of her.

"Okay." Dr. Bay nodded. "I'll wait for her to wake up and ask her. Once I've assessed her, we'll go from there, but I'll probably admit her into an inpatient facility for at least a week to stabilize her." She placed her hand on my arm. "She'll be okay. She's in the right place to get the treatment she needs, and she'll come out on the other side."

I nodded, hoping she was right. "When can we see her?"

Dr. Bay looked out of the windows behind us. The sun had long since risen, and we were verging on lunchtime now. "Once I've assessed her. I'm hopeful she'll wake in the next couple of hours."

"Okay," I whispered, afraid to talk too loud. She was alive. She was breathing. She was still here.

Dr. Bay left the room, the door clicking shut behind her, and as soon as it rang out, Jan darted toward me. "Why the hell is Aria on medication? And why are you her emergency contact?" Her hands gripped my arms, and I yanked them away from her.

"She's bipolar," I blurted out. "She needs the medication to stabilize her moods. She's been on it for a month or so now."

"And why do you know?" Jan stared at me, her eyes probing for information, and I wasn't sure what she saw, but when her nostrils flared, and she ground out, "What the hell have you done?" I knew she knew. I knew I couldn't hide it from anyone anymore—not that I wanted to.

"Jan," Lola called, walking closer to us. "Why don't you sit down—"

"Did you know?" Jan asked, twirling on Lola.

"Know what?" Lola frowned, her gaze batting between the two of us. "I don't understand…"

"She doesn't know," I told Jan. "No one knows."

"Not true," Ford interjected, raising his hand in the air. "I knew."

"You knew what?" Dad asked.

"Could someone please explain what the hell is going on right now?" Sal demanded.

Everyone was looking at me, waiting for an answer, and I knew it was time to give it to them. We'd wanted to do it together. We'd wanted to tell everyone how we felt about each other, but Aria hadn't given me a choice. They had to know now.

"I'm in love with Aria." I paused, waiting for their reactions, but they all continued to stare at me. "And she's in love with me. We're together. We have been for months."

"Months?" Jan asked, backing away a step. "As in, when she was seventeen?"

I cringed, and even though I wanted to deny it, I couldn't. "Yes."

"Fuck," Ford spat, but it was Dad who came to stand next to me and placed his hand on my shoulder.

"You took advantage of my daughter!" Jan screamed, raising her hand and then slapping me across the face. The burn of her palm didn't register for several seconds. "How dare you! How dare you—"

"How dare I?" I laughed, but it wasn't humorous in the slightest. "How dare I look after the girl who you basically abandoned? How dare I show her some love? How dare I make sure she wasn't destroying herself more and more each day? How dare I be there when she needed someone to talk to? How dare I? *How dare I?*"

"I think we all need to calm down," Dad said.

Sal wrapped his arms around Jan, whispering something to her, and then he looked at me. "I'm taking Jan outside for some air." He paused, his chest lifting on an inhale. "Thank you." I frowned, not sure what he was thanking me for, but he continued, "Thank you for looking out for her when no one else did."

Jan stared up at him. "Sal—"

"No, Jan." He looked down at her. "We failed her. Look where we are right now. We fuckin' failed."

"But he took advantage—"

"You don't believe that," Sal interrupted her, placing his hands on either side of her face. "Deep down, you don't. You're looking for someone to blame, that's all. No one is to blame. Have we made mistakes? Yes, but we can't do anythin' about the past now. We just gotta look forward. Ri is getting help, and we'll be there every step of the way."

"But..." Jan's shoulders drooped. "You're right. I...I need some air."

The two of them walked out of the room, whispering to each other, and closed the door behind them.

"Well..." Lola cleared her throat, and the tension in the room dissipated. "I'm guessing it was Aria you were talking about at the cookout all those months ago?"

I turned my head to face her, a small smile lifting at my lips. "You'd be correct."

"Thank god." She leaned to the side against Dad. "I hated that Willow chick. She was…" Lola shivered, and I knew the feeling. "Aria and Cade." She grinned wide. "Should have seen that one coming from a mile away, huh?"

They should have seen it because, from the moment I'd laid eyes on Aria, I knew I would do anything in my power to protect her. I just hadn't realized how much. But now we were out in the open, and I never wanted to go into hiding again.

"It's fate, darlin'," Dad told her, wrapping his arm around her shoulders. "Ain't nobody in this world who can defy fate."

He was right, which was why I would obey it for the rest of my life. Fate had brought us together, and I'd never let her go again.

————

ARIA

I clasped my hands together on my lap and twisted the sleeve of my long-sleeved top over my fingers. My heart hammered in my chest as I waited for Dr. Bay to come back inside the room. Today was the day I confessed everything. Today was the day all the lies would be smashed to pieces.

Cade sat next to me, his hand on my thigh, squeezing in reassurance. From the time I woke up three days ago in the hospital bed, he'd barely left my side. He was only allowed here during certain hours in the day, but he was here every second he could be.

My hands shook as I remembered my gaze landing on his when I'd woken up. I'd nearly ended it all. I'd nearly taken my own life just like *he* had. I'd been stupid, so stupid to act on impulse, and all it had done was make it clear that I needed the help I was getting.

And that it was time to come clean to the people who mattered most.

I stared down at Cade's long fingers and his short nails, not daring to move my gaze off them as the door creaked open. I didn't need to turn and look to see who it was. I didn't know what I expected to feel, but it wasn't the nervousness rolling through me. I'd seen my mom several times since I'd woken up, but the conversations had been stilted and fake. Now was the time to put a stop to it.

Mom's red hair came into view as she sat on the sofa opposite me and Cade with Sal sitting beside her. Her lips quirked as she tried to smile at me, but it didn't quite reach her eyes. Did she think I was like my dad? Was she scared I'd do what he did?

Dr. Bay sat in the chair between the two sofas and cleared her throat. "Aria, I've explained to your mom and Sal what the purpose of today is for, but I'll tell you again so we're all on the same page."

I glanced up at Dr. Bay and out of the windows directly behind her. When she'd first said I was being admitted into an inpatient facility, I was sure it'd be like in the movies with white hallways and nurses strapping people to their beds to force medication down their throats. But it was nothing like that. In fact, in here was the calmest and most at peace I'd felt outside of Cade's home.

"Today is the first step in the road to rebuilding your relationships. The four people in this room are a family, and we need to remember—"

"He's not my family," Mom said, her lips lifting into a sneer as she narrowed her eyes on Cade. "He's just someone who took—"

"Mom," I ground out, already thinking this was a bad idea. Cade was it for me, and if she couldn't accept him, then she couldn't accept me. It was on the tip of my tongue to tell her that, but Dr. Bay held up her hand.

"Jan." Dr. Bay paused and waited for Mom to look at her. "Cade has been there every step of the way during Aria's journey. He has been a tremendous support, and while I can understand where you're coming from, today is about making amends and being open and honest with each other. If you don't have it in your heart to do that, then I suggest we leave today's meeting until—"

"No," Sal demanded, his hand covering Mom's on her lap. He glanced at her, and she let out a breath. "We talked about this, Jan."

His gruff voice had my shoulders relaxing, and it was the first time I understood that I needed all three of the people in this room. I'd pushed them all away at various stages, scared to admit I needed them, but I did. Dr. Bay had told me several times over the last couple of days to not keep things pushed down anymore, so I opened my mouth and told everyone, "I need you all."

All their gazes swung my way, and I felt the heat spreading over my cheeks. "I've pushed you all away, but now it's time I told you why." I took a breath. "Mom, I know you don't understand what Cade and I have, but it's real." His hand squeezed my thigh. "It wasn't a sordid affair. It wasn't him taking advantage of me. I love him more than anything. I need you to accept that because I need you both in my life."

Mom's gaze dropped to her lap, and her shoulders moved up and down rapidly. I knew she'd be upset, but there were worse things to come, I wondered if she realized that.

"Jan," Dr. Bay said, leaning forward in her seat. "Do you understand that you need to accept Cade and Aria as a couple to be able to move forward?"

"I do," Mom croaked out, and finally glanced up. "I just…" She sniffled, and I felt my chest constrict. "I'm jealous." She blinked several times. "I'm jealous she went to him and not me."

"She didn't," Cade said, his deep voice soothing the ache in my chest. "I found out by accident."

"You did?" Mom asked, and Cade nodded. "I can see why you're good for her. I just wish I could be good for her."

"That's why we're here today," Dr. Bay said, a small smile lifting on her face. "Today is the first step in that." Dr. Bay glanced over at me. "Aria, why don't you start with telling your mom how you've been feeling since the death of your dad?" She wasn't mincing her words, and I was glad she'd jumped right in there because Mom and I were skirters. We skirted around the issue and pretended everything was okay, and I could see now how much we both needed this.

"I...I can't explain it." I placed my hand over Cade's, needing more of his touch to center me. "I guess it goes back to the first time you caught me cutting." Mom's eyes filled with tears, but I continued, "I told you I wouldn't do it again, and even though you saw the few other scars, you just believed me. You accepted my word and didn't question it one bit."

"I didn't think I had to," Mom said, her voice low. "I've never doubted you, honey. You've always been my rock. The one person I could depend on, but…" She bit down on her bottom lip, her shoulders shaking. "I can see what a huge mistake I made. You lost your childhood before your dad died, and afterward…after that you became the one person I didn't have to worry about."

"I didn't want you to worry about me," I told her as every muscle in my body begged me to walk across the light-yellow rug separating the two sofas.

"But that's the problem," Dr. Bay interrupted. "And that was why you didn't confide in your mom."

Mom and I stared at each other, so much pain showcased in each of our eyes. I was surprised we were still standing. I'd thought she was okay after what had happened with my dad, but I can now see that she'd been putting on a front, just like I had.

"I wish I'd have known, Ri," Sal grunted, but I could hear the crack in his voice. "I'm sorry we didn't notice. I'm sorry I didn't…fuck." He slapped his palm on his chest and cleared his throat, trying to hold himself together. "I love you like you're my own daughter, Ri. And the thought of you living your life each day in so much pain. Fuck, it about breaks me."

A lump built in my throat, one I wasn't sure would ever dissipate. I'd caused this pain but…I hadn't started it. This was the aftereffects from my dad, a decade after he'd taken his own life.

"I didn't want to kill myself," I blurted out. A tear rolled down my cheek. The pain was pouring out of me, and I didn't want it back. I didn't want to live my life the way I had. I didn't want to resent Mom for being happy. I didn't want to avoid Sal because I knew he was a better man than my own dad. And I didn't want to push Cade away in case he got too close. "I just needed relief, and I…I lost control."

"I get that," Sal said, his eyes shadowed with darkness. He'd lived a rough life, one full of pain too, and I should have known he would understand me better than anyone else. I had no idea what he'd gone through growing up, but pain like ours knew each other without a word needing to be spoken.

"What happens now?" Mom asked, her gaze veering to Dr. Bay.

"You all need to take ownership of what you did wrong. You need to acknowledge it, and then all of you need to let it go. This needs to be a clean slate, one where support and love is the backbone of all of your relationships."

The silence stretched inside the small room, and I realized no one wanted to go first. But we were here because of what I'd done, so it only made sense for me to go first.

"I should have asked for help." I looked at Mom and Sal, then finally Cade. "I should have trusted you all enough to come to you with my pain. I should have been more vocal."

"I should have paid more attention," Sal said. "I should have known something wasn't right when we moved into the house, but…I ignored it."

Mom cleared her throat, her gaze meeting mine as she whispered, "I should have been a better mother." I opened my mouth, about to tell her she'd been the best mom she could have been at a time where nothing was certain in our lives, but she didn't give me the chance. "You're my baby, Aria. I think deep down, I knew you weren't okay, but the older you got, and the more time that passed, I had no idea how to approach it with you. You've grown into one of the strongest women I know, and I'd like to get to know her. I'd like the opportunity to be the mother to you I should have always been."

"I'd like that." I smiled, the first genuine smile I'd had in days. I'd been covered by clouds of darkness, and now they were drifting apart, allowing the sun to shine through and give me hope for the future.

"I want to apologize," Cade said, sitting up straighter. I frowned at him, but he wasn't looking at me, his attention was focused on Mom and Sal. "I should have come to you that first day. I knew when I saw the scars I should have reported it, but…" He heaved a breath. "I thought I was protecting Aria. And then things kind of snowballed, and I got a little lost. I got angry at you for not being there, but I wasn't thinking about the fact that Aria had pushed you away too." He swallowed, and the room was so quiet, you could have heard a pin drop. "I love your daughter, more than anything else in this world, and I know I need to show you both I can be trusted with her. I intend to prove it every single day."

"I don't doubt you love her, son," Sal said, his lips quirking at the corners. "For anyone to go at Jan the way you did in that waiting room tells me that much. Fuck, even I wouldn't answer her back like that." He chuckled, and Mom couldn't stop the small smile and eye roll she gave him.

"I wanted to show you all how serious I am," Cade continued. "Which is why I quit my job this morning."

My eyes widened. "You did what?" My mouth was open in shock, and I couldn't quite believe the words coming out of his mouth.

He turned to face me, his hands drifting up to the sides of my face as he stared into my eyes. "I quit. We're in the open with nothing to stop us. Nothing else compares to you, baby. I'd climb the highest mountain in the goddamn world if it meant I could spend five minutes with you." He leaned his forehead against mine, and this time, a tear absent of pain but filled with happiness rolled down my cheek. "I love you, so damn much. Today is the first day."

"The first day of what?" I asked, my voice a broken whisper.

"Of the rest of our lives, baby." He pressed his lips to mine—a simple, closed-mouth kiss, but it was everything. It sealed the promise he'd made, one that I had no doubt he would keep forever.

Epilogue

ARIA

"Aria Sayer."

I lifted my robe and took the steps slowly. My stomach dipped with nerves as I floated across the stage and accepted my high school diploma. Cheers rang out, but I couldn't look out into the crowd—not yet anyway. There were so many people here, sitting in the chairs which lined the field, but there was only one person I wanted to see. Cade.

I wrapped my hand around my diploma and looked into the crowd. A row of people was standing, but they weren't just any people—they were *my* people. Uncle Brody, Lola, Belle, and Asher were the first I spotted, and then Ford, but it was Cade sitting next to Mom and Sal I zoned in on.

Since the first meeting in the inpatient unit, we'd

started having the sessions once every two weeks as a family. It had taken Mom a couple of months to come around fully to the idea of Cade and me being together, but she'd gotten there eventually, and now we were a real family.

I'd wanted to move into Cade's house when I'd been discharged out of the unit, but he'd told me he thought I should stay at home until the school year was up, and I was sure that was the first thing Mom approved of. He'd been right in his suggestion because Mom and I were now closer than ever. We hadn't rebuilt the relationship we had, we'd simply created a new one. One where we talked openly about the past. One where we remembered the happier times and laughed at some of the weird things Dad did.

I smiled over at all three of them, feeling my eyes burning with tears. We were a family—a real one which I didn't want to escape from. Mom waved like crazy as I walked across the stage and down the steps and right into Hope's arms.

"Can you believe this?" she screamed into my ear. "We're high school graduates!"

"I know!" I hugged her harder than I ever had. We only had today, and then she was off on tour with her boyfriend's band for the summer, but luckily, she was going to attend the local college, which would mean I'd see her all the time.

Once I'd gotten home from the hospital, I'd seen

the envelope stamped with Shire Oaks College on the front and tore it open. They'd offered me a full-ride scholarship, and even though it was my dream to go there and turn my running into something more than I ever thought it could be, I had hesitated. I didn't want Cade and me to be in the same position as we'd been in the last school year, but he'd told me he wasn't coaching the track athletes, so we'd be fine.

I let Hope go and grinned at her. She was my best friend, and even though I'd also pushed her away, she understood once I'd told her everything. This time I hadn't left anything out. I'd told her every little detail, and she'd sat and listened to it all then hugged me for what felt like hours.

"I'm going to miss you," I told her.

"Psssh." She waved her hand in the air, but I could see the tears shining in her eyes. "You won't even remember me once you've moved in with lover boy."

I chuckled. She was probably right. When Cade and I were together, we lost all sense of time. He said it was a side effect to our love, I just thought it was because he was so damn consuming.

Arms wrapped around me from behind, and I squealed as I was lifted into the air and twirled around. I couldn't help the laugh that burst out of me because I knew whose hands they were. "Congratulations, baby," Cade said, and I was aware of eyes burning over our skin, but I didn't care one bit. He planted me on the floor and spun me around to face him. He dipped down and pressed his lips to mine. We were out in the open, and I wasn't sure how we survived before it was like this.

"How long do you think we'll have to wait until you can move in?" Cade asked, his dark-blue eyes hopeful.

"Well, I'm officially graduated now, so…tonight?"

His lips spread even wider as he lifted me off the ground. "Sounds perfect to me."

"What sounds perfect?" Belle asked, bounding over to us. "Ew, stop kissing, it's gross." She screwed up her nose and made a gagging sound.

My head flung back, and I laughed harder than I had in weeks. I hadn't seen Belle much lately, but now that summer was here, I had every intention of spending as much time with her and Asher as I could.

Cade placed me back down onto the grass, and I crouched down in front of her. "Shakes," I said. "Shakes sound perfect."

Her eyes widened. "Oh! Can I come?"

I grasped her hand in mine and stood, my gaze flicking over to Mom and Sal. They'd both cried this morning when I'd put my cap and gown on, even though Sal had tried to cover it up. "We're all going. I think it's time we celebrated as a family."

"Couldn't have said it better myself," Uncle Brody said. "Proud of you, baby girl." His eyes shone, but I could tell he wasn't only talking about me graduating. They said it took a village to raise a child, but it also took one to support one too. They'd all been there for me, ready to listen and ask what they could do to help. When the simple fact of the matter was, them just being there was more than enough.

"Thank you," I croaked out and flicked my gaze down at Belle to distract myself. "Let's go get shakes." I wiggled my fingers to get her attention, and she whipped her head up to face me. "I vote banana."

"Ew." Belle shook her head and pulled me away from the crowd. "Everyone knows strawberry is the best."

I glanced back at everyone as they followed us off the school grounds and spotted Hope pushing through everyone to get to Belle and me. "Shakes, here we come!" She clasped Belle's other hand. "Hey, Cookie Monster."

"Hey, Hopeful." Hope laughed, not fazed by Belle's nickname for her one bit.

Cade grasped my other hand, and I glanced up at him, seeing the love shining in his dark-blue eyes. We'd not had an easy road to get here, but I thought it made us stronger. Together, we were unbreakable.

Together, we could master any situation and come out the other side hand in hand.

"Love you, baby," he whispered, bringing my knuckles to his lips and planting a kiss on them.

I would never tire of hearing those words coming out of his mouth, and I would never get tired of replying, "Love you, too."

Acknowledgments

This story became so much more than I ever thought it would. When I started Cade and Aria's book, I never imagined it would become what it is today. The journey has been epic and emotional.

My first thank you needs to go to Paige. You're the most awesomest Alpha Reader and PA. Thank you for loving my stories as much as I do, and generally just being you!

My second thank you needs to go to my husband and daughters. This book became such a huge part of my life, and I can't thank you enough for putting up with my weird ways.

I'd liked to say a huge thank you to my BETAs readers: Nikki & Yvonne. You ladies are amazeballs and I couldn't do this without your continued support!

To my bestie, Dan. Thank you for always being there for me, no matter what. You're the besets friend a girl could ask for! Love you long time!

To my ARC team. You ladies are simply amazing and I love for each and every one of your messages! Thank you for taking the time to ready my stories, I appreciate so much.

To the bloggers who help share EVERY-THING. I love you so much, and I can't put into words how grateful I am! You are a special bunch of people who continue to put a smile on my face.

Linda, thank you soooo much for everything you do. You're always there no matter what, and I'm not sure what I'd do without you! You push me when I need to be pushed, and tell me to slow down when I need to stop. You save my ass more times than I can count, and I love you!

To my editor, Jen, thank you so much for everything you do. You make me a better writer with each book, and you're so much more than an editor. You've become my friend, and I wouldn't be without you!

My proofreader, Judy. Thank you for putting up with me! I continue to use commas in the wrong places and you continue to correct me. Never leave me, because I'd be lost without you!

To all the authors in the community. You continue to support me and I can't thank you enough for that. I love our little slice of heaven, and wouldn't want to be anywhere else!

Lastly, I want to say thank you, to you. Thank you for taking a chance on this book. Thank you for reading. And thank you for being awesome!

Also by Abigail Davies

MAC Security Series (Alpha Security/Military)

Book 1: Fractured Lies

Book 2: Exposed

Book 2.5: Flying Free (Standalone Spin-off)

Book 3: The Distance Between Us

Book 4: ReBoot

Book 5: Catching Teardrops

Six Book Boxset

The Easton Family

Fallen Duet (Forbidden Angst)

Book 1: Free Fall

Book 2: Down Fall

Confessions Series (Romantic Comedies)

Book 1: Confessions Of A Klutz

Book 2: Confessions Of A Chatterbox

Book 3: Confessions Of A Fratgirl

———

A. A. DAVIES (Darker, alter ego)

Verboten (Extreme Taboo. Inferno World Novella)

———

Broken Tracks Series,
(co-authored with Danielle Dickson)

Book 1: Etching Our Way

Book 2: Fighting Our Way

———

Destroyed Series,
(co-authored with L. Grubb)

Destroying the Game

Destroying the Soul

About the Author

Abigail Davies grew up with a passion for words, storytelling, maths, and anything pink. Dreaming up characters—quite literally—and talking to them out loud is a daily occurrence for her. She finds it fascinating how a whole world can be built with words alone, and how everyone reads and interprets a story differently.

Now following her dreams of writing, Abigail has found the passion that she always knew was there. When she's not writing: she's a mother to two daughters who she encourages to use their imagination as she believes that it's a magical thing, or getting lost in a good book.

If she's doing neither of those things, you can be sure she's surfing the web buying new makeup, clothes, or binge watching another show as she becomes one with her sofa.

Connect with Abigail

Reader group—Abi's Aces
Newsletter

www.abigaildaviesauthor.com

facebook.com/abigaildaviesauthor

twitter.com/abigailadavies

instagram.com/abigaildaviesauthor

goodreads.com/abigaildavies

bookbub.com/authors/abigail-davies

amazon.com/author/abigaildavies

pinterest.com/abigaildaviesauthor

Printed in Great Britain
by Amazon

29768241R00188